"I am well aware of what Glasgow is like, Mr. McAllistair, and I am sure I will be given opportunity to come and go as I please."

Logan took her hand and slid it through his arm, keeping his hand over hers as they walked to the inn. Nothing out of the ordinary escorting a lady like this. He truly longed to make her more than a friend. Having her to hold pulled at his heart.

How would he watch her with another man? He tightened his grip on her arm, as if he could stop her from leaving him. Sheena was betrothed to Mr. Mackenzie; that fact never left his thoughts. Betrothals equaled marriage. Only the formalities remained. How could God's plan for them come to this? Logan stopped, making Sheena stumble backward a bit.

"Sheena." Logan looked at her with an intensity he felt surge from his core. "You cannot marry Mr. Mackenzie."

EVA MARIA HAMILTON

found true love online. She has been married for over twelve years and has a beautiful daughter. An enthusiast for lifelong learning, Eva's studies span diverse fields of academia in both Canada and the United States. With a diploma in human resources management, a bachelor of arts degree in psychology, an honors bachelor of arts degree in history, and a master of science in education, Eva realized her studies focused on one thing: the human condition. What better way to share this knowledge of and passion for humanity than by writing about it? Part of a close and loving family, Eva would like to embrace her readers as friends. With computers playing such an important part in Eva's life, you're invited to connect with her on her website at www.EvaMariaHamilton.com.

EVA MARIA HAMILTON

Highland Hearts

Love Inspired

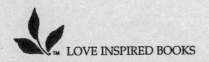

™ LOVE INSPIRED BOOKS

Recycling programs
for this product may
not exist in your area.

ISBN-13: 978-0-373-82910-1

HIGHLAND HEARTS

Printed in U.S.A.

My lover spoke and said to me, Arise my darling,
my beautiful one, and come with me. See!
The winter is past; the rains are over and gone.
Flowers appear on the earth; the season of singing
has come. The cooing of doves is heard in our land.
The fig tree forms its early fruit; the blossoming
vines spread their fragrance. Arise, come,
my darling; my beautiful one, come with me.
—*Song of Solomon* 2:10–13

I dedicate this book to my immediate and extended family, especially my mother-in-law, Josie, father-in-law, Joe, sister-in-law, Yvonne and the Tomasevic and Perri families, with a special thanks to my husband, Jason, daughter, Michelina, parents, Lina and Bob, brother, Bill, and grandmother Angelina for all their help, encouragement and support writing this book.

Acknowledgments

Thanks to the Toronto Public Library for hosting Deborah Cooke as their Romance Writer in Residence extraordinaire. Deborah, thank you. And thanks to Missy Tippens who introduced me to the lovely F.A.I.T.H. Girls and talented writers and friends of Seekerville. Your camaraderie, along with friends at Harlequin.com are invaluable. To my wonderful editor, Emily Rodmell, and everyone in the Love Inspired family at Harlequin, including Tina James and Krista Stroever, you have my gratitude. Plus a special thanks to Carolyn Graziani and everyone in the art department, including Sam Montesano, for creating a beautiful cover. And to God, whom I thank daily for all my blessings, thank you for always filling my life with such outstanding people.

Chapter One

Callander, Scotland
1748

Sheena Montgomery stood completely still at the top of Bracklinn Falls. The sound of rushing water filled the gorge. The rock underfoot felt hard and cold, a mirror image of her heart.

Alone, she looked past the tip of her toes dangling dangerously over the edge of the steep cliff. Several yards down the water crashed against the soft pudding stone, wearing it away. With all its fury, the water fought, eking out a way through the world. Pushing forward, not caring what it hurt in its path.

"Sheena?" a man's voice leapt out of the silence behind her, making Sheena whirl around so fast she lost her footing. In shock, she waved her arms frantically trying to regain her balance.

The man raced forward. His strong arms pulled her

away from a certain death. "There now, I've got you. You're all right."

Sheena stood staring at the man's face, his raggedly long brown hair and beard unfamiliar to her. But his eyes, those deep brown, soul-piercing eyes. Unforgettable.

Sheena's voice caught in her throat for a fleeting moment. "Logan?" Her eyes surely fooled her. She envisioned herself succumbing to her father's mental illness. Because Logan McAllister had left Scotland five years ago. He couldn't be here. She never thought she would see him again.

"I hoped to find you here, lassie." Sheena just looked at Logan. In all the years he'd lived in the Americas, he'd never sent word. Not one letter saying he was still alive.

But she wasn't losing her mind and wouldn't die the same way her father had this past autumn. Logan's arms cradled her against his warm chest. Her senses heightened. His smell, his touch, his very being, raced through her with dizzying speed. She stared at his lips, remembering their warmth.

"In our special place," he told her, and Sheena couldn't deny the meaning this place held for them. She remembered only too well all the times they had come here hand in hand, talking about the day they would wed.

Since the day he'd left, she'd hiked miles up this crag. Like a pilgrimage site, it became a shrine to their relationship. A place where she felt close to him again, like being in his presence, even though he was in another country.

But weeks stretched into months and then years and Sheena gave up on her silly girlhood dream, forced to acknowledge that Logan never meant to ever come back to Scotland. And yet, he stood in front of her now, grinning as if no time had passed and nothing had changed. Anger welled up in Sheena.

"Mr. McAllister." She pulled away from him. She couldn't say his given name as she always had before—he stood before her now almost as a stranger. Calling him *Logan* would show closeness, something she could no longer attest to. Besides, she would never give him the satisfaction of knowing how much she had pined for him during his absence or how much he had hurt her when he chose to leave.

He apparently didn't agree with her logic. "We're a little past formalities, aren't we, lassie?" Logan's lips formed a wry smile under his thick beard. A spark lit up the light golden flecks in the brown eyes Sheena had once adored.

"Nay, Mr. McAllister. I don't think so." A gust of wind sent Sheena's auburn hair into an annoying flurry that blocked her vision. She raised her hands quickly to get control of it.

"You are a sight for sore eyes." Logan's wry smile turned into a full grin. "Five years left you even more beautiful."

"Five years," Sheena repeated, her irritation erupting,

as she pulled roughly on her unruly locks to keep them in place.

"I still remembered how to get up to our waterfall." Sheena furrowed her brow at Logan's words, but Logan didn't seem to acknowledge her anger. "It's just as I remember." He closed his eyes and took a deep breath. She didn't move, hardly dared to breathe as she watched him to see if he did indeed look just as she remembered him.

He still wore the same socks that didn't slouch an inch lower than his knees where green ribbons held them up, but instead of his kilt he now wore brown breeches. The color had faded somewhat, and they looked as well-worn as his brown shoes.

His buttoned-up brown vest could do with some mending, not to mention how much scrubbing the collar of his white shirt needed.

Maybe in another time and place she would have offered to do such work. But not now. Not as she watched him draw in another seemingly peaceful breath. The pleasure he derived from his surroundings radiated from him and it infuriated Sheena all the more. Especially his apparent oblivion to her feelings.

"That's wonderful that your memory didn't fail you," Sheena said in an uncharacteristically sarcastic tone. "But this waterfall is one of the only things left that didn't change in your absence."

Logan's eyes opened and she looked directly into them only to hear, "God has the ability to change everything, lassie, and yet keep it the same."

"Maybe in your world, but surely not in mine." Since

Logan left, not one single thing in Sheena's life had remained the same. "Let's start with the year you left Scotland, Logan. In 1743 the military built a road right through Callander, just in case they needed to use it to pacify any Highlanders who sought to rebel." And in 1746 when the Jacobites did rebel, a bloodbath ensued.

This example stood as only one of many things that had changed in Sheena's life over the past five years.

But surely Logan knew about this. It was only Sheena he didn't know anything about anymore. He had made it very clear by his absence that he could live without her.

"Besides all this political nonsense, what else has changed in your life? From where I stand, everything looks the same to me as it did in the past."

"Logan, you don't understand. Everything has changed. The past is just that and I live in the present." She bent down and snatched up her black shoes.

"And what of that?" Logan stepped closer, giving Sheena no recourse. She couldn't back away from him, unless she wanted to meet her Maker. And as tough as life got, she would never succumb to that.

Sheena pushed her way around Logan. "I am sure the details of my life are of no interest to you."

"Let me be the judge of that, lassie." Logan followed her away from the edge of the waterfall to a rock she leaned against for support to put on her shoes.

She scowled at him as she walked away, jutting her chin high into the air. "Do as you wish, Logan. You always do anyway." Her underlying contempt for him and his actions snapped through the chilly air. She never wanted him to leave Scotland, but he had done so anyway.

"And you don't?" Logan kept up, even with her brisk pace.

"We both know that a man is given that privilege, while a woman is not."

"Since when have you not lived and breathed for yourself?"

"Since you left." Sheena stopped dead and faced him.

"Then you must tell me what happened to you in the past five years, lassie, so we can reverse it."

"I already told you, it no longer matters. Events are set in motion. Forces beyond my control and even *yours,* propel me toward a future that no longer resembles the past." Sheena held fast to her skirts and walked on.

"Sheena." Her even stride faltered at the sound of her name coming from his lips. "Whatever has happened can be undone. Nothing is ever final, not even death." He came up beside her again. "I am here now. We can fix this."

But Sheena couldn't argue any longer. Being livid, she didn't trust what would come out of her mouth. She knew cementing her new path in life after he left meant she couldn't turn back time now. If she felt gracious, she could thank God he lived to tell of his journey, but she wouldn't listen to his tales.

It hurt too much seeing him.

"My life is no longer any concern of yours." Tears welled in Sheena's eyes. If only he'd loved her enough to remain in Scotland. But he ignored all her pleading. Did what he wanted. Left. And now that he had returned, nothing remained the same.

"You are wrong. It is. It always has been and it always will be." Logan reached out for her hand, but she pulled away.

"Nay." Sheena turned swiftly. "Nay, it isn't." She ran from him.

Logan could see over the whole village of Callander with his feet planted on the crag. He knew exactly which path Sheena was taking to her house, but he couldn't follow her.

He sighed. He wanted the separation from Sheena to end. Already spending five years away tortured him enough. But evidently, she needed time to get used to the idea that he had returned. That took him completely by surprise.

He'd dreamed about his homecoming every day since the day he left the Highlands. He'd amassed so many versions of their reunion and yet none of them played out like this. In his dreams, Sheena ran to him, wrapped her arms around him and professed her undying love. Somehow, he needed to figure out a way to make her react like that.

If only he could tell her why he'd left Scotland five years ago. But he couldn't. To do so would go against her father and the secrecy he'd sworn Logan to uphold.

And Logan knew, if he breathed a word to Sheena about what had transpired five years ago before his departure, her father would never allow Logan to marry her. Not then. And not now. Not ever. And Logan couldn't let that happen.

So he never told Sheena he'd met with her father to ask his permission to marry her. And he never told Sheena that her father had demanded that Logan prove his worthiness to marry her by risking his life to accept an indenturement in the Americas. Nor did she know that as a measure of good faith, her father had given Logan a Montgomery family heirloom. It was a wooden box with leaves carved all over it that housed a letter her father had written, telling Logan he could marry Sheena after he made the treacherous voyage back to Scotland.

But tearing himself away from Sheena to accept his indenturement in the Americas had ripped Logan apart. The shock and betrayal in her darkened amber eyes had agonized him. Hearing her plead with him to stay, seeing her tears, watching her anger develop had pained him. But he couldn't see another option. Not when he had been dirt-poor and had nothing to offer her besides his love.

He had hoped they would wed. And yet there he had stood at the top of their waterfall, their most special place, telling her he would leave Scotland for an indenturement in the Americas.

He knew it didn't make any sense to her. He knew he'd hurt her. He only prayed the situation didn't turn into something irreparable. He would go and talk to her father right after he made amends with Sheena and, of course, after he dug up that wooden box containing the hidden letter he kept to remind her father of the promise he'd made.

However upset Sheena was now, after his explanation she would know he'd never meant to hurt her. She would understand that everything he'd done he'd done to secure their future together. She would forgive him. At least he prayed it would be so.

Turning his attention toward the countryside where he grew up, he walked down the treeless crag, to the barren land beneath, with his life's meager belongings hardly filling the slim bag he flung over his shoulder.

Logan's shoes sank into the damp earth as he walked home, their wet sound his only accompaniment. Not even a bird greeted him. If only his reunion with Sheena had turned out differently, with her love the same as it had been their whole lives. Maybe then the five years he'd spent away would seem like nothing more than a bad dream. But he couldn't ignore or wish away the reality of the situation. She despised him for leaving. And his return marked the beginning of atonement, rather than triumph.

Sheena came down the crag like a woman running from an attacking poisonous adder snake. Gasping for breath, she leaned against a rock at the edge of the village to steady herself. Glancing back up the crag, she saw nothing but the steep cliff. Logan hadn't followed her.

The tears she ran from stormed out. She fell to her knees in the soggy moss, not caring when the cold wetness soaked through her skirts. Logan's unexpected homecoming caused too much pain. He thought they could just pick up from where they'd left off five years ago. Not possible.

Reliving all the hurt he'd caused her, she cried until she completely exhausted herself and couldn't shed another tear. Taking a long, deep breath, she turned her face up toward heaven and wiped her tear-streaked cheeks with her hands. Standing slowly, she forced her mind to focus on the here and now. The supper hour loomed, and her attendance would be mandatory. Duty and obligations beckoned her. As they always seemed to do.

After shaking her green, sodden outer skirt several times, she gave up. The chances of her drying those skirts before reaching home stood as high as the skirts themselves coming to life and saving her from her impending engagement. An impossibility.

Walking as if an executioner awaited her arrival, she spied her white two-story house far too soon. Smoke wafted up from the chimneys on opposite ends of the house, signaling the use of all the fireplaces therein. The numerous windows on each floor winked at her in the sunlight, mocking her foul mood.

Sheena stopped outside the main entrance and took another deep breath. The walk home had returned her breathing to normal, but her mind remained in turmoil with every thought of Logan. She needed to stop thinking about him. To compose herself.

She hesitated longer, not wanting to go in. She didn't

know if she could maintain her composure. Although, she reasoned, no one would see the inner workings of her mind if she just kept her expression calm. Not that she would get any sympathy anyway. That, she knew only too well.

Moving forward, she shoved Logan out of her mind. And not just for supper. She needed to push him out of her life for good. Her future didn't include him.

She thrust the door open. "Well, it's about time," her aunt Jean shouted, even before Sheena closed the rest of the world out.

"I'm sorry, Aunt Jean," Sheena called automatically as she quickly took off her dark blue woolen shawl. She forced one foot in front of the other, propelling herself to the drawing room.

"Where have you been for this long?" Jean continued.

"No doubt out roaming the countryside," Sheena's mother piped up in her usual tone of resentment, not even bothering to look up from her embroidery.

Sheena hastened over to her mother's chair. "I'm sorry, Mother." She kissed Tavia on the cheek.

"And what about your aunt? Do I not deserve the same respect as…"

"Aye," Sheena interrupted Jean's tirade, kissing the woman's cheek as well, then crossing the room to sit close to the fire, hoping her skirts would dry before anyone noticed.

The chair's hearth location served an extra purpose in keeping her at a more guarded distance from them. Dealing pleasantly with the pair of sisters on a good day took every ounce of concentration. After seeing Logan mere moments before, Sheena highly doubted she was up to the task today.

If only she could run straight upstairs to her bedroom, but what a verbal lashing she would receive for behaving in such a way. Best to try and sit quietly until supper got served momentarily, and then she could spend the evening alone, as she did every night.

"Why do you persist in going out in the countryside, child? What a filthy place," Jean said, scrunching her face as she took in Sheena's green skirt. "Just look at yourself." Sheena tried laying her hands over her knees, but she couldn't cover the stains taking hold of the woolen fibers. Just as she couldn't hide from herself the scar Logan had stained onto her heart.

And to her annoyance, Tavia picked that moment to feign interest and look up from her needlework. "Sheena, do you know how long it's going to take the maid to scrub that out of your skirt?"

"I can do it myself, Mother."

"I know that," her mother clucked her tongue. "But you will not. You cannot behave like a servant. How many times do I have to tell you that?" Tavia wagged the needle at her. "And now the maid must waste unnecessary time on your clothes, when she could be doing other, more important chores."

Her mother always insisted on Sheena acting like a lady and keeping company with her own wealthier landowning class, even though no one else in the region did and Sheena didn't even hold the title of Lady. Nevertheless, Tavia had always hated Sheena's friendships with Logan and his brother's sister-in-law, Cait. Even when they played as mere children. And it all came down to money. Logan and Cait lived a poor life in the countryside, farming the land. Thus, Tavia considered them useless, due to their inability to help raise Sheena in society. A goal Tavia now neared fulfilling.

And Sheena remembered well enough her mother harboring ill thoughts toward Logan for constantly "being about" as she put it. But Sheena and Logan always remained careful never to let her mother, or anyone else for that matter, know how much more than just friends they had become. Her mother would never stand for such a match and Logan and Sheena agreed to wait for the perfect time to break the news that they loved each other. Although Sheena knew only too well now that the time had never come. And never would.

Logan had wanted to do everything properly back then. He never asked Sheena to marry him, because he said he must ask her father first. But instead of following their plan and meeting with her father, Logan had met with Sheena and told her he'd accepted an indenturement in the Americas and would come home in three years, so instead of a wedding band, Sheena received a green moss agate stone to remember Logan by before he boarded a ship and sailed away.

Sheena's head had spun for days trying to understand why Logan hadn't followed their plan to ask her father for her hand. If Logan had, they would already live as husband and wife now. But it didn't matter. Not now that she had turned twenty-three and Logan twenty-four. It was all so very long ago. When she still believed in fairy tales and love and Logan with all his promises.

Now, however, she knew better. She wore the scar Logan etched onto her heart. But try as she might to throw away that green moss agate stone, she never could. She'd convinced herself she didn't hold on to it as a reminder of him, rather for the protection people believed the stone brought to the carrier.

Sheena looked to Jean, knowing she needed to clear her thoughts, and she couldn't endure another lecture from her mother right now. The shock of seeing Logan had exhausted her.

She couldn't love Logan now. And not just because she didn't trust him anymore. Her future didn't include him. He'd left and hadn't even returned as he promised after three years. For all she knew he'd married another woman during his time away. He'd forfeited all rights to be included in her future plans and that is exactly what happened.

"Aunt Jean." Sheena got her attention. "Walking in the countryside is very good exercise. You should try it, at least once." Jean's facial expression gave every indication Sheena wouldn't persuade her.

"Nothing good ever comes from the countryside, child. Oh, just thinking about some of the people who live out there makes me want to call for my smelling salts." Tavia laughed at her sister's theatrics before turning her eyes back down to admire her handiwork. But Sheena only half listened. She succeeded in getting Jean on another tangent, but the fight within her own mind raged.

"Just take that terrible MacDonald boy who is always spitting. Why didn't his parents teach him any manners? And just yesterday, I ventured as far as the village and had the misfortune of running into that Murray woman and she just about talked my ear off. Don't people know when they've said enough?" Jean looked to her sister for confirmation, and began again when she met with her sister's acceptance. "Then there was that McAllister fellow. Remember him? Terrible lad. Good for nothing." Sheena flinched, her insides tense. Why did her aunt have to bring up his name? All she wanted to do right now was forget about him.

"Now, Jean." Tavia laughed. "Even I would say that's not very charitable."

"Maybe not, but true nonetheless." She held her embroidery tight in her hands, but from what Sheena could see, her work didn't possess many new stitches since this morning. "I said good riddance to him and I will say the same to all the rest of the poor Highlanders who get cleared out of Scotland."

"Then, Aunt Jean, you may have to add a *welcome home* when they return, as well." Sheena couldn't bring herself to say Logan's name, but she would defend her fellow clansmen. Poor or not, they were her brethren.

"Really? That lad made it home?" Jean scoffed, raising her eyebrows.

"He is well past the age of being referred to as a *lad*. But aye, he returned."

Sheena held her temper in check as her aunt spewed forth her distaste of Highlanders. "Why on earth would he come back? There is nothing for his kind here. Just goes to prove my point about *those* people. No sense. Do you know how much it costs to travel by sea? No wonder his people are so poor. They have no idea how to make or save money. Dreadful waste. It is like a different world up here in the Highlands. I so miss Glasgow. And civilization."

The sound of a servant entering the room diverted their attention. "Supper will be served now," the parlor maid said as she curtsied awkwardly, fleeing the room the second her words escaped her lips. Sheena didn't blame Cait for rushing away—she only wished she could, as well.

"See what I mean." Jean pinned her needle into the cloth. "You must be thankful your fate is tied to a notable house Sheena. You will only have to suffer these people as your servants. You shall be forever grateful to me for that, child." Jean laid her embroidery aside and rose with an air of dignity to lead the way to supper. Sheena didn't argue. Her aunt wouldn't understand why Sheena considered Cait her best friend.

"Aye, Jean, we are very thankful to you and Kyle for finding such a suitable match for Sheena." Tavia took her sister's arm, creating a wall in front of Sheena that made her unable to sidestep them. "Arranging your betrothal to Ian Mackenzie was the best thing your uncle and aunt could have done for you Sheena. Ian is the son of one of the richest tobacco lords in Glasgow—you will be set up in the nicest house…"

"Estate," Jean corrected her.

"Aye, estate." Tavia grinned. "And Sheena, you will have all the finest things. You will want for nothing."

Maybe one day Sheena would feel gratitude for Jean and Tavia's interference into her life, but not today. Not after seeing Logan at their waterfall. And surely not after he stirred all those old emotions she'd painstakingly buried inside the locked chambers of her heart.

Yet with her dowry bestowed upon Ian, to whom did that heart belong?

Chapter Two

Weary from his long journey home and his ensuing argument with Sheena, Logan finally smiled as the thatched roofs from huts came into view ahead of him. His family didn't even know he walked these moors. Logan almost laughed aloud; his surprise appearance would surely bring rejoicing. And he could use some of that.

"Uncle Logan?" A lad with the same brown eyes and hair as Logan jumped down from a rock after a moment's hesitation.

"Aye." Logan waved, his heart swelling.

"Uncle Logan." Ewan's shriek sailed across the moor. Logan dropped his bag and scooped up his ten-year-old nephew. "Uncle Logan, you're home."

"Aye." Logan laughed, noticing how much his nephew had changed in five years.

"As I live and breathe." Nessia stood before them wearing the same married-woman's kertch upon her head and looking nearly the same at twenty-seven as she had at twenty-two when Logan had last seen her. "You've come home." She embraced Logan. "Angus is out back. Come, you have to see your brother." Nessia grabbed Logan's hand and rushed him around their one-room dwelling.

Ewan ran ahead of them. "Da, Uncle Logan has come home."

"Logan?" Angus rose slowly from the mucky soil he farmed, even though at age twenty-eight he could no doubt easily jump to his feet. Angus's apparent shock as Logan approached changed into a facial expression that mirrored Logan's thoughts. It had been too long; coming home felt right. "I don't believe it. This is a great day." Angus hugged him. "Praise the Lord Almighty."

"You must be famished, Logan. Come inside. I'll get you something to eat." Nessia ushered them around to the sole entrance at the front of the hut.

The walls, nearly three feet deep, held an open wooden door swinging in welcome. Logan stepped through, seeing only black as his eyes adjusted to the dimness. Even though the spring sun shone at seven at night and wouldn't go down for a couple more hours, the one small window in the dwelling didn't seem keen to let in the sunshine.

"Duncan, this is your uncle Logan." Angus knelt down on the earthen floor to his youngest son's eye level. "You were just a wee lad when he left."

"This is the brother you always talk about?" Barefoot, Duncan eyed Logan and Angus nodded.

Logan didn't like that his nephew didn't remember

him. Wee Duncan wouldn't even recognize him if they walked right past one another. But what did he expect? A lot had happened in five years. Only a fool would think it a short time. Look at all he'd missed.

He definitely missed taking care of Sheena. And he understood her anger toward him. But he didn't share it. Not given what her father had forced him to do. He had needed to go to the Americas to secure their future.

He'd obeyed her father and taken the only step he could that would allow Sheena to one day become his wife. And he would never regret that. He returned worthy to wed her. But he also accomplished a lot more than what he'd set out to do—he'd amassed the means to offer her a decent life, something he couldn't have done five years ago.

But what if she wouldn't accept him now? Even after he explained. Without her… Nay. God saw him home safe and for that he should celebrate. He'd win Sheena's love back. With God's help. Somehow.

Logan held out his hand and Duncan took it. "You look like my da when he's ill and doesn't trim his beard and moustache for a very, very long time." Duncan's innocence made the room erupt in laughter. Despite the age gap of two years, eight-year-old Duncan could be mistaken for Ewan's twin. McAllister men evidently shared a striking resemblance.

"Come, sit." Nessia ladled broth into a wooden bowl from a black cauldron over an open flame. "Eat." She put a wooden spoon in the bowl and handed it to Logan.

He didn't need to be told twice. "Thanks. It's been

a long time since I've eaten a good meal." His compliment produced a grin from Nessia before she turned to dish out the lads' meals. "Is there cow's meat in this?" Logan knew his clansmen hardly ever ate meat.

"We lost another cow a couple days ago." Angus downed his drink from a large pewter tankard before refilling it and handing it to Logan. Logan smiled. One drinking vessel for the whole household. Could his family cope with a richer life outside Scotland?

"So tell us everything." Angus leaned toward Logan.

"Let him eat first, Angus," Nessia chaffed. "He's starving."

"All right, but I'm excited. I want to hear all about the Americas."

"You'd like it, Angus," Logan said. But he didn't elaborate after receiving a stark look of warning from Nessia.

He wanted to tell Angus everything though. His travels had opened his eyes to the larger world. Scotland lagged behind in many ways. He could benefit his brethren by sharing all he learned. Like telling them to end this nonsense of fearing trees and stop digging them up as soon as wealthier men planted them.

The farmers here would never produce good crops until they learned to block the wind and let trees and other plants with deep roots dry up the soil. He wished he could show them. The Americas grew acres of trees and yet the land also yielded bountiful crops. Food that people here didn't even know existed. Food that could fatten up their chronically skinny cows and sheep. Food that would stop the starvation.

"Would you like more?" Nessia offered after Logan finished his last spoonful of broth.

Sitting back, Logan patted his stomach with both hands. "As delicious as that was, I'm full." And yet, even if his stomach still growled from hunger, he would never take more than his share. Nessia and the lads came first.

"Great, then. Now that he's finished, it's high time for talking." Angus winked at Nessia, who shrugged off his playfulness.

"Just make sure Logan gets to bed soon. He's had a long journey and needs his rest. His eyes look like he can barely keep them open." Only three years his senior, Nessia never could help acting like his mother.

"Aye," Angus agreed and Logan couldn't argue as he put his hand over his mouth to cover a yawn. "Let's sit nearer the fire, Logan." Angus stood and kissed each of his lads on the head, wishing them a good night. Logan grinned. His brother didn't care about the criticism he received for acting affectionate, even when told by his clansmen that his behavior would ruin his children.

And Logan didn't, either. His nephews didn't seem the least bit spoiled. He watched as Nessia ushered the lads toward the end of the room with one on each side of her full brown skirt. The lads crawled through the opening of a high-sided wooden box that housed a straw mattress and lay down beside each other as Nessia placed one blanket after another on top of them.

Logan didn't wait to watch Nessia pull the curtain closed. Instead, he picked up his stool and followed his brother a couple feet nearer the fire that burned up from the floor where Nessia had just stood cooking. "It's nice to be home again." Logan watched the sparks dance to their own crackling sound as the peat moss burned.

"You should've never made the journey back." Angus lowered himself onto his wooden stool with a slow exactness. "It was far too dangerous."

"You knew before I left I had every intention of returning." Logan unbuttoned his brown vest.

"Aye. You did say that. But there was always a chance that you would change your mind."

Logan paused in his undressing. "Nay Angus, there wasn't."

"Then it is true. You really love her."

"Aye. I'll always love her. I just saw her now. She's upset at me, but with God's help that will change." Logan finished taking off his vest and laid it across his lap before stretching out his arms to feel the warmth on his overworked, calloused hands. "I would face the darkest evil and travel to the most decrepit of places if that's what it took."

"I imagine you have." Angus turned from the flames to his brother.

"Aye, I worked hard in the Americas, and crossing the sea is not easy. We lost Gordon McDougall on the voyage home." Logan closed his eyes and said a quick, silent prayer. "Gordon was ill before he boarded the ship.

I told him not to make the journey, but he wanted so badly to come home."

"Gordon was a fine man." Angus joined him in a brief silence. "A tragedy."

Logan rubbed his brow, remembering the pain and despair surrounding Gordon's death. "I couldn't bring Gordon's body back. I could only bring what little he had with him and I'll take it to his family first thing tomorrow with the news."

"Logan, it wasn't your fault he died. God has His own plans for each one of us and it's not for us to understand."

"Fair enough." Logan eyed his brother. "But I have plans of my own, as well."

Angus shot a look at him as Logan stood to stretch. "Before you go to sleep, Logan, tell me about these plans."

"Let me save that until tomorrow. Nessia was right, I am tired and in need of sleep."

Angus pursed his lips but consented. "Aye, tomorrow after you take Gordon's belongings to his family we'll talk about these *plans* of yours."

"Thanks." Logan held his brother's shoulder. "It really is good to be home."

Sheena rubbed her right eye as she walked into the village. Lack of sleep and tears shed over Logan last night irritated more than just her eyes.

Her whole body felt off, as if it wanted to shut down.

But she had promised to bring a basket of food to the McDougall family today.

At church last Sunday, she found out Ailsa McDougall had fallen ill and the women of the church picked days to bring whatever they could over to help the family. Today was Sheena's day, on behalf of the Montgomery household, because her mother wouldn't dream of walking into the countryside herself and already declared they couldn't spare a single servant for such matters, either.

Switching the basket from her left hand to her right, Sheena looked down as she rubbed her other eye. The cool breeze made her eyes tear up and sting. If this kept up, fairly soon they might refuse to stay open altogether. Sheena couldn't live like this. She needed sleep and to do that she needed to banish Logan from her mind and let the past go.

Sheena turned around the corner of the last building that stood on the village of Callander's main dirt road. Shutting her eyes tight to try to stop the stinging when another cool breeze assaulted her, she bumped into something and jumped back, startled and alarmed.

"Sorry, I wasn't watching where I was going." Sheena knew that voice—she didn't need to feel his hands holding on to her shoulders or see him clearly to know who stood before her. "Sheena," Logan's voice sounded full of concern. "Why are you crying?"

Sheena wiped at her eyes harder this time. "I'm not crying." She pulled back from him.

"Then why are there tears running down your cheeks? Here." Logan handed her a handkerchief.

"I didn't sleep well last night and my eyes hurt. There. Does that answer your question?" Evidently, it answered more than that as a grin spread over Logan's lips.

"Does that have anything to do with me?" Sheena didn't answer. She handed him back his handkerchief with a "Good day" before marching off. Never would she own up to him about that truth.

"Not so fast, lassie," Logan spun around and caught up to her. Patting his clean-shaven cheeks and chin, he asked her with a wink, "How do I look?" Her lips curled slightly and Logan didn't miss the nuance. His grin broadened, even as she hurried past him. "Where are you going?"

Sheena stopped and stared at him, her chest tightening with annoyance. Better to tell him and get rid of him now than allow him to follow her all over the countryside as he seemed likely to do.

"I am bringing this basket to Ailsa McDougall. She's ill." Logan's smile fell from his lips and he ran his hand through his brown, shoulder-length hair. He looked away for a moment into the distance at the crag that led to their waterfall.

She didn't mean to hurt him, but what could she say now?

"I have to visit the McDougalls myself, lassie." The light golden flecks in Logan's eyes no longer shone brightly and worry furrowed his brow.

"Logan, I do not need a chaperone." But what she

really did not need involved Logan standing near her and playing havoc with her emotions. Her future belonged to Ian Mackenzie.

"Be that as it may…" He seemed impatient, as if he wanted to tell her something, but couldn't bring himself to do it.

And even though Sheena knew that as Ian's future wife she needed to distance herself from Logan, she couldn't stand it any longer. "Logan, what is going on?"

Logan's gaze met hers and the intensity with which he looked at her made her hold her basket tighter. But she couldn't look away. She knew Logan, even after all these years. And as much as he'd hurt her, she could still read every one of his expressions. And something definitely ate away at him.

The fact that he'd left her instead of marrying her *should* eat at his innards, but something else troubled him. And as angry as she felt toward him, she would help him now if she could. Any Christian would. At least that's what she told herself.

"I have to tell the McDougalls their son Gordon died."

Sheena's hand flew to her mouth. "Gordon," she murmured. She needed to sit down. Gordon was too young to die. Everyone expected great things from him. The community would be crushed. His family would be devastated. She felt Logan's arm drape around her shoulder.

"He died on our ship, traveling back to Scotland."

"Why did he try to come back here? Why didn't he just stay in the Americas?" Sheena heard the note of irritation in her questions. Yet she didn't expect any answers.

But Logan didn't know that. "He must have had a good reason to risk his life. Just as I did."

Sheena looked up into Logan's face and searched his troubled brown eyes. Had love motivated his departure? Or did he just find he hated living in the Americas? She pulled herself away from him. It didn't matter now. Not since her mother had betrothed her to Ian.

"We'll tell them together." Sheena's voice achieved a calmness she had yet to feel.

"I am truly sorry," Sheena told the McDougalls before she hugged them all one last time. What else could she say? After Logan told them all about how bravely Gordon faced his illness at sea, that phrase was all he could utter, as well.

Logan smiled at Sheena as she approached him, standing by the wooden door. How kind of Sheena to help him break the news of Gordon's death to his family and stay to comfort the family as they let out their shock and grief.

"God bless you," Sheena turned to say one last time before leaving the McDougalls' hut—an exact replica of the one-room dwelling where Logan's family lived.

Logan stepped out into the sunshine beside her. "Thank you, Sheena." She stopped to look up at him. Her unsmiling face showed signs of stress and she simply nodded, folding her arms around herself, before turning and walking away from him again.

Logan desperately wanted to walk Sheena home. To gain even an extra few minutes to talk with her and remain close by her, but he couldn't. The McDougalls still needed answers to questions about Gordon that only Logan could provide.

Alone and ready to retire for the night, Sheena rubbed her green moss agate stone as she walked up the wooden staircase to her bedroom. Being with the McDougall family as they learned about Gordon's death brought her own heartrending emotions to the surface.

Yesterday, Logan's return and today the news of Gordon's death had left her emotionally distressed. Too much to handle in such a short time.

She sent up a prayer, not only for herself, but for Gordon, the McDougalls and Logan. How difficult for Logan to tell the devastating news to Gordon's family earlier. She could barely listen to him choke out the words. And Gordon's mother's screams still reverberated in her ears.

Sitting on her bedroom chair, Sheena tucked her distaff under her arm. She knew her mother hated her spinning wool like the servants, insisting she do embroidery instead. But Sheena preferred this type of work. And, as she repeatedly told her mother, everyone, whether rich or poor, spun wool. So her mother couldn't consider this activity beneath Sheena, even if her mother chose not to do it herself.

By now Sheena usually picked up her drop-spindle

to hold in her left hand, but something stopped her from picking it up and transforming that wool into yarn.

She just couldn't put the green moss agate stone down. Rolling it over between her fingers, the smooth rock usually soothed her. But tonight she grabbed it tight within her fist, squeezing it as if she meant to crush it into powder.

Forget spinning wool, she needed to talk to Cait.

Finding Cait finishing up her parlor maid's duties for the night, Sheena calmed her temper enough to ask her to join her in her bedroom for a cup of tea.

Did servants usually share tea with their employers? Nay. But to Sheena, Cait became her best friend as a wee lass and would always remain her best friend, so she never saw any problem with it.

"It is so nice to relax after the day I had." Cait dropped into a chair.

Sheena began pouring their tea. She didn't want to belittle Cait's complaint by putting her own problems ahead of her friend's, so she listened to Cait voice her troubles, before broaching her own.

"Cait, do you know why my aunt Jean came here on Monday?" Sheena stirred the sugar that settled to the bottom of her teacup.

"Aye, to bring the news that your dowry to Ian Mackenzie has been paid and you are now officially betrothed to him."

"Aye. But there's more to it than that." Sheena set down her spoon as Cait sat up to listen more intently. "My aunt Jean also brought the news that I am to visit the Mackenzies in Glasgow to meet Ian and his family before the wedding ceremony that they agreed would take place in two weeks."

"Two weeks?" Cait stood to take off her white apron, before sitting back down more comfortably. "Everything is happening so fast, Sheena. Just last week I knew nothing about any of this."

"I know." Sheena's teacup rattled in her hands. "When my mother first told me about Ian, I didn't even mention it to you, because I didn't think anything would happen until I met him. But according to my mother there was no need for that, because Jean met with him and thought he was perfect."

"No doubt because he's swimming in riches." Cait picked up her teacup and eyed Sheena over the rim as she took a sip.

Sheena stared down into the steam rising from her own teacup. "There is something else I never told you, Cait." Sheena glanced at her best friend now. "Yesterday, Logan came home."

Cait nearly choked on her mouthful of tea. "Logan? My sister Nessia's brother-in-law? Here in Callander?" Sheena nodded at each question, watching the smile lift Cait's entire expression. "I have to go and see him." She put her teacup down and sprang to her feet. "But wait. Logan's home…" She sank back down slowly into her chair, not bothering to fix her skirt into place beneath her as she should. "And you're betrothed to Ian now."

Sheena nodded. She knew Cait assumed Logan had come home because he loved Sheena and wanted to marry her, but Logan had never told Sheena that. And now it was too late, Sheena thought.

"Oh, Sheena. What are you going to do?" Cait reached across the empty space and put her hand on Sheena's knee. And Sheena put her teacup down, too, fighting back more tears as she unknowingly rubbed her green moss agate stone.

"I haven't told Logan about my betrothal to Ian yet." Cait opened her mouth to speak, maybe to offer to tell Logan for Sheena, but Sheena kept talking. "Please don't tell Logan. I want him to hear it from me." If Logan could tell the McDougalls that Gordon died, Sheena could tell Logan about her betrothal.

Cait nodded and Sheena straightened her skirt, forgetting she even held the green moss agate stone in her hands; it slipped out and fell onto the hardwood floor with a clunk before it rolled away from her.

Chapter Three

"How are the McDougalls?"

Angus handed Logan the family's only pewter tankard as Logan sank onto a stool beside him.

Logan took a long, slow drink. He felt numb inside. "As best as can be expected. They're devastated." Angus clapped Logan on the back, but said nothing. What could he say? No one could bring Gordon back to the McDougalls and that is all they truly wanted. "Angus, you must understand one thing."

Angus folded his hands in his lap, moving his eyes to watch the fire burn down lower on the floor. "Even though Gordon met with a tragic end at sea, healthy people can and do make that journey. Gordon was just too sick to attempt it."

"Why are you telling me this, Logan?" Angus's glare fell on Logan now.

"Because I'm going back to the Americas. And I want you to join me."

Angus nearly fell off his stool. "What?"

Logan reached out to steady him. "You heard me. Your lads are old enough and if you're all healthy, there shouldn't be a problem. Not with all of us going together and looking out for each other."

"Even if that's so, Logan, how on earth would we pay for that? I am not about to sell myself as an indentured servant." Angus's face reddened. "I will not be a slave to another man."

"You won't have to." Logan remembered the earful he'd received from Sheena about becoming an indentured servant; hearing it now from his brother made him a trifle annoyed. "And by the way, not all indentured servants are treated so unfairly."

Angus scanned Logan protectively. "I'm hoping you're speaking from experience."

"Aye. There are opportunities in the Americas that we don't have here." Angus sat quietly, no doubt thinking about everything Logan had just told him. "I don't want to scare you by what I've heard."

Angus stared at his brother. "What do you mean? I have no enemies." Logan watched his brother fume.

"Nay, of course not, but Scotland is changing." Logan leaned over and threw some more peat moss into the fire. "I was on board with some in the landowning class and you cannot rest assured that the land you live on today will be the land you live on tomorrow. You are a tenant farmer. Your landowner can and will—trust my words—take this land away from you. And then what will you do, change how you earn a living? Relocate your family to the coast and become a fisherman?"

Logan poked at the fire with a stick, sending sparks flaring into the darkness.

Angus wrung his hands, staring down at them. "This is very grave indeed. But you're right. The government did seize the Duke of Perth's estate."

"Aye. You may face a very bleak future here, but after all you've done for me, I want to help you. I want to offer you hope for a better life. A place where you own your own land and no one can throw you off it."

Angus turned toward Logan again. "You speak of the Americas as if they were the Promised Land."

"I speak from experience." Logan leaned forward to rest the stick against the dirt wall beside the fire. "I worked as an indentured servant for three very long years." Logan breathed in the heavy air, letting the smoky scent he missed at sea fill his nostrils. "I was blessed with a good master and I thank God for that every day. But I never took it for granted. When I was freed, my master kept his promise and gave me some money. However, that money wouldn't have been enough to come back with, so I spent two additional years guarding the town of New Inverness, in return for a land grant."

A smile overtook Angus's shock. "You own land?"

"Aye. *Out of the darkness,* my brother." Logan smiled back. "And I want to share it with you. Together we can farm the land and live a good life."

"Logan that's all very well, but I have no money to pay for our voyage." Angus stood to add even more peat moss to the fire.

"I may be the little brother by four years, but you must give me more credit. I wouldn't have returned without a means to get us all back. I've already taken care of that. Without family in the Americas, I did little else besides sleep and work."

"No doubt." Angus sat down again. "You must put some meat on your bones before you attempt to cross the sea again." He leaned over and squeezed Logan's arm in assessment. Logan smiled, knowing Angus had changed his mind about the perils of leaving Scotland. And Logan moved one step closer to making his dreams a reality.

"Any spare time I found while in the Americas, I spent making extra money however I could—farming, stable work, jobs that no one else wanted to do." Logan laughed. "But I had a purpose and that got me through it."

"And now you've come home to offer me and mine all of this?" Angus stood again and this time Logan stood to meet his brother.

"You are my family." Logan hugged him. After his day with the McDougalls, it felt good to look toward the future.

Life may remain unpredictable. And only God knew why things turned out the way they did. But with whatever time God gave Logan to live, he wanted to make sure he made his life count for something. He needed to start living his dreams, instead of just thinking about them.

"We must take care of each other, Logan."

"That's what you always told me. And I'm happy to finally be able to pay you back."

"Logan, you don't have to."

"I know." Logan squeezed his brother's shoulders. "I want to."

Angus laughed. "Let me talk things over with Nessia." He took hold of Logan's shoulders now and brought their heads close. "Thank you for your offer," he told him solemnly.

Logan smiled. "You can thank me when you see your new home. They're made differently in the Americas. There's wood aplenty—no importing it from Norway for huge sums of money." A knock on the door interrupted their conversation.

They looked at each other and then at the door. Angus dropped hold of Logan and strode over to it. Who would come knocking at this late hour? Logan watched Angus carefully for any sign that he needed assistance. But none came.

"Cait, this is a surprise. Please come in." Angus stepped aside to let his sister-in-law into his dimly lit home. "We only ever get to see you on Sunday at church. And here it is well past ten on a Saturday night. How did you get out of the house to come all this way?"

"I finished my duties and then I snuck out." Cait took her soaking wet, brown shawl off her head and un-wrapped herself from its woolen security before hand-ing it to Angus. "I couldn't help myself. I heard Logan was home and I'd rather see him than sleep."

She let out a gasp of delight when she spotted Logan

standing by the only light source in the hut—the fire. Without a moment's hesitation, she hurried over and embraced him.

"Look at you, Cait. All grown up." Logan surveyed her at arm's length.

Cait blushed uncontrollably, as she gave him the most awkward curtsy he ever saw. He stifled a grin. Some things didn't change. "That's right. I'm not the little girl who used to pester you day and night."

"Cait is in training to be a parlor maid." Angus laid her brown shawl near the fire to dry.

"Is that so?" Logan couldn't help teasing her. As Nessia's little sister, Cait felt like his little sister, as well.

"Aye," Cait nodded proudly, her straight brunette hair shaking off droplets of rain where the wetness had managed to evade her shawl.

"And how is it to be a parlor maid?"

"Most of the time, pretty scary." Cait rolled her eyes. "Except when I get to cater to Sheena. She's always very nice to me."

"Sheena?" Since when did Cait work for Sheena? Surely in the time since Logan's homecoming Angus might have mentioned something that important. He shot his brother a look.

"Aye," Cait answered.

"The two older women can be a bit brutish." Angus wrinkled his nose as if their behavior bore a foul odor.

"But not just to me." Cait looked from Angus to Logan. "They're pretty horrible to Sheena, too, when it suits them." Logan's face fell.

"What two older women?" His brain tried to put the puzzle together, but he couldn't without all the pieces. And apparently, after five years away, he couldn't assume anything anymore. Not even something as simple as Sheena still living with her parents in the house where she grew up. Sheena told him everything had changed. But what exactly did that entail?

Angus's voice brought Logan's thoughts back to the present. "The two older women are Sheena's mother, Tavia, and her aunt Jean." That only brought to light more questions. If she lived with her mother and aunt, where had her father and brother gone?

Cait spoke up then. "I'd like to give Tavia and Jean a good tongue lashing one of these days."

"You'd better not." Nessia wrapped a floor-length shawl around her nightgown as she moved into the circle. All the commotion had awakened her. "You mind your place in that house, Cait. It is a good station for you."

"Aye," Cait replied, as a reprimanded child would to her mother.

"Logan, may I have a word with you?" Angus nudged his head in the direction of the door and Logan nodded.

"But I've just come," Cait pouted.

"We'll have time together." Logan pinched her cheek. "You don't think we'd let you go anywhere alone at this hour, do you?" Logan stepped toward his brother. "I'll take you back. So we'll catch up then, right?" Her good humor resurfaced before she turned to face her older sister.

"I know this is asking too much, but what about Cait?" Angus whispered, safely out of earshot. "We could never leave without her. And we have practically nothing to sell to raise money."

"Angus, I've made arrangements for seven of us to go. I would never think of leaving Cait behind. I've always considered her my family, too." Logan squeezed his brother's shoulder, but Angus looked strangely discomfited.

"I don't understand." Angus stared down at his fingers, using them to calculate something. "I count one extra person. We're only six." He looked up at Logan, his face full of confusion. "You, me, Nessia, Ewan, Duncan, and Cait. Six."

Logan smiled at him. "You've forgotten Sheena."

Angus took a small step back in bewilderment. "You expect her to go with you?"

"I expect a lot from her, and marrying me is at the top of that list."

"Logan, Sheena's mother never thought of you as a good match for Sheena. You'll have a difficult time convincing them otherwise." Angus shook his head.

"Aye. So I've come to find out since being back." Logan's mind floated to his meeting with Sheena at their waterfall. "More than you know." Logan lowered his head toward his brother to make sure he would hear him even in his hushed tone. "I might as well tell you now. We've only got two weeks left in Scotland before we set sail."

Angus's jaw dropped, but Logan kept talking. "A

few of us promised the other men we'd bring letters back to their families, so we divvied them up and I took the bunch for Glasgow. I should have already delivered them, but with Gordon McDougall's death, I had to come straight home to Callander. Now we have just about a week to say goodbye to this village before we head to Glasgow. Our ship departs from there and I need time to deliver these letters."

"A week. Only a week?" Angus raised his eyebrows. But Logan didn't even know if Angus could keep up a coherent conversation anymore, because he just kept mumbling, "a week." Nevertheless, Logan nodded once to Angus's rhetorical question before Nessia broke into their huddle.

"I don't know what you two are talking about, but Cait must be returned to the Montgomerys' house immediately. She's only allowed a limited amount of free time on Sundays. I can't believe she risked her job to come here on a Saturday night. She should have just waited to see you in church tomorrow, Logan. If someone finds out she is missing, she will lose her post. Then what will she do?"

Angus and Logan exchanged a knowing look. They knew exactly what they wanted Cait to do.

Chapter Four

"So what are the Americas like, Logan?" Cait asked as they made their way to the Montgomery household.

"I stayed mostly in a place they originally called New Inverness, and even though it shares the same name as Inverness, not much else is the same as the Highlands. For one, it's a lot warmer there." Even on this spring night, he hugged himself against the wet chill soaking into every inch of his body. "Anyway, now they call it Darien, and it's in one of the most southern colonies in the Americas, known as Georgia."

"I can't even imagine it." Cait shivered as she sighed. At least it had stopped raining. "I wish I could envision it all."

Logan looked over at her. "Would you like to go there?" He broached the subject carefully.

"Are you joking?" Cait rolled her eyes. "I'd give anything to be able to live life the way I want to. Have my own home with a husband and children, instead of working in someone else's house as a parlor maid." Cait blushed. "Like Nessia."

"Aye, Nessia and Angus are lucky." Logan looked straight ahead into the darkness—he wanted the same blissful life with Sheena. "You're still young, Cait. Do you even have a young man?" Immediately Cait looked down at her shoes, shaking her head. "You don't?"

"I think I would know if I did, Logan." She crossed her arms. "Please don't tease me about it. I already feel terrible that in all my twenty years no man has ever seen me the way Angus looks at Nessia."

"Cait, I didn't mean to tease. The right man will show up someday." Logan smiled at her. "But I am happy to hear that you're unattached."

"Logan, you are not the type of person to take pleasure in the unhappiness of others." Cait still didn't look at him.

"Nay. You know me well enough. But you do not know my plans." Logan let out a whistle into the quiet night air.

"Please tell me." Cait grabbed his arm, making Logan unable to keep her in suspense any longer.

"I want us all to go to the Americas together. Angus, Nessia, their wee ones, you and Sheena. I'll pay your way, Cait, if you want to come with us."

Logan watched Cait's expression and she beamed. "If Nessia's going, so will I."

"Perfect." Logan's face shone, too. "Angus still has to consult with Nessia, but hopefully she'll see it as we do. It will be a better life for all of us. And there are lots of unattached men in the Americas, so you'll have your pick of eligible bachelors."

Cait shot him a less-than-amused look, but perked up quickly enough. "This is like a dream. It just doesn't seem real." Logan thought she might actually break into a jig. Not that he would stop her.

"We're leaving Scotland." Cait giggled. "I don't think I'll be able to sleep tonight."

"I'm glad to hear it." Logan's spirits lifted. "Not the sleeplessness—that's not what I meant." He laughed, but Cait didn't even notice, as she seemed deep in thought about something else.

"I can't believe Sheena never told me anything about these plans. It was only too kind of her to tell me that you came home, but she left this part out entirely."

"That's because she doesn't know yet. I haven't actually been able to talk to her about my idea." Logan lowered his voice. "It seems a lot has changed with her since I've been gone."

"Aye. You hurt her so much when you left. But you must not give up on her. Get her to forgive you. You have loved her your whole life. And I know she loved you, too. You must get her to love you again."

"So you know she does not love me anymore?" The words tasted bitter coming out of his mouth.

"Nay, I think she still loves you. Even if she may argue differently." Cait stopped and grabbed hold of Logan's shoulder. "Logan, I must let her tell you herself what has become of her, because she swore me to secrecy. But I can tell you this, on Monday her aunt Jean came from

Glasgow to visit for a week or so. Jean's been doing this on and off for almost a year now. But this time Jean brought Sheena some news that changed the course of Sheena's life."

Cait let go of Logan's shoulder, shaking her head. "If only you had come a month earlier, Logan. Then maybe none of this would have happened to her."

Logan couldn't bear waiting to find out what news Cait withheld. But he couldn't ask her to break Sheena's trust. He knew what keeping a secret entailed. He'd kept one all this time at Sheena's father's behest.

"Don't look at me like that, Logan. I can't tell you. But Sheena will. Just give her a chance, and remember—when you do find out, nothing has been done that can't be undone."

Logan nodded unenthusiastically. Winning Sheena's love back seemed harder than he ever imagined. Was this change the one Sheena had alluded to at their waterfall? The event that had changed her whole life? He must find out.

"Don't despair, Logan." Cait squeezed his hand. "God will help you. I know He will."

They fell silent as they neared the quiet two-story house. Creeping up behind a mound of rocks several feet from the white house, they sought to avoid peering eyes, if any existed.

"Cait? Is that you?" a whispered voice called out from the darkness.

Cait called back just as quietly, "Sheena?"

"Aye." Logan heard Sheena's footsteps making their

way toward the sound of Cait's voice. He kept silent. He didn't want her running away again. He wanted so badly to get near her. To talk to her, see her smile, hear her laugh. He missed her so much. Why did the sight of him at their waterfall send her running away, crying?

As Sheena's footsteps grew louder, Logan grew more tense. He desperately wanted things to work out between them. He needed to explain, to do whatever it took to win back her love.

He kept still and listened to her talk to Cait, waiting for the right time to make his presence known.

"I've been standing guard ever since you slipped out. I left the door open for you to get back in." Logan smiled to himself. Finally, the Sheena he knew and loved.

"Sheena, you didn't have to wait out here. You've put yourself in peril for me. But I won't let my foolishness be the cause of you getting into any trouble," Cait told her.

Sheena shrugged off Cait's concern. "Not to worry. We could stay out until dawn and no one would be the wiser."

"If that's so…" Logan's voice startled Sheena and she let out a squeal. In a fraction of a second, Logan grabbed her and put his hand over her mouth so that her sound wouldn't carry to the windows above. His whispered words came out calmly, even though he hardly felt serene. "I suggest you and I take this opportunity to talk, lassie."

"I'll stand guard by the door." Cait didn't give Sheena a chance to refuse her offer.

"Harrumph." Sheena's exclamation sent heat into Logan's hand and he released her mouth instantly.

"Sorry." He remained close to her. It took all his willpower not to kiss her. He'd wanted to from the moment he saw her standing on the edge of their waterfall and now with her so close, he wanted her even closer.

"It's all right." Sheena tried to gather her auburn hair and Logan wished she wouldn't. He liked it hanging loose. "I didn't know you were here. You could have said something earlier."

Logan could see the muscles on Sheena's face tighten in the moonlight and it made him smile. "So far since I've been back, lassie, I've stopped your heart two or three times."

"Aye." Sheena pulled her dark blue woolen shawl taut. "You need to learn how to introduce yourself properly."

"Apparently." Logan laughed, even though he did so alone.

"Thank you for bringing Cait home safely." Sheena stretched out her hand. But Logan didn't take it. Even though an excuse to touch her held tremendous appeal.

"Cait thanked me herself. No need for you to, lassie." He wouldn't let this fortunate circumstance end so quickly. After five long years away from her, he never wanted to be away from her again. Not even for five minutes.

"You must stop calling me lassie. I am not your sweetheart."

He leaned toward her. "Since when Sheena? You have always been my lassie."

"Since you left. I've already told you—everything

changed when you left. We can't keep revisiting the past." She gave him her back.

"We can, and we will, until I change your mind." Frustrated at her rejection of him, he knew he sounded too harsh, but he couldn't help himself. She'd never talked to him like this before. Never treated him with so much contempt. Had he lost his best friend—the soul mate he felt God had put in his life?

"You can't just come back here and expect that nothing changed in five years. There have been battles and death, and so much else." The wind picked up again and Sheena whirled around trying to tame her hair. It looked as fiery as her temper and just as unmanageable.

"You left, Mr. McAllister. No one made you. You just left." Sheena pointed at him and then shook her head. "Nobody comes back from the Americas. Once you left, you were as good as dead to me." Why didn't she just stick a dagger in him? It would hurt less.

But he wouldn't slink away and give up on her. He would fight for her. He just needed to figure out what exactly to fight. "Sheena, I told you I would come back. Did you not believe me?" Logan inched ever closer to her, fearing she would dart away at any moment.

"I didn't receive anything from you. I didn't know if you were even still alive." So his absence had scared her, and that angered her. At least she felt something. He could use that, push further.

"There was no way of sending you information," Logan pleaded. He couldn't waste any money writing a letter her mother would probably rip up before it even reached Sheena. He had to stay in the Americas and work an extra two years past his three-year indenturement to be able to save enough money for seven sea voyages to the Americas.

"But you were only indentured for three years. After that, why didn't you come home?" Sheena looked impatient with him.

"I couldn't." He knew how bad that sounded.

"You couldn't or you wouldn't?" Sheena crossed her arms, shifting her weight to rest on her left leg, waiting for his answer. If she tapped her right foot, he didn't hear it.

Logan hesitated, knowing she wouldn't like his answer. "Both." He didn't lie to her. He'd never do that.

Sheena's arms dropped and she shouted, "You could have come home, but you didn't."

"Keep your voice down. Do you want to wake up the whole house?" Yelling in the face of possible detection from her family proved just how deep Sheena's feelings ran. If she didn't love him, his indenturement and extended stay in the Americas wouldn't have bothered her this much.

But then why did she keep pushing him away?

"Logan, why are you doing this?" Sheena lowered her voice to a snarl.

"Why am I doing this? What do you mean? Why did I keep my promise to return? You know me, Sheena. You know I always keep my promises." He reached out his hands and this time she didn't step away.

Touching her gave him more confidence. She let

him in. He moved another step closer, pulling her to him. "I'm sorry. It took longer than I thought before I could return. But I never forgot about you." He brushed a strand of her auburn hair behind her ear, as he lowered his voice. "Don't turn your back on me."

Logan saw emotion flicker across her face. She fought with herself. He didn't know what she fought, but he knew he somehow got through her barrier. She softened. "Logan, you left before all the fighting broke out. I expected you home in three years. But instead, the year you should have returned, I lost my brother. He died at the Battle of Culloden in 1746."

"I'm sorry." Logan rubbed her arm, but she shrugged it off, turning away.

"Nay, it's not your fault my brother died. He supported Bonnie Prince Charlie's claim to rule Britain and died trying to regain the monarchy for the House of Stuart. But whether he was right or wrong to give up his life for a cause that failed, he was my parents' only son and his death killed a part of my father." Logan saw Sheena's hand reach up toward her face, wiping tears away. "My father never recovered."

Logan stepped forward. He wanted to hug her. To hold her and make all her pain go away, but he knew he couldn't. Too early. He needed to win her trust back. So he gently clasped her shoulders with a caressing gesture.

At first, he felt her shoulders rise and stiffen, but then they relaxed and he rubbed them both, trying to comfort her. "Is that why your aunt is here?" He spoke quietly, his face inches from the back of her head. He almost couldn't stand the sweet smell of her hair. How many times did he dream about this closeness to her? He loved her so much that holding back hurt.

"Aye. Nay." Sheena shook her head as if confused. "After my brother's death not even our livelihood mattered to my father anymore. It's progressed to the point now where we only have enough to run our household to the end of this month. We have no money left, Logan. My father just kept sinking deeper and deeper into his own world and we lost everything, along with him."

Sheena turned back to Logan, hugging herself snug in her dark blue woolen shawl against the encroaching mist. Logan let his hands drop to his sides. "This past autumn he fell ill and we tried everything to make him better. We even bought him spa water to drink from Bath in England, but it didn't help him. He died."

Logan couldn't believe that Arthur Montgomery had died. When Logan left five years ago, Arthur ran the Montgomery household as efficiently and astutely as any great man. By now his age would accumulate to fifty years—surely everyone had expected him to enjoy many more good years.

And yet, Arthur's death had other repercussions, as well. Only he and Logan knew about what they'd discussed at that meeting when Logan had asked to marry Sheena. And only they knew about the Montgomery's heirloom box that housed the secret letter Arthur had given Logan, promising that Logan could marry Sheena if he returned to Scotland after his indenturement in the Americas.

What would become of Arthur's promise to Logan if he was no longer alive to enforce it?

Maybe it didn't matter anymore. Logan loved Sheena and as soon as she forgave him, perhaps they could go back to the way things stood between them before he left. Maybe Logan could convince Sheena's mother that he would take good care of her. Logan had by now amassed enough money to satisfy Tavia's wishes for her daughter to live a good life. He just needed Sheena to love him again.

"I'm sorry, lassie. And I'm sorry you had to witness the McDougalls' grief today. It must have brought back many of those painful memories. If I had known, I would have spared you that experience."

Logan knew that pain. Having lost both of his parents at a young age, he was aware that nothing ever filled that void again. Try as they might, Angus and Nessia never could.

"Today did bring it all back, Logan, but I can't hide from death. It's a part of life and, besides, the McDougalls needed us to comfort them."

"Your comforting words meant everything to me today, too."

Sheena gave Logan a little smile. "I'm glad."

Her opening up to him eased the pain in his chest, giving him some hope for their future. "I hope your father, brother and Gordon are at peace in God's home."

Again, Sheena wiped a tear from her cheek. "Thank you. I pray for that every day."

Logan hated seeing her unhappy. "I'll pray, too. Just

as I pray you forgive me for coming back two years later than I planned."

Sheena's expression changed. "Logan…" She said his name with the sparkle he remembered seeing in her amber eyes before he'd left Scotland five years ago. In that moment, he knew he had a chance. She couldn't hide that spark. He took hold of her shoulders and leaned in even closer to talk with her.

Tenderly, he whispered his words to her, "I wish I could have been here to comfort you through your brother's death and your father's illness. But I had to stay on in the Americas."

Sheena interrupted him before he could tell her about his plans to take everyone to the Americas. "You wouldn't have been able to change anything anyway." Sheena tilted her head down toward the soggy ground. Her head almost touched his chest. It wouldn't take any effort to deepen their embrace. And his muscles flexed as he fought the urge to do so.

"Maybe not, but I could have made it easier for you to live during the difficult times." Logan reached out and gently pushed up her chin to level her eyes with his. "I've always been poor. I know how to make do. I could have shown you," he said, smiling.

She opened her lips to say something, but then closed them. He felt her sweet breath against his face and fancied smelling her delicate scent. He wanted nothing more than to comfort her and be her protector.

"I could show you which weeds won't kill you." He made fun of himself, knowing just how many times his family did eat weeds at mealtime. But Sheena turned her head away from his hand.

"My mother is not about to admit that she's poor, let alone live like the poor." Sheena drew in a long breath as if she wanted to apologize for Tavia.

But her words didn't shock Logan. They didn't even hurt him. He knew very well what Tavia thought. Some things never changed and Tavia's dislike of the poor would always be one of them. Indeed he knew Tavia's hatred so well that five years ago, his only option in ever marrying Sheena included selling himself as an indentured servant.

The scariest and most humiliating thing Logan ever did, and hopefully would ever do in his life, involved letting someone buy him. But he did it. And he would do it again, because he now possessed the means to offer Sheena a decent life as his wife. He just needed her forgiveness.

"Logan, just after my father died, when we still looked like we were wealthy…" She looked up into Logan's face, her amber eyes filled with worry. No sparks now. In their place Logan saw a look of pity. What had caused such a quick change in her demeanor? "…my mother spent the last of our money on my dowry and betrothed me."

The news hit Logan with the force of a fist. And all too soon, rage ran through his blood. "You're betrothed?" he shouted. "To whom?"

"Logan, your voice." Sheena grabbed his hand and pulled him down toward the ground.

"You can't be betrothed to someone else." Logan took hold of her arms.

"It's true," Sheena whispered softly, and Logan just stared at her. He couldn't understand what she'd just told him. Did she mean to hurt him, out of revenge or simply to break his heart for good?

Her insistence that he quiet down came too late. A light shone out from one of the rooms upstairs. Someone had woken up.

"You must go. Now. No one can find you here. Not out here at this hour." Sheena pried his fingers from her arms, talking as if seized by anxiety. "Go, Logan. Please." She sprang away from him, jogging toward Cait.

Logan tried to reach for her again, but didn't catch her in time. Impulsively, he thought about chasing her and carrying her away. She couldn't love another man. She couldn't want this betrothal.

God, why did this happen? It couldn't truly be Your plan to let me live through two sea voyages and five long, hard years of labor, just to lead me to the knowledge I gained tonight.

The light from many more candles began to shine through the windows on the main floor, interrupting Logan's thoughts as he realized people from within the household were approaching. He ducked farther behind the rocks. He didn't think he could remain still. His insides beat hard against his skin, trying to burst out. Life as he knew it had ended. And he couldn't do anything about it.

Chapter Five

Sheena just reached Cait's side when the door of her family's home flew open. She grabbed Cait's hand quickly to reassure her. But Cait's hand shook and Sheena knew the chilly damp night air didn't cause her trembling. Sheena felt her insides churn with guilt; she hated putting Cait in such a predicament.

She thought of pulling Cait to hide, but Tavia and Jean would send servants to look for the source of the noise. Someone would find them. And then, what if they discovered Logan, as well? That would make the situation even worse. Her family wouldn't welcome Logan, even in daylight.

Sheena inched in front of Cait to shield her as light from too many candles shone out through the darkness. Sheena and Cait stood motionless. Waiting. Someone obviously had set off quite an alarm, because everyone who slept in the Montgomery household now stood outside on the soggy grounds in their nightclothes.

"Cait? Sheena?" Jean's voice shattered the quiet of

the night as soon as she spotted them. "What is going on out here?"

Tavia came around to her sister's side. "Sheena, what on earth are you doing out of doors at this hour?"

Tavia didn't even finish her words before her sister broke in. "Cait, you foolish girl. You are not to be out of the house. You may as well stay out."

"Aunt Jean," Sheena rushed to Cait's defense. "Please, you cannot send Cait away. She was out here because of me." Sheena couldn't let Cait take the blame. Her inability to resist talking with Logan caused all this. Why couldn't she just walk away from him? He'd hurt her too deeply and her life had shifted course.

She shook her head, putting her thoughts at bay, as her mother pointed a finger at her. "Cait's out here because of you?" Tavia's voice hit a high note of accusation.

"Aye, Mother."

"Sheena, I am out of patience with you. It is not even dawn yet. I need my sleep. Instead, I am standing outside in the dampness. I could catch my death." She tugged at the red woolen blanket that almost swallowed her tiny frame whole.

"I'm sorry, Mother," Sheena said, only vaguely listening to her mother's lecture. Her attention remained fixed several feet away. She prayed God would help Logan stay hidden behind those rocks. Her mother would go crazy if Logan appeared. And then what would she do to Sheena?

Tavia already thought little of Sheena. They'd never

nurtured anything resembling a close mother-daughter relationship. Sheena always seemed to disappoint her mother. They thought and acted as opposites in nearly everything, and though she knew her mother wanted nothing more than for Sheena to behave just as she did, Sheena never could.

"Explain yourself, child," Jean bellowed and Sheena panicked. What explanation could ease the situation? She couldn't lie and yet she couldn't tell them the truth, either. "We're waiting." Jean stamped her foot.

"Why are you not speaking?" Tavia raised her right hand and slapped Sheena firmly across the face. "Such insolence. Answer your aunt." The blow knocked Sheena off balance.

Touching her flaming-hot cheek, Sheena felt tears swell at the sting and pain, but she stood bravely to face her mother and aunt. She had endured worse. A slap would not stop her from seeing to Cait's well-being.

"I needed some fresh air." Sheena didn't lie. Leaving a rock to keep the door ajar for Cait didn't quench her need for the open air. It beckoned to her, making her go outside to sit and think about Logan. Forcing her to confront her upside-down life.

"Is the air in the house not fresh enough for you, child?" Jean pressed. And Sheena had barely glanced at her aunt before her mother started again.

"Why didn't you just open your window?"

"I'm sorry. I will do that next time." With spring advancing she would need to, because soon enough the midges would come out in droves and make it impossible for people to sit still outside in the dark, unless they wanted to get bitten repeatedly by those annoying insects.

Sheena looked around at everyone's faces. "I apologize for having caused such commotion and awakening you all." Some servants looked too tired to care, obviously longing for their beds, while others seemed full of sympathy. But a few, all of whom belonged to Jean, seemed completely amused, and that callousness irked Sheena.

"Can you imagine what would happen if news of this incident reached Ian Mackenzie? I will not have him thinking you are a wild Highlander who runs about in the night. Until you are married to Ian, this foolishness of yours must stop. I will not tolerate it. Then I don't care what you do. Ian will have to deal with you on his own. However he sees fit." Tavia's words stung, just as much as her slap.

"Aye, Mother." Sheena bit her lip. "I'm sorry." She bowed her head not wanting to look at anyone. The only person who mattered couldn't see her face anyway. Even though he likely heard every word. And although she wished she could, she couldn't prevent that. She knew she'd hurt Logan deeply only moments before and now her mother forced him to hear about her betrothal again.

Her insides felt as if osprey hawks dove into them. Logan's stricken face flashed in front of her eyes and would likely remain permanently etched into her memory. He had looked utterly devastated. For him, for her, for the future they'd planned so many years ago that now lay in ruins.

As angry as she was, she never thought she would be the one to deal such a savage blow. Tears pricked at the thought.

But hurting Logan served a purpose. Maybe now he would understand she could never love him again. He needed to know she belonged to another man. She couldn't hide that from him. He needed to forge a life for himself without her. Just as she did when he hadn't come back two years ago.

She'd begun to believe that Logan had never intended to marry her in the first place. That he'd never planned to come back to Scotland at all. Maybe his guilt in telling her lies had caused him to flee the country.

"Let us all go back to bed and not talk of this ever again. I will not have word of this incident getting out." Tavia eyed the staff, much of which were on loan from Jean to keep their house functioning.

"If word of this does get out—" Jean stared them down "—all of you will be dismissed. You are all replaceable." At that, Tavia grabbed Sheena's arm and dragged her into the house, as Cait scurried into the throng of servants.

Hastily, Sheena wiped tears off her cheeks. Tavia would never know the true cause of those tears.

Logan remained painfully still. He knew if anyone saw him, Sheena and Cait would face a much more brutal fate. Crammed against a rock, his anger raged, steaming into the cold night air.

When Tavia hit Sheena, he almost ran to her defense, but something held him back. Even if it killed him to stay hidden, he'd rather give up his own life than sacrifice her future status.

Not being able to defend Sheena filled him with hate. As a Christian, he shouldn't feel that way toward anyone, but he couldn't help it. Tavia slapped Sheena when Sheena did nothing to deserve such punishment. What kind of mother behaved like that? One who didn't care whether her daughter's husband beat her or not. And one who seemed to welcome that fate for her daughter.

Logan remembered Tavia being cold toward Sheena her entire life, but never to this extent. At least Tavia had never conducted herself in public this way before. But maybe she couldn't in front of Sheena's father. He wouldn't have allowed it. But now with him gone, Tavia's true feelings were revealed, and Logan feared them for Sheena's sake.

Chapter Six

As the door to the Montgomerys' house closed, Logan thrust himself from the rock to stand at his full height. Only then did he realize his hands bled. He stared at them for a moment in disbelief. He'd injured them on the jagged edges of the rock that separated him from Sheena as he leaned against it, pushing with all his strength to maintain his self-control.

The bloody cuts annoyed more than they hurt, serving as a reminder of the hate coursing through his veins. He held his hands up trying to stop the bleeding, using his sleeves to dab at the blood as he made his way home.

"Logan?" Angus's voice whispered from the dim light of the fire when Logan came through the door.

"Aye." Logan went over to his brother's side by the dying flames and sat on the wooden stool next to him. He welcomed the solitary walk home, for it had given him time to calm down.

But in place of the anger came despondency. He felt like a soldier on the losing side of a battle. "I'm sorry if

I woke you Angus." He leaned forward, putting his head into his bloodstained hands and closing his eyes. He kept his head down. Did he make everyone's life more miserable? It certainly seemed that way.

"Nay. On the contrary. I've been too excited to sleep." Angus's enthusiasm glowed brighter than the flames. "Nessia was in complete shock when I first told her of your plans, but after I explained everything you'd said, she agreed. She sees the advantage. It's an opportunity for a better life. Did you talk to Cait about it? Is she coming? Because we can't leave her behind."

Despite himself, Logan's lips twitched slightly upward at the pair of opposites they made: Angus, with his hope for the future and Logan with his belief in a future devoid of anything worthwhile.

Resting his face on his weathered hands, because he couldn't summon the energy to lift his head, he answered, "I spoke with Cait and she will be onboard."

Angus just about jumped off his stool. And that made Logan look up. "Angus, you must contain yourself." Irritation tinged Logan's voice, even though he would never begrudge his brother his happiness.

Hopelessness wrapped itself around Logan's heart, leaving him more fatigued than any day of hard physical labor had ever left him.

"Aye. Did Cait make it home all right?" Angus's solemnity touched Logan. He didn't want his brother to set his own happiness aside for him. And he surely did not want anyone to pity him.

"Aye, no harm came to her. I wish I could say the

same for Sheena, though." Logan shook his head as if he could somehow shake away what happened.

"Sheena?" Angus looked at Logan without understanding. "What did she have to do with Cait tonight?"

"Sheena was looking out for her and got herself into trouble." Logan stared off at the dark sod wall. "Actually, I got Sheena into the whole mess." How could he forgive himself for being the cause of Sheena receiving such torment?

"You?"

"Aye. It's a long story. One I don't want to relive." Logan stretched out his legs and then his arms. "Angus, why didn't you tell me Sheena's father and brother had died?"

"I didn't get the chance. With you so upset about Gordon's death and needing sleep, you seemed to have enough to contend with. I thought it could wait."

"Aye." Logan understood his brother's reasoning. They hadn't had nearly enough time to talk since he'd come home. Plenty of other things probably still remained for Angus to tell him from his five-year absence.

And besides, Logan had never told his brother about his private meeting with Sheena's father or the letter. Back then and even now, Angus would never have let Logan accept Sheena's father's terms. And Logan had been desperate to prove his love.

"I found out something tonight that almost made my heart stop beating." Angus leaned closer. "Sheena is betrothed."

"Betrothed? To whom?" Angus's gut reaction met with an unnatural laugh from Logan.

"That is exactly what I said." Logan tilted his head back until he looked up at the thatched roof. "Only you were able to keep your reaction in check, so as not to wake your whole household, and I shouted at the top of my lungs, like a madman."

"Logan, I am deeply sorry. This must have happened just this week or Cait would have told us last Sunday at church. I definitely would have made the time to tell you that. Are you sure about this?"

"Aye. His name is Ian Mackenzie." Logan rubbed his eyes. "And I'm going to guess that he's a wealthy gentleman."

Angus frowned at Logan's tone. "Have the terms of the marriage already been agreed upon?"

Logan nodded. "Sheena's dowry has already been paid."

"Logan, you know that a betrothal cannot be broken. She is as good as married." Logan sat motionless, not wanting to hear what his brother said, even though he knew the truth behind it. "She won't be coming with us to the Americas." The still darkness of the night crept over them as the flames in the fire died down and almost ceased. "I am so sorry, Logan."

Angus reached over to pat Logan's arm, but Logan didn't want Angus's condolences. Being told the life he always imagined living with Sheena couldn't ever come true struck Logan, jolting him out of his stasis.

"Angus, I did not come this far to give up." Logan

leapt off his stool with such force that Angus almost fell from his. "I know that Sheena is supposed to be my wife. I will put my trust in God." Logan paused. "I think I still may have a way to end all this." And hope blossomed within him again.

"What?" Angus sat transfixed, looking up at him. "You cannot break a betrothal, Logan." A huge smile tore across Logan's face.

"In most cases that is true, but not in mine."

Angus looked as confused as ever as Logan told him about the box Sheena's father had given him.

"Aye. If we can find that letter, it'll prove that Sheena's father betrothed her to you first and make her betrothal to Ian void. But without Sheena's father to substantiate your claims, what if the letter doesn't hold any legal force anymore? Someone could argue that it's a forgery."

"Maybe, but I'll show it to everyone from Ian to Tavia. Someone will care enough to honor Arthur's wishes that I marry Sheena. And if no one else does, I have to believe that Sheena will accept the letter."

"Then let's take advantage of what little night there is left. We can start looking for it in the morning." Angus patted Logan's back. "I'll pray for you, Logan. And for Sheena. I suspect you'll both need all the help you can get from God."

"Aye. God won't desert us now. He can't."

As the sun rose to new life on Sunday morning, Logan crept out of their one-room dwelling quietly, not wanting to awaken anyone. He'd awoken refreshed, even though he didn't sleep nearly as much as he thought his body required.

But how could he waste time sleeping? He would leave Scotland in two weeks. Filling his lungs with cool morning air he surveyed the green-and-brown countryside. The ground, solid and steady under his feet, felt good. Too many days sailing across the Atlantic Ocean with the boat's constant rocking motion made him appreciate the stillness of the morning shining before him all the more. He walked around to the back of their hut to find a shovel.

"Uncle Logan." Ewan's voice carried across the field sometime later to where Logan stood near a hole in the earth.

The lad ran as clumsily as if he trod on needles. "Uncle Logan." Ewan's chest heaved when he reached Logan, a good distance from their small hut.

The lad obviously only wore footwear for Sunday service and they irritated him. "Ma said that if you don't come now you won't be ready for church and then we'll all be late."

"Is it time already?" Logan asked rhetorically, stifling a laugh at how worried Ewan looked that Logan risked trouble from Nessia.

He jammed his shovel into the dirt as hard as he could to mark his place for when he returned. He knew he would come back and dig for as long as it took. This is where he'd buried the box before he left for the Americas five years ago. Why couldn't he find it?

Logan sighed. "We'd better go." He rushed back home with Ewan to humor him. A fine lad—Angus and Nessia had done something right.

"There now. We're all dressed and ready to go." Nessia moved Duncan's hands away from his shoes and stood him up straight. He obviously didn't wear shoes regularly, either. "We must hurry so we won't be late." Nessia looked at each lad sternly.

"Aye, Ma," the lads said, almost in unison, and Logan led the way through the countryside toward the church so they wouldn't see the smile he couldn't suppress.

Nessia definitely knew how to keep her children in line. A skill Logan could attest as invaluable for a voyage to the Americas. And Logan pictured them all in the Americas, happy. He hoped he had the chance to have his own family with Sheena.

"Logan." He heard his name called so many times he lost count. And his arms didn't fall to his sides until everyone he had known since birth received a hug. The enormous welcome left him with a pang of guilt. How could he not feel sad, knowing he would leave again so soon? And not just him this time, but his whole family. He wished he could take all his clansmen with them. These good people deserved better than war and impoverishment.

"You must stay after church, Logan," said Mrs. Buchanan, Callander's most beloved matron and one of his family's oldest and dearest friends. "We will celebrate your homecoming." She spoke from a group of people gathered by the door.

Logan nodded. He wanted very much to speak to all of them, too. To tell them about the farming practices he'd learned in the Americas. He hoped he could persuade them to change their farming methods and better their lives here.

When the time came, the members filed into the church, leaving Logan standing by the entrance. He didn't intend to go in yet. He would wait for Sheena's family. Tavia may live as a monster at home, but that wouldn't stop her from attending church. She'd keep up appearances. Logan almost spat on the ground in disgust, but the sight of Sheena's carriage stopped him. It parked out of sight, on the other side of the church. Logan waited.

Hope rose in his chest as it always did whenever Sheena neared. He wanted to go to her. But that wouldn't happen, not with her mother nearby. However, it wouldn't stop him from trying.

"Mr. McAllister." Jean Kerr's large frame came around the corner first and bustled past him into the church with a curt nod. Logan stretched his lips politely, amused Sheena's aunt Jean remembered him after all these years. She'd aged a little, but unfortunately her dreadful personality remained intact. Time hadn't changed her for the better.

"Mr. McAllister." Sheena's pint-size mother parroted her sister. Neither gave Logan time to respond as they scurried away from him. But that suited Logan just fine, seeing as he couldn't come up with anything nice to say to either of them anyway. They'd always treated him with rudeness, but he never imagined they behaved that way toward Sheena until he saw it for himself last night.

More servants passed him before he spotted Cait. His eagerness now remained barely under control, because he knew he would find Sheena near Cait. Sheena must have been the last one out of the carriage. And then he saw Sheena. His eyes met hers, the only ones he longed to see. The reason his heart still beat in his chest. "Good morning, lassie." Logan stepped in front of the doorway and grinned at her.

"Mr. McAllister." Sheena spoke too seriously for Logan's liking. If she was embarrassed by last night, she shouldn't be. She'd acted honorably. She didn't deserve to get hit. And she didn't warrant Logan's ire for telling him the truth.

He wouldn't let her feel uncomfortable around him. How could he ever win her back if they weren't on speaking terms?

"I'm sorry about last night."

Sheena ripped her eyes from his. "I'm sorry, too." She entered the church without another word.

Maybe she didn't hate him. Probably didn't even blame him for last night, either. For as long as he could remember, Sheena never got angry and never held a grudge against anyone. She always saw the good, or at least tried to work the good out of people.

But would she forgive him if he went into the church right now and yanked her out in front of her family? He so wanted to talk to her. Get her alone again. End her betrothal to this Ian Mackenzie. His heart screamed for him to do it, but his mind yelled louder. And he knew he couldn't kidnap her from church today.

Logan turned, with a smile for Cait's benefit. She grinned back at him encouragingly as he took her arm and led her into church.

"It's nice to have you home." Cait squeezed his arm and he knew she understood his pain and tried to cheer him up.

Logan longed to sit with Sheena. But he never did that. He always stood.

The separation from Sheena in church had never bothered him before. Their bond always seemed to extend over the distance and left it meaningless. However, today, for the first time, he actually felt the gap. Now he found himself in a position where he must fight to regain that stronghold.

And then an idea struck him. Did Ian attend this church? Logan looked around to see if he noticed anyone eyeing Sheena. But he only met with smiles and nods from neighbors.

Everyone looked at him, except Sheena. What could he do to change that? His thoughts turned to God. If ever a man needed help, it was now.

"Amen," the congregation said in unison. Exiting the stuffy building, Logan wanted to head straight for Sheena, but he couldn't. Everyone nursed a healthy fascination with the Americas and wanted his attention.

So what could he do? He talked while keeping an eye on Sheena. He didn't know how or when he would get another opportunity to see her again. He couldn't just show up on her doorstep. He didn't know her wedding date. Surely, she wouldn't marry without telling him? But why not?

Turning his eyes downward, Logan wrestled with his thoughts. Did Sheena see him as a childhood friend? A first love? Nothing? Logan's stomach lurched. She meant everything to him. Without her... Nay. He couldn't even think about his life without her in it. Absolutely nothing to live for.

"Logan, tell us more about New Inverness." Mrs. Buchanan stressed the word *new* comically, but it still didn't raise Logan's eyes from the dirt.

"Aye, Logan." He almost snapped his neck, looking up so fast into the only face who could own such a sweet, melodic voice.

Chapter Seven

Sheena broke into the group huddled around Logan. Not an easy maneuver on her part and he was impressed. How many people did she skip around to get to him?

All the same, there she stood smiling at him with a teasing expression. "Please, Logan, do tell us more about the Americas." Logan stared in disbelief. She came to him. He could only hope she came by the same force that always propelled him to her, love.

"What more can I say? Beautiful." His eyes sparkled and danced after seeing her cheeks flush. He hoped she knew he spoke of her.

"There must be more to it than that," Mrs. Buchanan broke in, oblivious to Logan's true meaning.

Logan nevertheless elaborated, without taking his eyes off Sheena. "It's warm, and opportunity abounds for those willing to work hard. A husband and wife can settle on a fair bit of land, build themselves a cabin and raise a family, living off the fertile earth. A married couple could be very happy there."

Sheena looked away. Did she know this description depicted his vision of their life together? She couldn't, he reminded himself. He'd never told her about his dream for their future in the Americas. And yet, her cheeks remained pink.

"Sheena," Jean screeched above the chatter. "It is well past time we go." Sheena started at her aunt's words, then waved a farewell to the surrounding company and made her way to Tavia without another glance at Logan.

"Cait, are you coming?" Jean barked at her.

"If it pleases you, I would like to stay on for a little while." Cait lowered her eyes while she spoke like a humble parlor maid.

"You will walk home, then. We will not send for you." Jean crossed her arms.

"Thank you." Cait curtsied, maintaining her cultivated servility. Logan held his tongue, knowing her employment under these conditions would soon end.

"Good day, then." Jean unfolded her arms and walked away without waiting for a reply.

Logan looked past Jean to Sheena, who stood at the foot of their carriage, waiting to be helped in. The words of his clan members broke into his ears again. "Oh, Cait, how do you put up with that tiresome woman?" Mrs. Buchanan spoke Logan's thoughts. As an equally wealthy woman of about the same age as Sheena's aunt, Mrs. Buchanan never treated anyone—rich or poor, in her employ or not—with any such disrespect.

"Well, Mrs. Buchanan—" Cait's mouth turned up

mischievously "—I'm not planning on putting up with her much longer."

"Is that so?" Mrs. Buchanan clucked, adjusting the brooch that held her shawl together on top of her purple silk dress. "Nobody told me. Are you to be wed soon?" Mrs. Buchanan's expectant expression caught Logan's eye, as it flitted between himself and Cait, making him smile at the absurdity of it as Cait frowned.

"Nay." Cait rushed out an explanation. "I'm going... Can I tell them, Logan?"

"You might as well." Logan hugged Cait's shoulder protectively, hearing the Montgomery carriage rattle away. He felt the emptiness surge through him, stronger than any gale wind that ever blew over the moors. He might as well help Cait if he couldn't help himself. He knew from his conversation the night before that Cait harbored a sensitive spot concerning matters of the heart.

"Logan, Nessia, their family and I are all leaving for the Americas in a fortnight." At Cait's revelation, Mrs. Buchanan gasped along with those gathered nearby. "Actually, we'll be leaving Callander in about a week."

Everyone looked from one to the other, astonished. "But you've just come home, Logan." Mrs. Buchanan couldn't contain herself. "Nessia's leaving?" She rushed over to her, shouting her name as she went, obviously surprised to lose a close friend.

"Cait, do you think Sheena will hear about this?" Logan looked in the direction where Sheena's carriage drove home and saw only emptiness. "I never got a chance to tell her." Another complication. If their problems multiplied further, he would need to write them down soon just to remember them all.

"Everyone from the Montgomerys' house went home except me, so if I don't say anything, they won't know until they meet up with people in the village tomorrow."

Logan exhaled thoroughly. He had some time, but not enough of it, especially when he didn't know how or when he would see Sheena again.

"I'd like Sheena to hear about this from me. But I don't know when I will get the chance to see her again. Can you help me?"

"Of course." Cait grinned up at him. "What are little sisters for?"

Logan laughed, squeezing her shoulder. A sense of hope filled him again. Why did he always doubt God? He should hold on to his beliefs. He and Sheena belonged together. They were destined for one another. Always. He shouldn't doubt that anymore. God would see to it.

"Come on, we'd better go see how Angus and Nessia are faring." Logan pointed his head to where Mrs. Buchanan wiped tears away from her eyes with her handkerchief. "Then I'll walk you to the Montgomerys' house."

The winds picked up as Logan and Cait neared the Montgomerys' house. Logan couldn't help thinking about the other night when he'd walked Cait home. His heart raced at the thought of seeing Sheena.

However, this time he wouldn't find her sitting outside, waiting for Cait to return. Their unplanned encounter last night wouldn't repeat itself. She probably was confined indoors to tend to her wedding plans. He stopped himself—he wouldn't lose hope. Somehow, he would see Sheena again and stop her wedding. And the sooner, the better.

But before he gave himself a full speech of encouragement, something in front of the Montgomerys' house caught his eye. "Is that Sheena next to that man on horseback?" He didn't want to believe he was imagining things, and looked at Cait for her reaction.

She strained to see for herself and shrugged. Logan picked up his pace—he needed to get closer to find out for sure. But no one else possessed auburn hair like hers.

And then his smile faded. "Is that Ian?" Logan didn't know what he would do if he met the man who'd stolen his bride.

"It can't be. He's in Glasgow." Logan looked back at Cait. Now that Sheena had told Logan about her betrothal, surely Cait could divulge other information. He would ask Cait to tell him everything she knew if he didn't find everything out from Sheena first.

The rider and horse galloped away before Logan got near enough to see the man's face. Clouds of dirt sailed across the flat land, whirling in the strong wind. Once on the other side of the gritty screen, Logan saw Sheena pacing back and forth, her posture irate.

Cait caught up to him and he put his hand behind her back, nudging her forward. Sheena clearly needed her best friend. Logan couldn't call himself the same anymore. He hated his current status as a thistle in her heart.

"Sheena?" Cait approached her as slowly as someone would a wild animal.

"Oh, Cait, thank God you've come home. I've been praying, not knowing what else to do." Sheena ran forward grabbing both of Cait's hands. Her failure to acknowledge Logan's presence bothered him even more. If she faced trouble, he wanted her to run to him with all her problems.

"Sheena, what is the matter?" Cait looked as worried as Logan felt and Logan couldn't keep his distance. He moved closer to Sheena. Always drawn to her. He'd help her if she would let him.

Sheena's words tumbled over one another. "It's my mother. She almost fainted when we got home from church."

"Is she ill?" Logan spoke, making his presence known. No matter what his differences with Tavia, he'd put his feelings aside to ease Sheena's burden.

"I don't know. I just sent Boyd to get the doctor." Sheena motioned with her hand in the direction of the man on horseback.

Remaining calm in spite of Sheena's frantic tone, Logan asked, "Where is your mother now?"

"She's in her bed." Sheena took a deep breath, as if she had forgotten to breathe until now.

"Sheena, you said yourself that your mother didn't actually faint." Cait eyed her. "And she seemed well enough all day today. Are you sure she's ill?"

"How could she pretend something like that?" Looking appalled, Sheena withdrew her hands from Cait. "She was in quite a state before she started complaining about feeling light-headed. She was so agitated."

"Agitated?" Logan couldn't help raising an eyebrow. "At what?"

Sheena shot daggers at him. "At me."

"At you, lassie?" Logan remained serious, fighting hard to resist his urge to sneer. "Whatever for?" He couldn't fathom anyone getting upset with Sheena. Not when she went out of her way to please everyone.

"For making her come out in the middle of the night yesterday when the weather was so disagreeable."

"Was she still talking about that?" Cait rolled her eyes and then told Logan in an aside, "She went on about it all morning."

"Oh." Logan wouldn't risk another argument with Sheena over this matter, but since she'd stormed off to her house ahead of them, she would never hear him confide in Cait. "I think Tavia is lying."

"Me, too." Cait didn't even take a second to think it over.

"She's done it so often, it's hard to believe her now."

"I know. Nessia and Mrs. Buchanan always said she feigned illnesses at church to get out of helping with group activities."

"And if I remember clearly, only Sheena's father ever believed her. Tavia is doing another fine job of pretending, only this time Sheena has taken her father's place."

"I don't like her sending Sheena into a panic like this."

"Me, neither." Logan's anger rose just thinking about it, but he contained himself by the time they caught up to Sheena. "We were all outside last night and none of us have felt any ill effects from the damp weather." He tried to get her to see reason.

"My mother has been very frail since my father's passing." Sheena lifted her chin, making it look like a rebuke. But he wouldn't let her cast him as the bad one, not when Tavia should hold that title.

"Aye, but she should be used to the dampness, as all true Scots are." Logan winked at Sheena, but she ignored his joke.

"I hope you are right, but I will feel better once the doctor examines her." Logan nodded. At least he'd succeeded in getting Sheena to entertain the idea that her mother was just putting on a show.

"He shouldn't be long." Cait patted Sheena's arm comfortingly, which diverted Sheena's glare from Logan.

"And neither should I have been." Sheena looked back at Logan, anger and worry in her eyes. "Thank you for your concern, but I must go tend to my mother now. Good day."

"I'll go with you." Cait took Sheena's elbow.

"And I'll wait here until I hear that everything is fine." Logan remained firm. He would not let Sheena dismiss him like a stranger whose presence only served the purpose of learning gossip so he could spread it.

"That is not necessary," Sheena told Logan.

Thankfully, Cait cut in. "I will bring you news as soon as I can, Logan." At least someone knew his true intentions. He stood helpless, watching Cait guide Sheena back inside the house.

Maybe he'd pushed too hard again. But time wouldn't stand still. Logan needed to take action.

Chapter Eight

Sheena and Cait remained quiet as they climbed the wooden staircase. Sheena would never even think of reprimanding Cait for going against her wishes with Logan. Cait was her best friend, first and foremost. And Sheena would never treat Cait as anything less.

Besides, she knew the closeness Cait and Logan shared. Long ago, she shared that closeness with them. But that didn't mean she wanted to see Logan or talk about him. She couldn't even think about him right now. Not while her mother suffered because of her. Why on earth had she approached Logan after church—to make amends? Their relationship brought her nothing but pain. And now her mother suffered needlessly because of that, too.

Stepping on a creaky floor plank Sheena cringed, hoping the noise didn't reach her mother. She didn't want her to hear her, especially if it upset her again.

"Sheena, is that you?" Sheena froze at Tavia's words.

She prayed all the way to her mother's bedroom. *God, help me help my mother.*

Two pairs of unaffectionate eyes—Tavia's and Jean's—greeted her when she entered the room. Sheena ignored them—she would do her duty and take care of her ill mother.

Leaving Cait standing just inside the doorway, Sheena quickly made her way to her mother's bedside, opposite Jean. "I sent the butler to get the doctor." Sheena looked down at the red blanket on Tavia's bed. The same woolen one Tavia had grabbed last night to keep her warm and dry before she found Sheena outside.

The thought that maybe Tavia was feigning her illness sprang to mind, since Tavia had been the most warmly dressed of them last night.

"You sent for the doctor?" Her mother bolted up in bed. "I do not need a doctor." Sheena fell back. "What I need is a good daughter. One who does what she's told and has some sense."

"Tavia, please. Lie back and rest." Jean rose briskly to take care of the situation. Fluffing Tavia's pillow, she turned on Sheena and Cait. "Leave."

Needing no further prompting, Cait ushered Sheena toward the door and closed it behind them.

"She seems fine to me," Cait said, throwing her hands into the air. Sheena ignored the remark. She didn't want to believe that her mother had lied.

Focusing instead on the bench in the hallway, Sheena sat down and straightened out the wool of her skirt.

Cait sat next to her and stilled Sheena's hand. "You

mustn't blame yourself for having your mother out of doors last night. That was entirely my fault. I couldn't wait to see Logan and I didn't think of the consequences." Cait moved a lock of Sheena's hair away from her face and Sheena knew Cait's heart held her best interest. She always acted like a sister to her.

Sheena didn't want Cait feeling guilty about Tavia's illness, either, so she changed the subject to the one thing she knew Cait cared about. The one person Sheena couldn't get out of her own mind anyway. No matter how hard she tried. "You're spending a great deal of time with Logan." Sheena looked sidelong at Cait, half unwilling to broach the subject. Yet Cait needed to know Sheena's thoughts on the matter, to understand Sheena's position. Sheena knew only too well that last night Cait played matchmaker. That kind of foolishness couldn't be repeated.

"I missed Logan so much." Cait squeezed Sheena's hand and then released it. "He is great fun to have around. And if I remember correctly, you used to think so, too." Sheena looked up into Cait's smiling face. She remembered clearly being inseparable from her childhood friends. But that hadn't stopped Logan from leaving.

"Cait, I know what you're saying. Need I remind you, I'm betrothed. Even if I had feelings for Logan when I was younger, I cannot dwell on them now. That was in the past. My future is with Ian. Everything has been arranged."

"Aye, but that was before Logan came back to Scotland." Cait moved to face Sheena.

And Sheena braced herself—this conversation wouldn't end easily. "It doesn't matter. I cannot break my betrothal."

"I know. But if you love Logan and not Ian, I would think you of all people would do anything to be with the man you love. How can you marry a man without loving him?"

Sheena's cheeks flushed. She'd loved Logan five years ago with all her heart, but he'd left her without a good reason. Actually, with no reason at all. Sheena didn't trust him anymore and a relationship without trust wouldn't work. So how could she love a man she didn't trust? She couldn't. Plain and simple. Everything he ever told her could be a lie. Maybe he never even intended to marry her in the first place and fled the country because of the guilt he felt about lying to her.

She needed to set her sights on her future husband. Ian never lied to her, made promises he couldn't keep or broke her heart.

"Ian may be a stranger now, but he will not be one for long. I will grow to love him as my husband, just as he will grow to love me as his wife."

"And what if that doesn't happen? I don't even want to think about the terrible life you could lead. What if Ian's an awful man who treats you horribly after you're married?"

Sheena found a crease on her skirt and pressed it with her hands again. "I think I can assume my aunt would make sure Ian was a nice man before my mother betrothed me to him." But Cait gave Sheena a knowing look, as if she doubted whether either Tavia or Jean cared enough to do that. And that annoyed Sheena further because she didn't know for certain. When her father was alive, he always kept her mother patient about Sheena's unmarried status. But after his death there was no one to see that Sheena didn't get thrown to the wolves.

Getting through to Cait turned out to be much harder than she thought. But she wanted someone on her side. She needed a confidante. Someone to stand by her.

"Just because my mother wants to move back to her hometown of Glasgow where her sister lives doesn't mean she would do anything to accomplish that goal."

"Sheena…" Cait grabbed her hands again, stopping Sheena from working out her tension on her skirt. Only this time, Sheena wouldn't back down.

"Nay." Sheena pulled her hands back from Cait. "This is the way it has been done for hundreds, if not thousands of years, and this is the way it has to be for me." Sheena tried her hardest not to raise her voice as she argued her point. Whether for Cait's sake or her own, she didn't know anymore.

"Sheena, I can't believe even your mother would be so heartless as to not consider your feelings. If you do have feelings for Logan, tell your mother. She won't want to see you unhappy." But Sheena doubted that. She knew perfectly well that if God gave Tavia the choice of who in her family should live or die, Tavia wouldn't even need time to think—she'd shout out Sheena's name and dance in delight at her husband and son coming back to life. Sheena's happiness didn't matter to her in the least.

And yet, Sheena felt compelled to defend Tavia. "My mother is still suffering from the loss of her husband and only son, not to mention her estate and way of life." Sheena shook her head. "We all must have great compassion for her in her situation." Cait's dark brown eyes almost looked black as she took in Sheena's words.

Nevertheless, Sheena couldn't stop. "My mother spent the last of our money on my dowry to Ian. If I don't marry Ian, she will lose that money. And then we will have nothing. We're already losing our house at the end of this month, but my mother has set it up so that I will marry Ian by then and we will move right from this house to his house in Glasgow. I don't think my mother could stand being poor and she will do anything to avoid living off her younger sister Jean's charity. We're already too close to doing that and she abhors it."

Cait folded her arms and raised an eyebrow, so Sheena tried a different tactic. "My mother sees this as a good match for me. Ian is rich and my mother has always wanted me to advance in society. Cait, my mother is the only immediate family I have left. I must obey her, as the Bible tells me to. Without her, I wouldn't be alive. Can't you understand that?"

Sheena rose in frustration and walked over to the window to peer outside. Enough talking. Cait would never understand her betrothal to Ian and it seemed senseless to continue discussing it. "Where is the doctor?"

Cait came to stand beside Sheena. At least Cait let her air all her thoughts on the matter without interruption. "Sheena, I think I hear hooves."

Their heated words evaporated as relief rushed through Sheena. She saw Logan run out of nowhere up to the doctor and take his horse, allowing the gentleman to reach the house more quickly. She thanked God for that. Easier to thank Him than Logan.

Tavia snorted, pulling her red woolen blanket up even farther under her arms and giving it a good pounding. "Plenty of bed rest," the doctor told her.

A look of anxiety came over Tavia's face. "But, doctor, I have a very important trip I must take these next few days."

"Then you must send your regrets. We mustn't take a chance of your getting any worse. Listen to your body and rest. Those are my orders." The doctor looked at his patient as a governess would a disobedient child. Did the doctor think Tavia feigned her illness, too? "I will be back in a couple of days to check on you, unless you feel faint, and then you must send for me again."

"Thank you, doctor." Jean shook his hand without letting it go. "Please come with me and I will have the cook fix you something to eat as payment for your trouble."

"That always suits me fine." The doctor nodded at Tavia and Sheena before following Jean out. Awkwardly,

Sheena stood at her mother's bedside alone. Cait didn't dare come back in this time.

"I guess you got what you wished for." Tavia didn't look at Sheena and fluffed the blanket around herself.

"Aye, Mother. I am glad the doctor was able to come right away and tend to you." Sheena stepped in closer to her mother. God only knew why. Did she really expect a tender moment with her mother?

"Not that." Tavia glared at her, waving her hands in the air, making Sheena edge backward. "But now that I am sentenced to bed rest, I won't be able to accompany you to meet Ian and his family tomorrow."

"We could postpone the trip." A glimmer of hope shot through Sheena's heart.

"Certainly not." Tavia sat up again. "I will not let anything get in the way of your marriage to Ian. God did not make you pretty for nothing. It is a gift and you must use it for something good." Advancing in society, raising their standard of living, setting them up comfortably. Everything marrying Logan couldn't accomplish.

Sheena looked at her feet. "Aye, Mother." She'd heard that lecture too many times before.

"It is just as well, though. There's a lot of packing to do before we move to Glasgow next week, so I will get Jean to stay here and see to it, while I recover. I'll just write you a letter to send with a servant to your uncle Kyle once you arrive in Glasgow, telling one of your cousins to meet you at the Mackenzies'. But that does not mean that you will go without a chaperone all the way to Glasgow. I will make sure Boyd stays with you at all times, and it will only seem respectable that a female accompany you, as well. So take Cait. For all they know she could be your lady-in-waiting or your cousin, rather than your servant. And she's useless around here anyway." Her mother pointed her finger at Sheena. "I will not let you ruin this. Your father always wanted to see you properly matched. And I believe this is a great match."

Sheena hated to look up, but she couldn't resist letting her mother know just how very much she loved her father. "I would never go against Father's wishes." If only her father were still alive. Sheena missed him so much. Would he approve of her betrothal to Ian?

"You will make a good match in Glasgow, just as your aunt before you. I thank God every day she found you a Glaswegian lad. Nothing will make you happier than being well provided for, as your aunt has been all these years."

With the memory of her father fresh in her mind, Sheena hated that her mother alluded to an unhappy, materially lacking marriage with her father. "What about you, Mother? You were happy, too."

"Money makes life easier, Sheena, and I did not have an easy life up here in the Highlands." Sheena couldn't believe what her mother was saying. She insulted her husband, Sheena's father.

"But you have more than most. Look at your house. You have servants, beautiful clothes and have never gone hungry."

"That is nonsense. There are those with much better

things than I have. You will see when you go to Glasgow. We live like the poor here."

"The poor?" Sheena's thoughts sprang to Logan. "Mother, the poor live in dirt huts with only one room, where they sleep alongside their animals in winter and spend their days laboring for a pittance. We have never been poor."

"I will not compare myself to *those* people. Do you know how the royal family lives? They live in castles. They have jewels and riches beyond our imagination. They can command men to do their bidding. The people you speak of do not even matter in the world. They may as well be animals. We are not like them. We are not savages."

"Neither are the poor." Sheena could not control the anger rushing to her head as she defended Logan. And, she reminded herself, Cait and all her other friends who lived in the countryside.

Sheena knew her parents married for love and she always thought they would want the same for her. That's why Sheena told Logan not to hesitate and ask her father for his permission to marry her. She believed her father would have given them his blessing if they told him how much they loved each other. Her parents always seemed so happy before her brother died and her father fell ill. But her mother seemed to forget all that now. Her focus narrowed to money alone.

"Sheena, listen to me." Her mother grabbed her hand to get her attention. And it worked. Tavia rarely ever touched her and it made Sheena fall silent. "We are different." Tavia emphasized her words with a quick release of Sheena's hand and it jerked Sheena's senses back to normal.

"Nay, we're not. Father was a Highlander. These are our people. This is our clan."

"Nay. Not anymore. Your father is gone and we owe these people nothing. Our new life is in Glasgow where I came from."

"But Mother…"

"Sheena, that is enough. Leave me to rest." Sheena hesitated. Her emotions needed time to settle before she did exactly what her mother asked. Even though she knew she couldn't argue any further. Her boldness already got too close to outright disobedience, and whatever she thought about the people of Callander wouldn't matter in a fortnight when she became Mrs. Ian Mackenzie of Glasgow.

Walking out of the room without looking back, she leaned against the closed door and paused for a moment to gather herself. Remembering the feel of her mother's dry, rough hands on her skin, Sheena didn't feel either extreme of temperature, only natural coolness, and that heightened Sheena's suspicions that Tavia had feigned her illness. How could her mother do that? And why would she lie to everyone? No wonder Sheena sending for the doctor upset her so.

Looking around, Sheena didn't see Cait. Just as well, Sheena thought. She didn't think she could summon any more strength to quarrel with anyone else. In the past couple of days, she'd argued more than she ever remembered doing her whole life. First Logan, then Cait, now her mother and, truthfully, herself.

Needing some air, Sheena went to the window. But before she pushed it open, she saw Logan below, talking with Cait. And she couldn't muster the willpower to leave the window and banish Logan from her mind.

If only Sheena and Logan had never fallen in love in the first place. Then she would never know the pain of losing such a fine man, such a perfect love. And even though it ended with abandonment and pain, the time they spent together when they promised to wed could only be described as blissful.

Sheena loved Logan with every fiber of her being back then. He was her world. And he made her feel as if she shone for him alone. They made so many plans, from their wedding to what they would name their children all the way to how they would grow old together, never wavering in their love.

How Sheena used to adore Logan. The sweetest, most handsome, chivalrous, kind and loving man. Ever since they'd met as children, they'd stuck together as close friends. And that friendship grew into so much more.

She wished at that very moment to change places with Cait and step into the past. To stand so close to Logan and look into his loving face. To feel him so close by. What she wouldn't give to change their past. Why did he leave her?

It didn't matter now. She needed to forget about Logan. She needed to start truly living by the words she'd just told Cait. Her future spread ahead of her, set in stone. She couldn't do anything to keep from marrying Ian. He would become her husband. Somehow, she must set her mind to leaving the Highlands in the morning. By evening tomorrow she would meet her future husband for the very first time.

What would Ian be like? She coaxed her mind in Ian's direction. In the direction her life was headed. Whether she liked it or not. She couldn't pine over Logan. He didn't hold a place in her life anymore.

Fortunately, Ian lived far enough away that after they married, Sheena would never run into Logan again.

She shouldn't even watch him now, with a gloriously beautiful sunset behind him.

And then Logan looked directly up at the window where she stood.

Tears fell from her eyes, faster than the droplets from their waterfall. Her Logan stood so close. And yet, she could never make him truly *her* Logan again.

Even if her mother hadn't already paid her dowry and betrothed her to Ian, Sheena couldn't trust Logan anymore. How could Logan guarantee her that he wouldn't suddenly just leave her again? It only stood to reason that if he left her once he might leave her again. His feelings for her obviously never ran as deep as her feelings for him had.

Chapter Nine

"The stagecoach will not wait for you, Sheena." Jean hovered in the entranceway as Sheena raced into the room, knowing her aunt would scoff at her unladylike demeanor. But today it didn't matter. Sheena would escape in two seconds.

"I forgot something and couldn't leave without it." She gave Jean an obligatory kiss, told her goodbye and continued running out the door to Cait.

Squinting at the sunshine outside, Sheena buried her green moss agate stone in a hidden pocket she'd made on the inside of her dark blue shawl. She didn't bother turning to wave goodbye as they made their way down the path. No one waited lovingly to wave back. Especially since Jean nearly hit Sheena with the front door as she closed it behind her.

Whether Jean believed Sheena had made Tavia ill or knew her sister lied and got upset at Sheena for calling a doctor didn't matter—Jean held a grudge. Jean didn't want to spend any more time in this village. She wanted to go home to her beloved Glasgow. But yet again, Sheena reminded herself these worries could wait until her return in a few days. And by then, hopefully, everyone would forget all about it.

From their vantage point, Sheena and Cait could see down to the center of the village and the road leading to it. But before Sheena's breathing steadied itself, Cait shouted, "I see the stagecoach."

"I hope you're up for running." Sheena grabbed Cait's hand and they descended the rest of the hill, laughing and panting. It felt so good to let loose and enjoy some fun. Sheena hadn't experienced anything that spontaneously joyful in a very long time.

"I need just as much water as those horses." Cait handed her bag to the coachman, who threw it up on the roof of the stagecoach with the other bags that needed to be tied down before the journey began.

"Aye." Sheena gave the man her bag, as well. "Where's Boyd? I know he left early this morning." Sheena looked around, but she couldn't see Boyd among the dozen or so people who had gathered. Everyone kissed and hugged family and friends in welcome or farewell and it caused some commotion. Happy commotion, for them at least. No friends or family wished Sheena Godspeed. She couldn't even find Boyd. "He should be here."

"I'll go make sure everything's in order." Cait left Sheena standing alone beside the large rear wheel of the stagecoach. The feeling of isolation grew in her.

"Excuse me, miss." A man stood before Sheena with

his wife and two lads. Sheena moved forward toward the smaller front wheel, giving the man enough room to help his wife onto the rear outside section of the stagecoach.

Sheena couldn't help watching as the man picked up each of his children and placed them in turn on the large wheel until their mother could assist them into their seats. They seemed like a loving family. Not having money couldn't take that away from them. Sheena looked away.

She knew she would sit in the most expensive seats inside the stagecoach. Not because of their safety or because they provided shelter from the elements, but because her mother would never allow people to see her sitting on the outside. Travelling in the cheaper seats on the roof with the bags, or beside the driver, or even on the outer back, where the nice family sat, would disgrace her whole family if anyone saw Sheena sitting in them.

Sheena hoped her mother and aunt tapped into their generosity and gave Boyd and Cait enough money for all of them to sit inside. But given her mother's state of health last night and her own tardiness this morning, Sheena missed the specifics of those arrangements.

"Need a hand, miss?" the coachman offered, and Sheena knew she'd be holding them up if she didn't at least board.

"Thank you." Sheena took his hand, putting her right foot onto the step and pulling herself up into the stagecoach. Moving over to the far side, she sat down and peered out the window, still unable to see Cait or Boyd.

As other passengers started boarding, she welcomed

them with growing anxiety, knowing she wouldn't get out of the stagecoach now.

Soon Sheena heard footsteps atop the roof as the next round of passengers climbed on. She leaned as far out the window as she could, but couldn't see anyone that way. And so she sat back down and pressed her dress with her hands, looking anxiously toward the door for Cait and Boyd.

Finally, Cait bustled into the stagecoach. "We had a little haggling to do to get these seats," Cait whispered to her once she sat down beside her.

"I can help you pay for them. You shouldn't be paying out of your own pocket. I have money," Sheena whispered back, not wanting the other passengers to hear such private details. "You wouldn't be going if it weren't for me." Cait just waved her hand, a smile spreading across her face.

Why the grin? Sheena didn't see anything funny about her relations treating their servants like second-rate citizens, but in the next moment, her concern turned to shock.

"Logan?" She spat out his name.

"Good morning, lassie." Logan squeezed past the other passengers into the seat across from Sheena. "Beautiful day, isn't it?" He smiled at everyone in the stagecoach. Everyone except Sheena nodded happily in agreement before going back to their own conversations.

"Where is Boyd?" Sheena turned to Cait, not understanding.

But Logan answered for Cait. "His father is ill and

his family needed him at home, so I came in his place."
Sheena looked from Logan to Cait and then back to
Logan again, since he kept talking. "Not to worry,
though. You're in good hands. I'm a wonderful chaperone. Just call me Boyd if you want." He paused, flash-
ing his white teeth at her in what he probably thought
was a perfectly charming grin. His brown eyes twinkled
mischievously and Sheena knew seeking answers from
him would prove hopeless.

She turned back to Cait. "Do my mother and aunt
know about this?" Cait shook her head with a smile.

And a laugh escaped Cait's lips as the stagecoach
sprang forward. "I thought we needed some time, just
the three of us. For old times' sake."

Sheena looked at Cait, trying to grasp the situation.
Cait had gone behind her back again, this time putting
Logan in Boyd's place. No doubt because of her inkling
that Sheena still loved Logan. When would Cait realize
it didn't matter?

Sheena asked for God's help. She couldn't believe the
journey to meet her future husband now involved her
former…

Her former what? Friend? True love? It all seemed
so crazy. How could Cait do this to her? Or to Logan?
Unless Logan willingly agreed to it. And if he did, what
did that mean?

Seeing her with her future husband would be hard on
him if he still loved her. Although perhaps Logan had
already accepted her life's path and put aside their past
relationship to come as a friend.

Oh, God, I am such a poor Christian. If the situation reversed, I could not do what Logan did. And yet I know 1 Corinthians 13 by heart. "Love is patient. Love is kind. It does not envy. It does not boast. It is not proud. It is not rude. It is not self-seeking. It is not easily angered. It keeps no record of wrongdoing. It does not delight in evil, but rejoices in the truth. It always protects, trusts, hopes, perseveres."

But she knew that look in Logan's eye, that tone in his voice and his mannerisms. His coming could mean that he did still love her.

Sheena broke off praying.

Each hoof that hit the dirt brought her one step closer to meeting Ian. The man she could not run from. She closed her eyes again and asked God to make Ian a good man who followed His teachings. As his wife, she would be completely and utterly at Ian's mercy.

"Please don't be mad at me." Cait sat pensively. She'd meant well. Even though she was wrong about anything concerning Logan and Sheena.

Logan leaned in toward them. "I have business to take care of in Glasgow anyway, so there was no need for Boyd to come when his family needs his help around the farm." Of course, Logan would do whatever he could to help a fellow clansman. Keeping his voice low, he continued, "Hopefully Boyd can stay out of sight for a few days."

"How many people were in on this plan?" Sheena suspected she knew the answer, even as she asked.

"Just about everyone." Cait grinned at her. Cait must

know the special place she held in Sheena's heart to try such a trick. And Logan… She couldn't think about that.

"I should have expected as much from the people of Callander." Sheena couldn't help shaking her head in amusement. "Besides planning Logan switching places with Boyd, did you also plan for the doctor to make my mother stay in bed?" She dared a glance at Logan.

"We're not that practiced at scheming." Logan chuckled.

"Nor that mean," Cait offered. "But you have to admit, we'll be more fun to have around."

Sheena smirked, turning to the window, unable to laugh with Cait just yet.

Watching the rocky crag pass outside the window, a numbness overtook Sheena. She would leave the only home she ever knew when she married Ian. Everything familiar to her, gone. Everything she loved, in the past. Her childhood held so many wonderful memories, but her children would live completely different than she had. They would grow up in a city. They wouldn't see rolling hills or the blanket of purple heather that covered the ground in autumn. They wouldn't get to run through the wide expanse of moors and up crags to beautiful waterfalls. She would make a point to show them. But that would make it an exception rather than a daily routine.

Sheena sighed, looking at Cait. She would forgive her only comfort and reminder of home. She would make sure Cait became her lady's maid so Cait's life would get better. Sheena didn't need Cait to wait on her hand

and foot—she just needed to see her. The sight of her would bring Sheena the comforts of home. Sure, her aunt lived in Glasgow and her mother would move in with Sheena and Ian, but they wouldn't remind her of all the good times. They loved city life. Glasgow beckoned them home. They didn't grieve at leaving the countryside.

The stagecoach jerked to a halt and Sheena flew forward out of her seat like a wooden doll. She landed hard, but not a scratch came to her, for she landed in Logan's arms.

Logan's expressive gaze softly bore into hers. She smelled the clean freshness of the country coming from his strong, lean body as his hands held her with assurance. Her heart thumped so loudly in her chest that she almost couldn't hear him speak.

"Are you all right?" Logan's words caressed her neck in a deep heat and Sheena lost her ability to answer him. His hand pushed her hair behind her ear and she shivered at his touch. "Did you get hurt?" This time she shook her head. The noise of the stagecoach started to fill her ears. Everyone grumbled and shouted over the mayhem. The children outside cried.

In anxiety, Sheena pushed against Logan's firm chest, freeing herself from his strong arms. Her best friend needed their aid.

The bedlam created from the other passengers' dislodgements made it hard for Sheena to locate Cait on the stagecoach floor. But as soon as she did, Sheena grabbed

Cait's hands and pulled her to her feet, falling back into Logan again.

"Sorry," she mumbled to him, managing to right herself after Cait stood on her own. Sheena straightened her dark blue, floor-length shawl before sitting back down on the edge of her seat to wait for the other passengers to jump out of the stagecoach one by one.

"Cait, are you all right?" Logan asked, and she nodded, wrapping her brown shawl around her and covering her head. Logan stood then and led them out. From the ground, he offered his hand to Cait and, as he helped her down, Sheena stuck her head out of the stagecoach, breathing in the open air so crisp and cool after their confinement in the stuffy stagecoach. When her turn came, she took Logan's hand in hers and felt him warm, gentle and strong. His essence. What made him Logan.

Sheena realized she hadn't asked Logan if he hurt himself or, worse, if she'd hurt him. She flushed. She couldn't bring herself to say anything to him about it. She only hoped she hadn't given him too many bruises. The thought of her weight thrust upon him sent her blood racing. And yet, he seemed no worse for wear.

Slowly, Logan let her hand go and then headed straight to help the other men gathered around the front wagon wheel. Sheena saw they'd crashed into a ditch, making the whole stagecoach lean to the right. The men would need to devise a plan to get it unstuck. At least the wheel hadn't broken.

Sheena couldn't watch Logan for long with all the rest of the pandemonium.

The chestnut-colored Chapman horses fretted and whined while the driver tried his best to calm them down. Having them bolt or rear up wouldn't do them any good. Nor would letting them kick somebody.

The family riding in the back turned their children this way and that, making sure they hadn't been hurt. A couple of the rooftop passengers praised God after getting thrown from their seats and landing in mud puddles that softened their falls. *Thank you, Lord, for helping everyone make it through this.* Sheena sighed with relief.

And yet, her heart raced even now. Shock, she told herself. Trauma from the upheaval. Not Logan. Nevertheless, her mouth felt dry and her knees felt shaky. She couldn't do anything to help so she walked over to a nearby rock and sat down with her back toward it.

She watched the men around the stagecoach. Her eyes zeroed in on Logan once again, as he pushed from the back of the stagecoach with the other men to right it. With a firm stance he strained his muscles as he pushed on the wagon. She closed her eyes again.

God, You must help me. Logan is just a man to me now, like any other. Ian is to be my husband. Please help me. She wanted to cry aloud, but pressed her hands together against her forehead in prayer.

God, You must help me to love Ian as my husband and take away these memories of Logan. She pressed her thumbs into her head as if that would knock the memories out. She couldn't live in the past. And she didn't want to be reminded of it anymore.

What she experienced with Logan ended long ago.

If it had ever even existed in the first place. He didn't love her enough to stay in Scotland and marry her then and he didn't love her now. Nor could she love him now. She couldn't forgive him for leaving her. She didn't trust him. And even if those reasons weren't enough, her mother had betrothed her to Ian. Ian held all claim to her heart. And then she heard the roar from the crowd as the wheel dislodged and the stagecoach regained stability.

She didn't feel joy or relief, as the others did, only regret. They would all go back on the stagecoach very soon, putting more miles between themselves and Callander, the village she loved. Why was thinking of Glasgow as her new home so difficult? Callander held some nasty memories for her. With hearing the news of her brother's demise at Culloden and her father's untimely death, she knew so much pain it didn't make sense that she couldn't abandon Callander entirely. She needed to let go of the past and open herself up willingly to her future. To Ian. *Please, Lord, set my heart and mind at ease.*

Sheena opened her eyes and looked up. Seeing Logan's brown eyes, she blinked several times. She could see them so clearly in her mind that she couldn't ascertain if she'd actually opened her eyes or not. Until he spoke.

"Are you sure you didn't get hurt?" Logan bent over her, his face full of concern as he sat beside her.

"Aye. Thank you for catching me." She stopped herself from looking away from him. She wouldn't let shame take over. "I hope I didn't hurt you." She didn't flinch or blush. Perfect frankness.

"You've never hurt me physically." He stood. Did she hurt him in other ways? "Come on. Everyone is getting back on." He reached out his hand to help her up and she took it without hesitation, just as she would take any other man's hand, and followed him back to the crowd by the stagecoach.

"Please take my place inside the stagecoach." Sheena offered her seat to the children as they stood by their parents in front of the back wheel. "I won't feel right sitting in there knowing the dangers that could befall your children out here." The husband looked at his wife, but Logan spoke before they could.

"Nay. Please have your children take my place. There will be room enough for them and you in the stagecoach, Sheena. I will remain out here with the two of you if you wouldn't mind." The husband and wife thanked Logan profusely, sending their children off in the direction of the stagecoach door.

"Logan, I am perfectly fine to sit back here," Sheena huffed.

"I will feel better knowing you will be safe." Logan motioned her toward the stagecoach door. "I am your chaperone, after all." He smiled.

Sheena refused to get drawn into that joke. "It's not as if we're going to get shot at by highwaymen." Sheena rolled her eyes, but didn't argue further. She wanted to put some distance between herself and Logan anyway. "But what if we hit another hole? Aren't you the least bit worried I might squish one of those wee children to death?" A laugh escaped Logan's lips more quickly than his hand offered to help her up.

"Regardless, they are still much better off inside than out here." He closed the door.

bel worsened. At all church age in three runs children to them. "A large rounded inched a her every gave of then the harm merged to help her saw.

"No," whatsoever, they are still naked down off inside then out out." All to and out last.

Chapter Ten

As the stagecoach trudged on, Logan spent his time thinking. Nothing else he could do.

Despite the dusty roads that took some getting used to, Logan planned to relish every moment of his time left in Scotland. He didn't even want to blink as he tried to commit everything to memory. And yet, some sights made him painfully aware of the terror Sheena and his family had lived through while he had worked off his indenturement.

The stagecoach had just passed the town of Stirling, but instead of seeing St. Ninian's church in all its former beauty, only the tower remained. Angus had told him the Jacobite rebels had blown the rest of it up. A church. Logan shook his head. A holy place on sacred ground. Another sign of the times. He didn't understand what had happened to his beloved Scotland. All this infighting. Sheena hadn't overstated the fact that everything had changed since he went away.

Even her love for him. Because if she still loved him they wouldn't be making this journey.

But now he sat out here on the back of this stagecoach on his way to meet her betrothed instead of remaining in Callander where he could spend his time digging to find that Montgomery family heirloom box with her father's letter in it to prove Logan's love for Sheena and put an end to all of this.

Thankfully, Angus had agreed to keep up the search, because if Sheena needed to go, Logan couldn't let her go to Glasgow without him. What kind of man would she meet in Glasgow? Sheena didn't know Ian. If he turned out to be horrid, Logan needed to protect her. And the only way he could do that was by accompanying her to meet her betrothed. Her father promised to protect Sheena until Logan returned from his indenturement in the Americas, but since her father was no longer alive, that role now fell to Logan.

If Ian possessed any faults, Logan would find out. In the meantime, he would try to see if Sheena still loved him, because if she did, even a wee bit, hope for them still existed. And he prayed for that. Along with all his prayers for his brother to find that box by the time they returned home.

Six long hours of riding on the stagecoach, it finally came to another abrupt stop. Thankfully, a planned one this time. They'd ridden almost twenty-four miles and Logan certainly welcomed the hourlong break for lunch so he could stretch his legs. The Chapmans needed changing over to fresh horses that would bring them to their final destination in another five hours or so, depending on how the last twenty-one miles of the journey turned out.

Logan jumped down from his seat wanting to help Sheena off the stagecoach, but his wobbly legs needed steadying before he could take those steps to the door. Luckily, most of the passengers inside had fallen asleep and that made them slow to exit the stagecoach. Logan waited for Sheena, who let everyone out ahead of her. But he didn't mind waiting. He'd wait forever until Sheena's beauty shone down on him. The arduous journey didn't diminish her radiance.

"How was the scenery from your seat?" She took his right hand and dropped her left foot down onto the step.

Logan reached up and took her other hand, looking into her shining golden amber eyes. "Awe-inspiring, as usual. God certainly knew how to create lovely things." Sheena's cheeks flushed slightly as she turned her face away.

Trying to climb down without looking, she lost her footing and Logan grabbed her around the waist to steady her. Sheena gasped as he lifted her to the ground. Her cheeks turned completely red now and Logan liked them like that—he knew he affected her. As much as she pushed him away, she felt something between them. Something they always shared.

"Oh, my legs." Sheena looked down at them, still holding on to Logan's shoulders. "I don't think I can stand on my own." She laughed, leaning against the stagecoach.

"You'll have to lean on me, then. Leaning there may not be safe." Logan pulled her away from the stagecoach, welcoming the chance to hold her longer. "They've got a lot of work to do with the horses to get us back on the road."

She nodded, making Logan once more thankful she didn't argue with him. Since his return, it seemed they'd quibbled more than in their entire life together. So this change felt good. Back when they meant more to each other than friends. When they loved each other and told each other so.

Realizing his staring at her made her cheeks an even deeper shade of crimson, he tried to ease her discomfort. "My legs were the same. You'll get feeling back in them soon enough." Logan wished that wouldn't happen though. He would love to stay this close to her, but he couldn't wish for the impossible. Too foolish.

"I don't think I can take sitting in that stuffy, cramped compartment again." Sheena finally stood up on her own, releasing him. Inevitable, he reminded himself, and held back a sigh.

"We can always walk back home." Logan knew the moment the words left his lips Sheena wouldn't like them. But he couldn't help himself.

"Or walk to Glasgow." She looked around at the other passengers lumbering toward the inn. "It is about the same distance." Logan grunted, stopping himself from saying anything further to her provocation. She seemed keen to hardly pay him any attention, since she looked everywhere but at him. "How did you ever manage being stuck on a ship for so long? I don't know if I could stand being away from the open fields, where one is free to walk and see all the natural wonders God put here for us to discover."

Her reprimand smarted more than he expected. "My time on the ship was limited. I knew it would end and I'd be able to roam the land again, so I never even thought about that. I was too concerned with my work on the ship and tending to sick passengers, all the while trying not to let myself get sick." He hadn't become an indentured servant for the fun of it. He lived, breathed and worked for her. "You, however, might be in for a bit of a shock when you get to the city of Glasgow. It isn't at all like the countryside you're used to."

"I am well aware of what Glasgow is like, Mr. McAllister." Logan flinched. When and why did she resort back to his proper name? He'd probably pushed too hard again. "And I am sure I will be given ample opportunity to come and go as I please." Logan dipped his chin. If the world turned upside down and Sheena wed Ian, he did hope for her sake that Ian treated her most kindly. She deserved nothing less. "I think we should follow the others to the inn. I don't know about you, but I am parched."

"Aye, I could use a little sustenance, too." Logan took her hand and slid it through his arm, keeping his hand over hers as they walked to the inn. Nothing out of the ordinary, escorting a lady like this. He'd done it too many times to count with Nessia and Cait, but for Logan the closeness to Sheena felt different—he truly longed to make her more than a friend. Having her to hold pulled at his heart.

How would he watch her with another man? He tightened his grip on her arm, as if he could stop her from leaving him. Sheena betrothed to Ian—that fact never left his thoughts. Betrothals equaled marriage. Only the formalities remained. How could God's plan for them come to this? It didn't make sense. *I'm sorry, God. It might be Your plan, but it isn't mine.* Logan stopped, making Sheena fumble backward a bit.

"Sheena." Logan looked at her with an intensity he felt surge from his core. "You cannot marry Ian."

"Excuse me?" She removed her arm from his, roughly putting some distance between them. "Who are you to tell me what I can and cannot do?" Her hostility took Logan by surprise.

"I am…" He wanted to tell her what he dreamed of being to her. Tell her about the land he owned in the Americas and the life he dreamed of sharing with her there. But he couldn't. Until she loved him in return, it wouldn't matter to her. Meaningless words. Or worse, it could further isolate her from him and even drive her deeper into Ian's arms. Something Logan certainly did not want. "Sheena, I have known you since birth. I know everything there is to know about you and you cannot marry a man you don't even know."

"If you truly know me, as you claim, then you must know that I am not a fanciful sort anymore. I do not hold on to romantic notions."

He couldn't deny her unspoken accusation. She

was angry that he'd left her. He'd wounded her deeply. She might even hate him now. Regardless, she stood beside him furious that he'd broken her heart because she thought he'd left her as a way to abandon her. He needed to get her to forgive him and trust him again so she could move past these feelings and love him again. He needed to find that secret letter from her father and show it to her. That could end all this. But without the letter what could he do to change her mind?

"I have always done my duty for my family and will continue to do so. My mother betrothed me to Ian and I can't break that betrothal."

Logan continued staring at her, as if she spoke a different language. What happened to the days where they stared at the sky, discussing amusing topics like which shape the clouds shifted into? The innocence of their youth seemed far behind them now with such serious subjects at hand. Sheena folded her arms in front of her, making her look even more inflexible.

Should he tell her about his meeting with her father? Would she believe him without reading the letter herself? She didn't seem to trust him anymore, and certainly didn't even seem to like him at the moment. He'd never felt lower in her estimation.

Logan searched for a hole in her armor. "Are you sure this is what your parents want for you?"

"Aye," she said with conviction.

"How can you be so sure when it is only your mother who arranged the betrothal? Maybe your father had other wishes for your future happiness."

"How dare you speak of my father as if you know him better than his own flesh and blood?" Sheena uncrossed her arms quickly as her fists tightly balled up and found their way to her hips. "He wanted me to make a proper match."

"He wanted you to be happy, unlike your mother who wants you to marry someone with money and social standing." Logan couldn't hide the bitterness in his words.

Sheena dropped her fists, a look of guilt on her face, but Logan wouldn't stand there like an object worthy of pity. He'd slaved away in the Americas. And for what? To still rank as only a poor man, not good enough for Sheena. He turned his back on her. Anger beat inside his skull. He lowered his head and closed his eyes.

"Logan." Sheena put her hand on his shoulder and tried to turn him around, but Logan didn't want to move. How could this happen? He opened his eyes to see Sheena's worried expression and Logan knew he could never just walk away from her. He needed to prove to her that if her father had lived, he would have accepted Logan as her husband. Hopefully by now Angus had found that box with the letter inside. Words would mean nothing to Sheena—Logan needed to show her the proof of his love for her. Only then would she believe him and her mother could no longer bar the way. Sheena would understand what Logan did and what her father wanted for her—love. With that, this maddening betrothal to Ian could end.

"I'm not as poor as you think I am." Logan looked

toward the inn where everyone now sat inside, eating and drinking.

"Logan, I didn't know. You never told me."

"Nay, but would that matter to you that I'm not so poor anymore?" he challenged her. "Have you changed? Are you only in search of someone with riches?"

"Logan, how can you ask me that?" Sheena took a step back.

"I'm sorry," Logan said, and Sheena just looked at him. Motioning for her to join him in sitting on a rock, Logan thanked God Sheena obliged him.

"I wasn't always poor, you know. Well, I was, but my family wasn't."

"They weren't?"

"Nay." He wanted more time to tell her everything. He needed Sheena to understand him and know him even better than she already did. But he especially wanted to show her, and yet he couldn't show her anything concrete until they got back home and he found what he dug so feverishly for. Nevertheless, he needed to start somewhere. "Maybe that's why I don't see money and rank as all that important. It can be here one day and gone the next. It is the character of the man that matters."

He searched for some understanding in her eyes. "It all happened before I was born. My parents never talked of it. Too scared of the government. So when Angus told me, it seemed like a fairy tale, rather than my family history." Logan approached a rather large rock and Sheena followed him intently.

"My father, rest his soul, is now united with my

mother in the Lord, but he wasn't always poor. Life beat him down." Logan peered at her sideways, as she sat down beside him. "When my father was younger, he was a man to be revered. I mean no offence, but from what I've heard, your house was the size of his stable. And that's why his adversaries cut him down. He was too powerful."

Sheena sat still, listening at Logan's side, and that comforted him. At least she listened. Maybe he could make her understand. Get her to change her mind about him. "My father was involved in the Jacobites' rebellion thirty-three years ago in 1715, and after it ended badly for them, he used to thank God he was still alive, but he used to curse the government for seizing his estate."

"They took everything?" Sheena held her hands together in her lap rubbing her thumbs.

"They spared the clothes on his back and his family and a few other things." Logan reached down and picked up a stone. "It could have been worse though—they could have imprisoned him or killed him." He threw the stone ahead of them at another rock and watched it ricochet into the dirt with a soft thud. "Instead, all they did was move him out of the way, down to our little village of Callander."

"Logan, how did your parents live through that?"

"Love." Logan took Sheena's hands in his. "That is all anyone needs." He grabbed his opportunity. "It's all we need." He couldn't keep his feelings for her hidden any longer. She needed to know he still loved her.

Sheena blanched. And Logan caught hold of her with

one of his hands holding her up. "Sheena?" He rubbed her back feeling it tight under her shawl.

She stood. "I'm fine."

"Are you sure?" Logan rose beside her, still holding on to her in case she fainted.

"Aye. All this traveling has left me a little light-headed. I think I need some nourishment." Logan consented, ushering her toward the inn. He didn't want to. But what else could he do? He couldn't force her to stay out here with him. Patience, he reminded himself. He had torn through one of her walls. Only how many more walls did he need to tear down before she would love him again?

Sheena sat in the stagecoach, watching Logan return to his former seat inside—no need for him to sit out back since the family with children stayed at the inn. New passengers greeted the adventure and their merriment rubbed off on Cait.

"Here we go again." Cait's cheery words flew out the window ignored. Logan didn't even acknowledge Cait or Sheena for that matter, as he turned his head toward the window. Sheena merely looked at Cait. Neither smiling nor nodding. Her uneasy mind and heavy heart didn't allow words to escape her.

This was the final leg of the journey. By nightfall, they would arrive in Glasgow. Sheena would meet Ian, her future husband.

Sheena needed time to think. And some room to breathe. But the stagecoach set off, trapping her in its cramped compartment which seemed much smaller than before. She couldn't even look out the window, because that would bring Logan into view and she didn't want to face him. Not now. Not ever. She looked down at her lap. If news of this change in plans ever got back to her mother and aunt, they would all pay dearly.

Sheena closed her eyes and rested her head in her hands. She still couldn't believe Logan had come back to Scotland. Let alone that he was sitting here traveling with them because of business in Glasgow. What kind of business could a man need to take care of in a city he never lived in, anyway? Especially after being out of the country for five years?

Sheena sat back up, opening her eyes. Instantly she regretted it as Logan's gaze met hers. She quickly turned to the window to capture the view of a moor for herself.

Why had Logan told her not to marry Ian? Logan knew why she must make this journey. Maybe he didn't agree with arranged marriages, but that didn't matter. Her mother had already paid her dowry. Sheena must go through with this betrothal or else she would lose everything. Her mother and she would then be completely at the mercy of her aunt Jean and uncle Kyle, hoping for their charity. Sheena couldn't do that to her mother.

Did Logan seriously try to tell her back there that he loved her? Is that what he meant? It seemed that way, but even if he did love her, that didn't change how he'd cast her aside.

Whoever said she wanted to break her betrothal to Ian? Logan had left her. She'd never forgiven him for deserting her. She'd begged him to stay and he hadn't. He didn't love her enough to stay five years ago and she couldn't endure that kind of disappointment and heart-ache again.

She might not have come to terms with Logan's abandonment of her five years ago, but that didn't mean their love still existed, either.

Both Logan and Cait didn't think she could love Ian, but what about love brought about by mutual companionship and partnership over the years? Sheena never thought of Logan as a romantic. She never even thought him the least bit sentimental, not after he left Scotland. That cured her of all her fantasies regarding men.

But if Logan had gained some romantic ideals, he needed to get over them. At least as far as they concerned her.

How dare he bring up her deceased father as if he knew his wishes for her life better than she did. Or her mother for that matter. Sheena had always maintained a close relationship with her father—he used to dote on her. He always tried to make her happy and show her he loved her.

Her sweet and caring father, God rest his soul, always wanted the best for her. He would get fiercely angry if he lived to hear Sheena tell him about all of Logan's promises of love and marriage before Logan abandoned her. Her father would hate Logan for hurting her. He would never forgive Logan and maybe she shouldn't, either. Of course, as a Christian she should, but God knew how challenging that kind of forgiveness was.

Sheena didn't know why Logan bothered trying to play with her emotions. She didn't trust him. He'd lied to her before, catastrophically, and she wouldn't let him make a fool out of her again.

Sheena folded her arms. Her stomach didn't feel right. It felt tied in knots. Every bump of the stagecoach made her clutch her middle tighter as she fought to keep her food and drink down.

She'd felt this way before. Nervous anxiety. Fear. And, worst of all, uncertainty. Forget Logan—she needed to deal with the most pressing matter at hand—Ian. If she felt scared to meet him, Ian might feel the same way. What did he think about their meeting tonight? Did he even want to marry her? And if he did, why? With all the women in Glasgow he should have already found a woman in the city. Maybe Sheena would find something terribly wrong with him.

Her temples started to throb and she released her stomach to massage them. She needed to turn her worries over to God. He would take care of her. She repeated that thought in her mind until she calmed down and passed into a restless sleep.

Groggily, she opened her eyes. "Sheena, we're here." Cait shook Sheena's shoulder. The stagecoach still swayed in motion, but the scenery outside the window had changed dramatically. Instead of wide expanses of moors and rocky crags, the tallest buildings Sheena ever saw surrounded her now.

Darkness hadn't descended on the city yet and rows

upon rows of houses and buildings, all perfectly uniform in their stone structure, lined the massively broad streets. She had never traveled to Glasgow before and the opulence amazed her. Now she could see what her mother meant. Their house didn't compare. And a one-room hut like the one Logan's family lived in would never be built within the city's limits.

When the stagecoach stopped, Sheena continued looking out the window. She would wait and get off last. But this time, it would serve another purpose besides following the teachings of Romans 15:1–3 that she should put others before herself. Most likely, Ian stood right outside the stagecoach to greet her, and she didn't know what she'd say to him or even how to behave in front of him.

And yet, she couldn't hide in here forever. After the last passenger left, she approached the open door. The air outside the stagecoach surged in, smelling like her stable at home. No doubt all the horses pulling people around the streets contributed to that stench.

As she peeked her head outside, Logan offered her his arm. She took his hand with only a mere thank-you and then looked away quickly. She couldn't focus on him now.

Standing near Logan and Cait among the throng of people who exited the stagecoach before her, she steadied herself. Her legs felt weak once again, but for more than the obvious reason of sitting so long. She would try to stay lost in the commotion, to hide out for a little while at least. Under any other circumstance, she would marvel at the beauty of the city, but not today.

Right now, she would meet the man she would spend the rest of her life with.

"Excuse me." A man with an accent much different from her own approached her. She couldn't describe him as tall or short, wide or thin, handsome or ugly. He stood exactly in between all extremes. The most distinguishable feature about him sat on top of his head—sunset red hair. "Are you Miss Sheena Montgomery?" he asked her, his voice neither deep nor high.

"Aye." Sheena could hardly breathe as she stared into her future husband's eyes. She couldn't quite make out their color, neither completely green nor blue.

"I'm Finnean Munro. Ian sent me to escort you to the Mackenzies' home." The man bowed low and Sheena put her hand to her chest in relief. *Not Ian after all.* Her lungs started to fill with air again. Sheena couldn't hide her relief. And not because this man turned her stomach. She just hadn't felt even a glimmer of love and she couldn't shake that vain hope. Because she didn't want to find out how long it would take her to grow to love a husband, or what she would feel for Ian in the meantime. Apathy? Is that how she would feel toward her life as well after she married him?

Sheena didn't want to think about the possibility and rubbed the front of her neck as Finnean stood. "I have two chaperones with me and our bags, as well." She didn't make eye contact with Logan or Cait as she introduced them to Finnean.

But the man's easy nature played well with Logan and Cait who would make fast friends under different circumstances. Finnean looked to be not too much older than her. And maybe Sheena should talk with them, but she just couldn't relax. Her throat tightened. Time bore down on her. Once the trio stopped joking, they would all get into the Mackenzies' carriage to bring her to her future husband, like a roast pig on a platter.

"This way." Finnean stepped forward to take Sheena's arm, but with a look to Finnean, Logan took it first. Without any fight left in her, Sheena didn't protest. She wouldn't let Logan anger her now. What did it really matter—holding on to Logan's arm for a few feet? Nothing life-changing could happen in that short span of time.

Chapter Eleven

"Sheena, you look scared. You don't have to do this, you know." Logan pulled her close, whispering in her ear. What did he think she could do? Hike up her skirt and run to the country? Stay hidden and live like a woodland hermit? How perfectly lovely to be pushed off on her own for the second time by this frustrating man.

"I only have to meet him today." She yanked her arm from Logan. "It's not as if we're getting married right now." She said the words aloud, but they didn't calm her nerves any.

They fell silent following Finnean, who now escorted Cait. And before Sheena knew it, they had climbed into Ian's elegant carriage. Her future carriage. The one she would use to ride around the city forevermore. Sheena didn't dare look at Logan, but she saw Cait sitting awe-struck and that irritated her. She didn't understand how her friend could seem so blissfully happy as her life was crashing down on her.

She straightened her brown silk dress. The undergar-

ments itched though and Sheena fought hard to sit still.
Jean had bought Sheena the outfit she wore as part of
her trousseau, together with a couple other outfits from
Glasgow. Her mother even made sure to lend Cait some
dresses, in lesser-quality material, of course. But Logan
would stand out. Sheena rolled her eyes.

Even though he wore brown breeches that fastened
below his knees, where they met white socks that he tied
up with his green ribbons, Logan didn't wear a man's
coat over his white puffy shirt and brown button-up,
sleeveless vest. His shirt also lacked the frills wealthier
men wore around their collar that cascaded down their
chests. And Logan didn't affix a pair of expensive buck-
les to his plain brown, well-worn shoes, either.

But Sheena couldn't do anything to help Logan.
She didn't possess the money to anymore. Besides, she
couldn't concern herself with him. For all she knew at
the time her mother betrothed her to Ian, Logan had
already entered into wedded bliss in the Americas. Of
course, she knew now that hadn't happened, but she
couldn't change that.

The carriage stopped and so did Sheena's heart.
She took a deep breath. They sat in front of the largest
home on the street and most likely in all of Glasgow.
She couldn't help feeling small and insignificant in com-
parison. Even the sun sank behind it as if defeated by
its enormous size. She wondered how this could be her
new life. Such wealth and nobility—could she manage
it? Surely, she never dreamed of marrying a real prince

who owned a castle, but this approached the fairy tales she'd heard as a child.

Ever since she could remember, her dreams involved marrying Logan. Knowing she wouldn't own every luxury money could buy always seemed like a good trade-off to her. Life with Logan—the man she had loved above all others—would have filled her days with the happiness money could never buy.

More servants than Sheena could count filed out the main doors, lining up in welcome. All this would become part of her new life. She fought back her negative thoughts with a prayer. *God, help me. If this is what You want for me, please stay with me. With Your help, I can bear anything.* But her time to pray ended almost before it began.

"Miss Montgomery?" Finnean called from the open door. Sheena looked around at the empty carriage. How long had she sat there contemplating all this luxury? How very foolish she felt accepting Finnean's hand and descending from the carriage. Thankfully, she got out on the side away from the house, where no one could see her, so she could use the extra moment to marshal her strength. She couldn't fall apart now. She could do this. She must.

Coming around the carriage, Sheena averted her eyes from Logan. She needed to keep her mind focused. She hurried in front of him so he could trail her in proper fashion. She couldn't even see the giant mansion or servants anymore, because her gaze snapped to the man at the bottom of the steps. The man her mother had betrothed her to, Ian.

"Miss Montgomery." He bowed as Sheena neared him. And she offered him her hand. With a smile upon his chiseled face, he took it gently and kissed it.

"Mr. Mackenzie." She curtsied, looking down momentarily and then straight back into his hazel eyes. Green irises so speckled with brown flecks she wondered if God heard her prayer. Did He give her this as a sign? *Here in your future husband's eyes I put the mossy land of your youth. The country and moors you loved to roam will now be yours to behold in his eyes.* Sheena didn't know what to think anymore.

"I hope your journey was agreeable?" His voice, low enough to make any woman swoon, interrupted her thoughts. But she couldn't help thinking how a man with Ian's looks and position in life couldn't find a woman to marry before now.

"Aye. Thank you." She noticed his height. A tall man with a rather large build. How a city fellow, who most likely never did physical work an entire day in his whole life could be so well built Sheena didn't understand.

"May I present Miss Cait Ross and Mr. Logan McAllister." Sheena took a step sideways, still not meeting Logan's eye as she felt him come and stand beside her.

"Miss Ross." Ian bowed in front of her. "Mr. McAllister." He shook Logan's hand. *Awkward* didn't begin to describe this. The man she always thought she would marry meeting the man she would be forced into marrying. "Hope you will both enjoy your stay with us."

Sheena just watched, keeping her eyes on Ian. She didn't know if she could look at Logan while Ian stood nearby.

"Thank you." Logan and Cait repaid his pleasantry before Ian turned his gaze back to Sheena.

"Please let me escort you inside to meet my family." Sheena extended her hand in acceptance and he took it in his arm. She couldn't see anything out of place about him, not even a strand of his short chestnut hair as he led her easily toward his home. "My family is waiting eagerly inside. They thought it only right to give us a few moments alone before you met them all."

"Very kind of them." Sheena couldn't even form a complete sentence as she looked up and saw his eyes twinkle at her and it made her uncomfortable. His eyes looked as if the sun shone over a field. But just because his eyes reminded her of home didn't mean God meant for this marriage to happen. And yet, what if He did?

Ian led her into a large vestibule and waited as she took her dark blue shawl and handed it to the butler, along with the letter her mother had written to her uncle Kyle, before taking hold of her arm again and leading her toward the parlor. He didn't seem as if he could behave like a cruel man. At least she prayed he wouldn't turn into one after they married.

As one of Ian's servants opened the doors ahead of them, a unified gasp floated into the air. "Ah, she has come." An older woman wearing a white powdered wig with three curls on each side of her cheeks shut her fan as if using it to clap with excitement.

A wide grin stayed firmly planted on Ian's face.

"Miss Montgomery," he announced needlessly as this cheerful woman lost no time in making her way to Sheena. "You are lovely." She stretched out each word as she beamed. And her enthusiasm became contagious.

"Thank you." Sheena curtsied.

"Ah, there's no need for all that nonsense." The woman, who looked close to her mother's age, took both of Sheena's hands and lovingly patted the top one. "You are to be my daughter-in-law. We're family. I will not have us standing on ceremony with one another."

Sheena smiled at her. This woman with green eyes whom she had only just met bestowed upon her more maternal warmth than her mother had in...who knew how long. Sheena chastised herself—she shouldn't call up such harsh criticism. Her mother possessed her own good qualities. Comparing her to others wouldn't help anything.

"Thank you Mrs. Mac..."

"Ah, now there you go again," Ian's mother cut her off jokingly. "Call me Mother, please. Or at least Mother Rose when your own mother is around." She laughed. A full, hearty laugh that would make anyone in the room want to laugh with her.

Sheena nodded; however, her laugh remained caught in her throat. She knew she should call Rose *Mother* right now to please her, but she couldn't. It didn't feel right. Not yet, at least. Sheena folded her hands in front of her, squeezing them tight.

"This is my daughter, Maggie. She's twenty-two, only a year younger than you." Rose reached over and grabbed the arm of a woman neatly dressed in a purple silk gown who stood in attendance. "My only lass."

"Pleased to make your acquaintance." Sheena held herself back from curtsying in front of Ian's lovely sister.

"Likewise." Maggie pressed close to her mother's side. How could Sheena not make comparisons? Sheena never got that close to her mother. "I've always wanted a sister," Maggie said quietly and Sheena pushed her lips up pleasantly. These women treated her so nicely.

"And this lovely lady is cousin Caroline MacNab." Rose waved for the only other woman to come.

"How do you do?" Caroline dipped her pointy chin and Sheena followed her lead, noticing how vibrantly her blue eyes shone against the blue silk of her dress.

"Very well, thank you. And you?"

Caroline's thin lips stretched slightly, but to call it a smile would only stretch things further. "Good. Thank you."

Caroline's neat caramel hair didn't move an inch as she went back to her seat on one of the upholstered chairs. And Sheena didn't mind Caroline going and hopefully staying far away from her. Sheena had encountered too many greetings as cold as Caroline's in her life not to know exactly what they meant. Finally a taste of home.

"Ah, very well. Now, then, this is Ian's younger brother, Reed." Sheena held her hand out to the man with his red hair pulled back with a black ribbon. And noticed that Reed's emerald eyes bore no resemblance to his older brother Ian's.

"And this is your soon-to-be father, Niall." Sheena met the oldest gentleman in the room. His brown eyes creased at the sides when he smiled. He, too, wore a white powdered wig that had been pulled back with a dark blue ribbon at the base of his neck.

"Welcome to our home." Niall bowed before taking her hand.

"Thank you." Sheena curtsied.

"And this is Miss Cait Ross and Mr. Logan McAllister." Ian winked at Sheena, baffling her. Maybe he meant to reassure her and encourage her with his family. That just made her tense up. She felt all the color drain from her face. Had he fallen in love with her? Because she hadn't. Sheena looked away from Ian as Logan and Cait rose from their compulsory bow and curtsy.

"Ah, my dear, you must be tired after your long trip." Rose's tenderness softened Sheena's heart. But before Sheena could utter her polite protest, Rose continued, "Please go and freshen up before supper. Our butler already took your bags to your rooms and he'll show your companions to theirs." She paused to smile at her son. "I'm sure our Ian would like the honor of taking you to your door himself." Rose's eyes emitted rays of motherly love toward her son. Sheena couldn't say she'd seen anything like it before. Not in her own home anyway. Fatherly love she knew, but her mother never looked at her like that.

Unconditional love. That's what it looked like. She'd heard about it often enough at church, since God showered this type of love on His children, but she never came close to feeling it from her mother. Is this what her family missed? Would Sheena now get a chance to receive this undying love from a mother? It seemed as if it could warm a person right through.

And if Rose projected this, then surely Ian knew how to love. His love for his wife could grow strong and unbreakable. She thought Logan and she had shared this same love once, but now she knew they didn't.

She remembered begging Logan not to go to the Americas. She'd pleaded with him. Tried everything—reasoning, promises, crying and, inevitably, shouting. He hadn't listened to her though. He'd left her. And she never wanted to feel that hurt again.

Ian seemed rooted here. He wouldn't go anywhere. He would never leave her. "It would be my pleasure to escort you, Sheena." Ian placed Sheena's hand on his arm again.

She knew all eyes followed them as they left the room and the doors closed behind them. The others would now freely discuss their thoughts and perceptions of the future Mrs. Ian Mackenzie.

"Your family seems wonderful, and your home is beautiful," Sheena told Ian as they climbed the wide staircase.

"Thank you." He let out a laugh as infectious as his mother's. "But this isn't where I intend to live." Sheena raised an eyebrow, but didn't interrupt him with all the questions leaping to mind. "My parents are having a house built for us down the street. It will be ready for the night of our wedding." Sheena didn't know what to say to that. "The house will be just as beautiful as this one."

"I'm sure it will be," she finally managed to say, keeping her propriety intact. "That was very generous of your parents, Ian."

Ian only nodded. "This is your room." He opened the door, but did not set foot inside. "I will come and escort you to supper at the bell."

"Thank you."

He loosened her hand from his arm and kissed it. "You are very pretty, Sheena." She looked down at her hand still in his and somehow it looked rather small sitting atop his much larger one.

"Thank you." She gently slid her hand away from his and took a step back into her room. He bowed and she curtsied, before the door closed. Turning and leaning her back against the door, she slid down to the floor.

It all happened so fast. Meeting Ian and her future family. Learning about the house she would share with Ian after they married. Talk of their wedding night. She closed her eyes and rubbed her head. *I need You now more than ever, God.* Sheena opened her eyes to the delicately decorated bedroom. Everything in it made her feel like a lady, which, at the moment, made her feel most uncomfortable. She would marry Ian soon enough, with all that entailed.

And to think she'd just met him for the first time a couple of minutes ago. *That's correct,* she told herself, she'd only just met him. She would stay here a few days and get to know him. That's all. She already knew he treated her as a gentleman should. A very good start. He seemed to have good character traits. Honorable. Courteous. All admirable in a husband.

And yet, as she steadied herself and stood, she knew none of her thoughts mattered—whether she fell in love with Ian or not and whether she knew him or respected him. Completely inconsequential given their betrothal. They would marry in less than a fortnight. She couldn't run from that fact.

Feeling tired from a long day of traveling and the tumult of those emotional waves battering her mind and heart, Sheena climbed into bed to rest. The pillow looked soft and beckoned her to lie down. But with a knock on her door, she bolted upright before her head even got close.

She stared at the door, as if she could see through it by sheer mind power and then went to open it. Her feet felt as heavy as her head. Moving this slowly, however, wouldn't stop the passage of time. The events in her life would happen on course and she couldn't do anything about that. Nor could she hide out in here. And yet, she didn't think she could muster the will to face everyone again.

"Oh, Cait." Sheena reached out with relief at the sight of her friend, pulled her into the room and closed the door.

"Logan told me you almost fainted before. Are you feeling faint again?" Cait's concern sprawled all over her face.

"Nay. I'm just a wee worn out from the events of the

day." Sheena turned her face away from Cait in case it revealed too much and walked over to the bed again. She did not want to talk about her feelings for Logan and it seemed that is all she and Cait talked about lately. And they couldn't anymore. Sheena knew she shouldn't allow any feelings for him to grow anew.

"Aye, Sheena. I dare say we are all tired of this." Did she speak for Logan, as well? Cait walked over to Sheena's vanity table. "But I'm afraid the day has not yet ended." She pulled the upholstered stool out. "We'd better get your hair tidied up for supper." Sheena reluctantly sat. At least she could rest a bit.

"Thanks." She looked at Cait, who immediately busied herself with Sheena's unruly auburn locks. "Where is your room?"

"Right next door." Cait flashed Sheena a smile in the mirror. "They must think I'm your cousin, because my room is so pretty. I feel like a princess in it." If only Sheena felt the same way. If only happiness flowed from her, as it did from Cait. But she couldn't help feeling more like a princess locked in a tower.

Regardless of her qualms, though, she must face up to her responsibility. She couldn't shirk her duty.

She felt shame. Like a child protesting her bedtime. But she ought to stop complaining. God held her best interest at heart. He knew best for her and if He thought this best, who was she to argue? *God forgive me. I will be most happy in the blessings of life that You have bestowed upon me.*

"I'm glad you're receiving a little pampering, Cait.

You deserve it." Sheena forced herself to smile and the effort it took seemed all too obvious for her lifelong friend.

"I'm right next door." Cait stopped fixing her hair and put her hand on Sheena's shoulder. "Remember that. If you ever need me, no matter what time of day or night, come to me." The seriousness in Cait's brow made Sheena force her smile even further.

Placing her palm over Cait's hand on her shoulder, Sheena looked with gratitude at her friend in the mirror. "I will thank God for you tonight, Cait, and pray that your dreams for life really do come true."

Cait squeezed Sheena's shoulder. "As I will pray for you." Cait went back to work on Sheena's hair and Sheena sat staring at her reflection. Did her reflection even look back at her? She felt so disconnected, as if she were watching someone else.

The bell tolled before a knock on the door rattled both women. Sheena turned in her seat. She took a long breath. Ready or not, her destiny awaited.

Chapter Twelve

Logan stood back near the wall, watching as Ian knocked on Sheena's paneled door. "Oh, hello, Cait. Are you and Sheena ready for supper?"

"Aye." Cait opened the door farther to reveal Sheena, a pleasant smile spreading faintly on Sheena's lips as she approached the doorway. Cait lost no time getting out of their way and taking Logan's arm so they could follow Ian and Sheena down the stairs to the dining room.

It came as absolutely no surprise to Logan that he sat at the far end of the long, wooden table away from Sheena, who sat positioned in the middle, while Cait sat on the opposite end. Someone had planned this out carefully in advance, because this arrangement offered complete interaction between the family and the newcomers.

From this distance, though, Logan couldn't hear any of the conversations Sheena delved into with those around her. Too many other voices filled the air between them. And so, he watched her, making sure to look at his food and talk to those around him from time to time so no one would notice how much he truly stared at Sheena. But every time Ian leaned in to talk to her and she laughed, Logan ground his food harder between his teeth. Resentment? Most definitely. Protectiveness? Of course. The whole situation proved pure torture.

"You seem to be enjoying the ice cream, Logan." Caroline looked down at the wee bit that remained of his serving. Logan nodded. So that's what the rich called this cold, sweet stuff that melted in his mouth. He'd never eaten ice cream before.

"Would you like some more?" Caroline sat ready to call over a servant, but Logan declined—he wouldn't impose. And Caroline smiled demurely at him. "How are you related to Sheena?" The question took Logan aback. He'd arranged to take Boyd's place so quickly he never thought this far ahead. He didn't know what to say about the matter. He couldn't lie. And yet, he couldn't say he came because of his undying love for Sheena. The fact that he planned to do everything in his power to stop Sheena's marriage to Ian probably wouldn't be the wisest answer, either. "We are fellow clansmen."

Caroline gasped and everyone's head turned in their direction. "Excuse me." She took a slow sip of her drink to hide her shock and everyone's attention went back to whence it came, except Sheena's. Her gaze lingered. "Are we allowed to use the term *clansmen* these days?" Caroline hushed her voice.

"I'm sorry if I offended you, Caroline. The old terms slip out occasionally." The Duke of Cumberland had succeeded in crushing everything dear to the Highlanders' way of life. Logan stared into Sheena's eyes, not bothering to look at Caroline, even when she dismissed the offense with her hand in an amiable manner.

Scotland's joining with England, as a result of the Acts of Union of 1707, obviously benefited a few like the Mackenzies, allowing them to trade freely with the Americas, thus opening up the opportunity for them to become wealthy tobacco lords. But it pit most of Scotland against itself, grinding almost everything beloved to the Highlanders. Logan's own life lay in ruins thanks to the blows his father had received in 1715. And Sheena lost her brother at the Battle of Culloden in 1746 and her father as a direct result of that.

Life would never have taken this terrible turn if the Treaty of Union had never been forged. Then again, if Logan's father hadn't lost everything, his family would have never moved down to Callander and Logan would never have met Sheena. Logan breathed deeply. Who but God understood why things happened in life?

Sheena turned away from Logan to Ian when he addressed her and to Logan's further dismay, Caroline brought up the subject again. "So tell me, Logan, does that term mean you and Sheena are cousins?"

Logan took a sip of his drink, stalling his response, "Nay. Not in the sense that you and Ian are. But we have known each other since birth." Logan wondered if he was offering too much information. He didn't want the knowledge of his coming here with Sheena and Cait to get back to Tavia and Jean.

The consequences could hurt Sheena and Boyd. Tavia and Jean would not believe or care whether or not Sheena knew of the scheme and they might punish her worse than he dared to imagine.

Logan had already witnessed Sheena get hurt as a result of his actions once. And Logan wouldn't let that happen again. "Reed." Logan turned to the man on his left, in hopes of ending the awkward conversation with Caroline. "A copy of Thomas Boston's *Human Nature in Its Fourfold State* lay on the night table in my bedroom. Have you read it?" The young man's eyes sprang to life. A man of books. *Thank You, God.* No doubt Logan could keep up a good conversation with him for the rest of supper and avoid Caroline. *I'm thanking You now, God, for all those lonely nights I dreaded when I missed Sheena and home and You provided me with books.*

"You must retire to the library with me so I can show you some of my other favorites." Reed downed his drink heartily.

"That sounds wonderful, Reed, but if you will permit me to postpone your invitation to another day, I would be much obliged." Logan noticed Sheena saying her farewells. She would retire to her room soon and he didn't want Sheena out of his sight for a second. "I confess that after today's travels I would not make good company." That certainly rang true as Logan fought to keep his eyelids open as Caroline played the pianoforte in the drawing room.

"Of course. We can continue our discussion tomorrow again over supper. And in the meantime, I'll set out some books for you that you might enjoy." Logan thanked Reed before Reed went to talk with Niall and Logan made his way to Cait's side.

"How is your evening going?" Cait whispered and Logan gave her a quick look. He couldn't answer fully, but he knew Cait understood his heartache as Sheena and Ian left the drawing room. Logan took Cait's arm to follow them, willing his feet to move as he climbed the grand staircase. What a terrible disadvantage these stairs seemed now in such a large estate house. At home, he could crawl into bed after only taking a few steps from anywhere.

"Wait." Cait pulled Logan's arm, stopping him before they reached the top of the stairs. "Look." She pointed toward the upper hallway with her free hand and Logan's eyes followed.

In front of Sheena's bedroom door stood Ian. He held before him a small box and Sheena took it. Logan's heart ached as she opened it. He knew what the box held. He wanted to give Sheena so much, but never could. And now he didn't know if he would get his chance again.

It angered him, watching Ian stand before the woman he loved with a gift. Having an abundance of wealth gave Ian the advantage in so many ways. He probably spent more on this one gift than most farmers made in a year.

A gold Luckenbooth. Ian took the brooch with two entwined hearts under a crown from Sheena's hand and pinned it on her. A far more elaborate brooch than Logan could ever dream of giving her. Ian probably even engraved the heart with some words of love or some memorable date, like their upcoming wedding day.

Logan hated seeing the brooch. He knew she would wear it during the most important times of her life, their wedding day, anniversaries, the birth of their bairns. Then she would no doubt pin it on their bairns. Logan could barely watch the two of them together. The thought of Sheena bearing Ian's children pained him.

But what could he do? He stood rigid. Completely motionless. Forced to watch another major milestone in Sheena's life take place right before his eyes. Another step leading Sheena further toward the altar to become Ian's bride. And Logan could do nothing to stop it.

"Did you enjoy supper?" Logan projected his voice to the point of nearly shouting at Cait as he pulled her up the rest of the stairs. Whatever crazy path they embarked on Logan wouldn't run away with his tail between his legs. He'd come to fight and he meant to win that fight. He'd stop this wedding. Somehow.

Overcoming her initial shock, Cait followed Logan's lead. "Aye." She looked directly at him as he smiled appreciatively back. "It was most wonderful."

"Aye. It was." Logan moved his head as if scanning the area, until finally resting on Ian and Sheena as if he just now saw them for the first time. "Oh, hello. Did you both enjoy supper?"

"Aye," Sheena responded in a much softer tone than Logan had used. He thought she looked embarrassed, like a child caught with something she knew she shouldn't possess. Did Sheena care to spare his feelings? It hadn't seemed like that today.

"Good to hear." Ian's knack for always projecting politeness irritated Logan. Because as much as Logan wanted to hate the man, he could seem to find no reason to do so. Yet.

Of course, Ian didn't know the situation between Logan and Sheena and only acted as any man would, but Logan would watch him. Closely. If Ian so much as let a hair fall out of place, Logan would pounce on him.

Logan released Cait's arm. "Did you need Cait's help tonight?" he asked Sheena.

"Nay." Sheena took a step back, passing the threshold into her bedroom and no longer standing in the hallway with Ian. "I am quite all right." Logan wondered if Sheena got upset at the intrusion, but he couldn't help it. Taking over for Boyd as her chaperone entailed making sure her chastity remained safe and unchallenged. And under Logan's watchful eye, that also meant no hugging or kissing. He would do his job or die trying. He would never let anyone compromise Sheena's reputation.

Who did he think he was fooling? Surely not himself. He didn't want Sheena anywhere near Ian. Not close enough to talk and definitely not close enough to touch. She would always remain his lassie. If only he could grab her and run.

"Good." Logan looked at Sheena and even though he meant to keep his eyes on hers, he couldn't help looking at her new brooch. Just as he thought, the expensive gold Luckenbooth shined. He looked back at Sheena and although her eyes flamed golden with anger, her cheeks turned red, as well. With embarrassment? Did she think her swain planned to buy her love? Did it work, despite her protest earlier that money didn't matter to her?

Ian stepped toward Sheena's door—obviously he didn't notice the difference in Sheena's composure. But why should he after only knowing her for just several hours? "Then I will take my leave of you, Sheena." Ian bent down and kissed her hand. Logan knew if he and Cait didn't stand between them Ian would take the opportunity to kiss Sheena since that desire was plainly written all over his perfect face. But thankfully, Logan stood there. Logan bit the inside of his cheek making himself stay quiet until Ian walked out of earshot. But before he could address Sheena, she told him and Cait, "Good night."

Logan didn't waste time staring at the outside of her closed paneled door. Sheena made it abundantly clear she didn't want to talk to them. *Be honest,* he scolded himself, she didn't want to talk to *him.* So he walked Cait to her room. "Until tomorrow, then." He tried to sound cheerful, but Cait would never fall for that. She knew his wishes too well.

"Logan, I hate to see you like this."

"I know, and I'm sorry I put you in the middle where you have to witness it all. But I didn't know what else to do, and I still don't know what to do. Until we get home, so I can unearth what I believe will end this sham of a betrothal, all I can do is play my part as her chaperone."

"Even if it kills you?"

"Aye."

Cait shook her head and kissed Logan's cheek. "Your poor heart, Logan." Worry creased every inch of her face. "Please try to rest it." Logan gave her a look showing her the impossibility of that. "Logan, Ian may appear perfect in every way, but anyone can see he's definitely not a novice with women. He operates a wee bit too smoothly. Although he hasn't won over Sheena's heart yet. If he ever will."

Logan left Cait to retire to his own room, where sheer exhaustion made him collapse onto his bed. His body might give out, his heart might ache, but his mind couldn't stop thinking about Sheena.

Did Logan's pursuit of Sheena as his wife prove that he harbored a selfish soul? He couldn't provide her with the kind of life Ian could. A fancy estate house, finely made clothes, abundant food and everything else she deserved.

Ian definitely stood out as a very wealthy man, even compared to the nobility. Logan rolled over, leaning his head on his crossed forearms. Logan didn't measure up. He did own a piece of land in the Americas, but as his wife Sheena would need to work hard alongside him to make a home on that land. Undeniably, her life would unfold more easily here with servants at her disposal. She would never have to lift a finger.

And more than just the material goods and ease of life, Ian also seemed every bit the gentleman and quite annoyingly fancied her. Chances are he would treat her well as a husband and would make a good father. The list continued to grow.

Ian's family seemed pleasant enough, but Logan's family equaled them on that account. Yet, in a sense, Sheena had never known the love of a mother, and in Ian's family, she would. Logan rolled over again, bracing himself for a very long night, because regardless of the negative thoughts swimming through his head, Logan knew he loved Sheena and always would.

Sheena opened her eyes and rolled over. She stared up at the window. The sunlight shone in. So morning came. But what time exactly, she didn't know. She felt anything but refreshed. Nevertheless, she couldn't go back to sleep. With only two days in Glasgow, Ian had scheduled both days full of activity. She couldn't help sighing. All the entertainment last night only lasted several hours, but it drained her. And another full day already presented itself.

God, please watch over me today and bless me with the strength to live my life. An image of Logan popped into her head and she couldn't hide it from God. *Aye, God, bless Logan in his life, as well. He used to be a very good man.* She smiled and then checked herself, remembering what she should pray for—acceptance of her situation and peace in her life. Squeezing her eyes shut tighter, Sheena hurried out her last thoughts upon hearing footsteps near her door.

A knock made her panic. It would take her some

time to get ready. "Sheena, are you awake?" Cait's voice whispered at the door.

Hiding behind the door, Sheena let Cait in.

"We've been waiting for you to get up." Cait held a silver tray in her hands. She set it down on the bedside table before going to make Sheena's bed.

"What time is it?" Sheena looked at the elaborate silver serving set with her own pot of tea and enough food for more than three people.

"It's well past breakfast." Cait pulled Sheena's blanket into place.

"Nay. That late? Ian had so many plans for today."

"There will still be time enough. Eat and then we'll make you beautiful."

Sheena interrupted Cait's soothing tone with her own sense of anxiety. "I can't. I've got to get downstairs." She raced to get ready.

"Good morning." Ian stood the moment Sheena stepped into the fancy parlor. *Oh, good, still morning.* She smiled back at him.

"Good morning," she said to Ian and then Logan. Logan? He nodded at her and her body froze. Logan and Ian sat here alone. What had they talked about? Neither looked upset or the least bit uncomfortable. How long had they held a private discussion?

"I'll just go see if Finnean's ready with the carriage." Cait excused herself.

"Where is everyone else?" Sheena looked around at

the empty room, noting how much larger it seemed without Ian's whole family in it.

"My father and Reed are working. My mother, Maggie, and Caroline had some charity business to attend to. And your cousin has to work all week but did say he'd be joining us for supper tonight and tomorrow. So that just leaves us." Ian stepped toward her.

"I'm so sorry I missed breakfast." Sheena didn't want to think about how pathetic she must seem to his family now. Sleeping well past breakfast could appear most lazy to those with full schedules. What would they think of her? She'd brought this embarrassment on herself. Exactly the kind of shameful behavior her mother would chastise her for. But Ian didn't seem disturbed.

"Traveling can be very tiring. So my mother gave everyone strict orders to let you rest."

"How very sweet of her."

Ian looked pleased. He held out his arm welcoming her to join him and Sheena took it. "I hope you got all the rest you needed, because I want to show you Glasgow, your soon-to-be new home." Ian squeezed her hand and Sheena nodded.

Could a romantic soul dwell within Ian? Nay, not possible. He'd agreed to an arranged marriage. Surely, a true romantic would never do that. She prayed again for strength today.

The splendor of Glasgow hadn't faded since yesterday and Ian seemed to know everything about this major port city. He made a wonderful tour guide, pointing out

buildings such as the University of Glasgow, the Tol-
booth and the Tron Steeple.

"Here's our stop," Ian told Logan.

"Thanks." Logan opened the carriage door with Cait
in tow and stepped down.

Sheena grew tense. Where had Logan and Ian agreed
to take them all to? "Shall we join them?" Ian offered
Sheena his hand and she took it not knowing what she
agreed to.

"That's Glasgow Cathedral." Ian pointed at the mas-
sive church. And that made Sheena's head feel light. A
mad rush of thoughts hit her. Did Ian's family attend to
all those things today? Didn't rich people just sit at home
and let their servants do all the work? That's how Tavia
and Jean lived and they couldn't even sweep up a crumb
of the wealth Ian's family owned. Did everyone await her
presence inside the cathedral? Would they surprise her
with her wedding ceremony to Ian today? Right now?

Chapter Thirteen

Sheena could hardly breathe. She steadied herself for the next couple of days with the thought of getting to know Ian. Not marry him. This couldn't happen. Not this soon.

Is that why he gave her the brooch last night? He couldn't wait? Did Cait know? Is that why she insisted on making sure Sheena looked extra pretty today?

Nay, her wedding couldn't take place today. Tavia and Jean hadn't left in time to get here. They would want to witness her wedding. Wouldn't they? They needed somewhere to show off the beautiful silk gowns they'd hired a seamstress to make for the occasion.

Sheena stumbled as she walked beside Ian. Surely, Logan wouldn't agree to this. Sheena looked past Ian in horror. Did she really expect Logan to stop her wedding to Ian? That was crazy.

No one could stop this wedding. Her fate lay sealed. Her mother had already paid her dowry—they would lose everything if Sheena didn't marry Ian. They would end up destitute, at the mercy of other people's charity. In addition, Sheena's mother would hate her, she would disappoint her aunt, who had arranged all this, wrong Ian and hurt his family. Could she live with herself after doing all that?

"Sheena?" She saw Ian's face before her, but it blurred. She couldn't take another step. She couldn't...

"Sheena." She heard her name called while someone tapped her cheek softly. She could smell ammonia and it made her eyes pop open and her nose burn. Forcing her head to turn away from the odor, she pressed her face into a heated brown vest while her numb body lay against its owner.

"Oh, thank you, God." Sheena recognized Cait's voice, proclaiming relief. The odor probably came from Cait's smelling salts. But why did she need... The realization that she'd fainted seized her as the memory of what made her faint came flooding back. Panic set in again. She clawed at the arms under the puffy white sleeves that held her. She needed to know what would happen to her today. Would she become Mrs. Ian Mackenzie?

"Open your eyes and look at me." Sheena didn't need to hear Logan's low voice whispering in her ear to know who held her. And she wished he hadn't said anything. Because now that she had come to, she couldn't avert her duty. She pulled her head away from Logan and looked up into his frightened face, but she couldn't utter a single word.

"Has she come to?" Sheena heard Ian blanket his concern over her.

"Lassie?" Logan searched her eyes for any sign of consciousness. Fully aware, she looked back into his softened brown eyes, thinking she saw love for her in them. But most likely, she told herself, she saw nothing more than mere concern for her well-being. If he ever loved her, he couldn't now. Not after watching her with Ian. And yet, she didn't speak or even blink as she stared at him. She felt safe in his arms. Protected. And she liked that. She missed it.

As his warmth radiated upon her, providing a sheltered haven, she couldn't help liking the gentleness of his arms around her. She couldn't deny how conscious she became of him holding her. Nor could she understand it. How did Logan come to hold her when Ian held her hand before she fainted?

"Lassie?" Sheena snapped out of it. She couldn't stay like this forever. She needed to answer Logan, let him go. She must marry Ian. Accept her place in life. And that place didn't include Logan.

"Aye." She forced her mouth to move. "Was I out long?" Logan squeezed her and kissed her forehead. His spontaneous emotional reaction made her blush uncontrollably. Maybe she did see love in his brown eyes after all.

"Long enough, lassie." Logan stiffened and made sure her strength returned so she could move. Sheena realized how odd she must look embracing another man in front of her betrothed. Being with Logan could hurt Ian just as being with Ian could hurt Logan.

"I'm fine." She pulled away from Logan. "Thank you." She couldn't look at Logan anymore and instead met Ian's mossy eyes, as he held his hand out to hoist her up.

Pressed against Ian, Sheena shook off the knowledge that she didn't feel the same way leaning against him as she did against Logan. Yet she quickly attributed that to nothing more than being more at ease with Logan. She'd known Logan her whole life. She hadn't even known Ian for twenty-four hours yet. She must stop her mind from racing to Logan and her body from remembering his embrace. Ian held her life and future in his hands. He could make it good or very bad. She couldn't provoke his wrath.

"I'm sorry, Ian." Sheena felt ripped in two. Torn between her future duty and her past love.

"No need," Ian quieted her. "I'm just glad you're well." He wrapped his arm around her more tightly. Whatever happened, Ian obviously wouldn't let her fall into Logan's arms again. "Let's sit down over here. We'll see about getting you a... Thank you," Ian told a woman wearing an apron who held out a tankard of water.

Glasgow, Sheena reminded herself. People everywhere. No doubt more than just her little party witnessed her faint. Shame on her. Did she make them fodder for the city's rumor mill? A hasty wedding and a fainting bride usually meant one clear thing to the gossips.

"Thank you." She handed the empty tankard back to Ian and he nodded his thanks to the kind woman, too.

"She's better now," Ian addressed the crowd loudly, to Sheena's embarrassment. She did not enjoy being the center of attention and definitely not at a time like this. "Thank you all for your concern." But when they appeared reluctant to leave, Ian gave them an explanation. "She's just a little worn out from traveling." This seemed to make sense to everyone and they slowly left the four of them alone. Sheena couldn't feel more grateful.

"You still look pale." Ian surveyed her face. "I'm going to find something for you to eat. I'll be right back. Don't move." Sheena nodded. She owed Ian more than just her cooperation. And he left her with an expression of worried concern.

"I think he's right." Logan stood in front of Sheena. "Just sit and rest until you get some nourishment." Sheena nodded. "You'll be fine in a couple minutes."

"I told you to have breakfast this morning." Cait didn't hold back.

"Aye," Sheena smiled into her best friend's loving face. "I should have listened to you."

Cait smiled back knowingly. "You should listen to me on a great many things." Sheena couldn't agree with her. She knew exactly what Cait meant and she didn't want to go over that argument about Logan once again, especially not in front of Logan himself.

Ignoring Cait, Sheena looked over at the cathedral grounds. The fear of having a marriage ceremony today passed. Not a single person came out of the Cathedral to tend to her. Obviously, she realized, because no one was hiding in there.

Just an ordinary day. How silly of her to give in to such crazy thoughts. An honorable man like Ian didn't deserve that.

"Here you are." Ian placed a triangular piece of oatcake in front of her and she took it thankfully. He cared for her already. That thought made her feel even worse. Up until now she hadn't acted like the woman Ian deserved. He warranted loyalty, love, friendship and a true Christian partner as his wife. What would she give him as a wife? A woman obsessed with her past? If she couldn't even act the part as his betrothed properly, how would she fare as his wife?

"While she's eating, I'll just go deliver this first one myself." Logan consulted Ian.

"I think that would be best." Ian approved of something Sheena knew nothing about. She wanted to ask what Logan referred to, what he must deliver, but she couldn't. Not her place. As the future Mrs. Ian Mackenzie, she shouldn't care.

But she couldn't squelch her curiosity, either, and kept her attention on Logan as he walked toward a house across the street. Who did he need to see in Glasgow?

She chewed her crunchy oatcake as she saw a woman open the door and Logan hand her an envelope. What did the envelope contain? She didn't know, but the woman hugged Logan and jumped around shouting. Sheena couldn't make out any words, but she could see the woman dabbing her eyes with her apron.

Sheena glanced down at the last piece of her rough-looking oatcake before placing it in her mouth. Peeking up again, she saw Logan walking back to them carrying something proudly in his hands.

Sheena swallowed the oatcake too quickly, scratching her throat before he returned. And yet, she started to feel better. Maybe her stomach was affecting her head. Not her head affecting her heart that made her faint.

"Would you like one?" Logan opened a towel to produce a bunch of appetizing scones. Sheena took one and smelled its delicious steam scent as Logan offered one to Ian and Cait before sitting down and eating his.

"I was just hungry." Sheena looked from Ian to Cait and finally to Logan once she finished her scone. "I am feeling much better now." She stood to emphasize her point.

"Let's take a walk, then." Ian rose and took her arm. "Logan has some more business to take care of." Logan led them down another street after getting directions from Ian.

"This is the house." Logan let go of Cait's arm and pulled another envelope out before making his way to the door. After knocking, he turned and smiled at Sheena, making it look as if he was smiling at all of them. But Sheena couldn't think about that, she couldn't help wondering if Logan contracted these people out for their food? Could he seriously get this excited about eating good cooking? Maybe. He surely didn't eat well when he lived at home. Sheena couldn't count the number of times she snuck food out to Logan when they played together as children. Amazing how such a skinny lad could grow into such a strong man.

"Hello?" a woman's harsh voice called through the crack in her door.

"Hi, Mrs. Johnson?" The lady nodded before Logan continued, "I've just returned home from the Americas and brought a letter from your son." Logan hardly finished his sentence before the woman yanked the door open shouting for her family and crying tears of happiness.

Logan held the letter out for her. "He was doing very well, last time I saw him." She hugged Logan. And Sheena wiped a tear from her eye. All of mankind understood missing a loved one. This mother's love extended to Logan as if hugging him equaled hugging her own son across the ocean. God surely knew how to create everyday miracles.

Before long, a little crowd of neighbors gathered from the woman's cries. And Logan produced more envelopes. Excitement at being able to deliver a letter to a man's family grew and soon Logan had been stripped of envelopes, while mothers, sisters, aunts, cousins and friends stood clutching the letters to their chests, some still hugging Logan. Seeing the beauty of God's work touched Sheena deeply.

She knew how happy Logan made these families. She experienced it firsthand when her family received a note from her brother only days before he got shot and died in the Battle of Culloden. Reading those last few words—*I love you all*—still echoed in her mind.

She wiped away another tear. How wonderful for Logan to set himself as God's messenger. Surely, God would bless him for this good deed.

They all needed to give themselves over to the will of God. He would fill their lives with happiness. They just needed to listen to Him. *Thank You, God, for making me understand that what You want for us and from us is love.*

And she saw Logan then. Really saw him. And he didn't appear any different than the Logan she had always known. A man who carried letters during a potentially deadly sea voyage and then all over Scotland just to help these families reconnect with loved ones abroad. She still didn't trust Logan, but neither could she cast him as the evil monster anymore.

Another day dawned. Logan grudgingly rose from his bed. He would dance attendance on Ian and Sheena once more, forced to watch them together as future husband and wife.

How long could he possibly keep up the charade as her chaperone? He wanted so badly to tell Ian he loved Sheena. But what would that accomplish?

Nothing. The man would no doubt throw him out or, at best, pity him. Ian stood in the path of righteousness. And yet, Logan almost fell apart more times than he cared to count.

"How much longer is he going to walk?" Cait whispered to Logan, as they followed Ian and Sheena down yet another meandering pathway. After their carriage

ride out of Glasgow, they had walked for what seemed
like hours over the countryside toward the water's edge.

"He just wants to hold hands with her." Logan tilted
his head in annoyance. Ian walked too close for Logan's
liking.

"He also wants to keep us at a distance." Cait leaned
on Logan's arm as her foot fell into a dip in the dirt.
Logan automatically steadied her without taking his eyes
off Sheena. Cait stifled a grin. "Logan, contain yourself.
I'm sure he won't try anything with the two of us always
so close."

"He'd better not get any ideas." Logan hurried their
pace more.

"You have to admit the man talks endlessly." Cait
looked up at Logan. "He'll have nothing left to say once
they're married. Sorry," she chided herself needlessly, as
Logan shook her comment away. He had already fallen
victim to a foul mood. Tomorrow they would return
home. Then he could see about his plan to end Sheena's
betrothal to Ian. He hoped Angus had found the box by
now, but if not, he would dig up acres around his home
until he found the Montgomery family's heirloom box
that housed the secret letter from Sheena's father. *God,
give me the ability to cope until then.*

"How thoughtful," Sheena told Ian as Logan and Cait
caught up to them. "Ian arranged for us to have a picnic
here." Her head moved around, taking in the scenery.
But Logan didn't look at it. He didn't want to remember
this part of Scotland.

"After yesterday, I knew I had to take better care of

you." Ian helped Sheena onto the blanket with a hopeful face, shining with happiness. Logan let out a long breath and pushed his weight onto one leg, restraining himself by throwing his arms across his chest.

Sheena busied herself with laying out her skirts properly. Making room for Cait to sit beside her, she also left room for the men. "Thank you," she told Ian as he offered her some refreshment first. "This is lovely."

"We'll have to do this regularly." Ian handed a goblet to Logan and then one to Cait. "Jean told me you are particularly fond of the countryside."

"She is correct." Sheena looked out onto the water while sipping her drink. But Ian didn't seem to see anything but Sheena. He probably wouldn't even notice if snakes made a home in his hair. Logan coughed and Sheena glared at him before Cait hit him needlessly on the back a few times. And entirely too hard, he might add. He would remember to mention that to her later.

"Why are you coughing?" He held up his drink to show the source of his discomfort before taking another sip and remaining quiet. He couldn't take too much more of this.

"You must stop clenching your teeth every time Ian opens his mouth." Cait held Logan's arm after their picnic.

"I can't help it." Again, Logan never removed his concentration from Sheena. "He's paying way too much attention to her, isn't he?"

"As I said last night, he's very smooth."

"Yes, he is. Ian seems a little too well rehearsed.

Compare Ian to Finnean, Ian's driver over there." Logan nodded in Finnean's direction as Finnean stood petting one of the carriage horse's manes. "Finnean seems very genuine whenever I talk to him, but Ian seems to have some secret he's trying to hide."

Cait looked at Finnean and choked out her reply, "I'll admit, I prefer Finnean's company." She looked up at Logan with flushed cheeks. "But maybe we're biased. Neither of us want to see Sheena marry Ian."

"No, we don't." Logan prayed God agreed with them.

"I thought we would ride back to the house. I don't want you overdoing it and fainting, as you did yesterday." Ian handed Sheena up into the carriage.

"That's very thoughtful, but I'm fine. Really. I am not prone to fainting," Sheena rambled on as Ian entered the carriage after her. "Yesterday was out of the ordinary." And if her mother ever found out about it, she would chastise Sheena for such a display of weakness in front of her betrothed, believing it one thing for a woman of her age and position to succumb to a spell and quite another for Sheena.

"I'm glad to hear it."

Sheena forced a smile for Ian. A truly considerate man. Charming even. And it seemed as if he did want to make the best of their marriage. God certainly had not sent her down here to rot. A perfectly pleasant and comfortable life awaited her here with Ian. She should welcome the stability as a very nice change.

But how could she concentrate on Ian with Logan around? The sheer sight of Logan threatened to bring back all her old feelings. He stood as a reminder of everything she held dear—her past, their village of Callander. Everything she would lose when she married Ian.

"We have only one small stop to make on the way if that suits you," Ian asked them all as everyone took their seats.

"Absolutely." Sheena's agreeable mood shone through.

"That's settled, then." Ian turned to Logan. "We will make that delivery stop on our way home." Logan dipped his chin and again Sheena did not like Ian and Logan sharing secrets, but at least this time she knew where they now headed.

Just thinking about another letter for a worried mother put a smile on her face. She loved delivering those letters. Logan's return to Scotland had turned into a blessing for so many. To the mothers and the men's families, of course. Not to her.

"I'll only be a minute," Logan told them before the carriage came to a complete stop.

"Nonsense." Ian held on to Sheena's hand. "We quite enjoy these little trysts." Sheena knew Ian spoke for both of them as a soon-to-be-married man ought to do, but nevertheless it shocked her at first, seeing as she had never experienced anyone holding such claim over her. Logan never spoke for her.

Not wanting to think about that anymore, she spoke up herself. "Aye. We cannot remain in here and let you

have all the fun, Logan, even though you do deserve all
the glory." Logan's face turned from Sheena sharply as
the carriage stopped, and he rushed out. Had she offended him? She didn't think she'd said anything that
bad.

Before Sheena even set her foot on the ground, Logan
knocked on the recipient's door. As if in a repeat of yesterday, a woman answered and teared up as Logan produced the letter.

"Thank God for sending you." The woman hugged
Logan. "You have made an old woman very happy. If
God called me home tomorrow, I could go in peace."

Logan told her he was happy to bring her the news,
as she reached in her apron pocket for a handkerchief.
After she wiped her tears, she looked at him squarely.
"My son's father passed away this winter. My son still
doesn't know. I'd like to send him a letter if you know
of anyone going back to the Americas."

Sheena's face fell. The poor woman stood very
much in the same situation as her own mother. Sheena
wouldn't dare ask about the woman's situation—she
didn't want to insult her pride. She could only pray God
surrounded this woman with the people and strength she
needed to get through something like this.

"If you can have a letter ready by next week, I will
make sure it gets to him." Logan patted her arm. Next
week? Would Logan come back all this way just for a
letter?

"But I don't have much money." The woman looked

inside her home anxiously and Logan began talking before she could say another word.

"Don't worry about that. We'll get that letter to your son."

"Oh, thank you, thank you." The woman clasped her hands together as if in prayer. "Bless you." She kissed his cheek.

"Be sure it's ready by next week," Logan called over his shoulder as he walked away from her.

"It will be." She waved her handkerchief in farewell. Logan waved back as they all began walking back to the carriage.

"So how do you like Glasgow?" Ian asked Sheena as they headed back to the street. Still enlivened, Sheena smiled. Her step much lighter. Her heart open. And her mind free.

"It is beyond my wildest dreams. It is exceptionally pretty. And the people are wonderful."

"I'm glad you think so highly of it."

"Oh, I do." They stopped talking to nod and smile as another couple passed them along the sidewalk.

"I hope you will be happy here." Sheena sensed Ian stiffen as he said this. Realizing his remark was the closest he had ever come to asking her about her feelings toward him, she needed to say something. But what? The delay in response grew too long. She couldn't offend him.

"I hope so, too." Maybe he hoped to hear something else. Maybe he wanted her to say *she knew she would*.

"I'll just go and get Finnean to take us home." Ian

helped Sheena into the carriage before leaving to find their driver.

"You are doing God's work." Sheena looked at Logan for a brief instant as he entered the carriage.

"Aye." Sitting down, Logan shrugged off the comment.

She forced herself to look at him again. "You've reconnected loved ones." Logan's gaze fiercely held on to hers and she fought the urge to squirm in her seat. Did he think of reconnecting their love? The carriage suddenly felt very hot and cramped. But she wouldn't let him make her feel uneasy. She would say what needed saying, if for nothing else than to praise God's work. "It was very kind of you to promise to get a letter to that woman's son."

"Aye," Cait agreed. "And all the women from yesterday were so grateful for that courtesy, as well." Sheena looked at Cait. She didn't know Logan had offered to send letters to the Americas for that many families.

"I know you said you weren't poor anymore, Logan, but that's a lot of letters. How will you pay for all those letters?" Sheena tried to calculate how many letters would need sending and how much it would cost. "I will help you pay for them," she offered, not thinking until the words left her mouth that he could take offense. Especially since he might think the money would come from Ian's pocket after she wed him.

"Thank you for your offer." Logan spoke through gritted teeth. "But I'll get the letters to the Americas myself."

"Fine, if you don't want my help," Sheena huffed, straightening her skirt.

"I don't *need* your help." Logan emphasized the word *need* in a low voice.

"It won't be a financial burden at all," Cait cut into the escalating argument with a frown on her face. "We'll just take the letters with us." Cait shot her hand over her mouth more quickly than Logan's eyes could widen at her.

"What do you mean—" Sheena leaned in closer "—take them with you?" Sheena saw Logan's eyes return to normal size as he faced her.

"I've booked passage on a ship leaving for the Americas next week and I'm taking my whole family with me."

Sheena couldn't believe his words, even though she heard him with perfect clarity. She stared at him. He planned to leave Scotland. Again.

"Cait?" Sheena looked for answers in her face when she uncovered it, but she started having a hard time seeing Cait as her eyes welled up. The air felt thicker and she couldn't quite seem to catch her breath. "You're leaving?" She heaved out the words as her chest grew and constricted rapidly. She would live alone in Glasgow. Her stomach knotted and twisted. Sweat beaded on her forehead. She felt hot and cold at the same time. "I need air." She fumbled forward and Logan caught her and returned her to her seat.

"Breathe," he repeated, until she listened to him. Her eyes shot between Logan and Cait. She would lose Cait, her best friend, and Logan again. Time raced ahead of her and she couldn't dig her heels in hard enough to stop it. "Come on, lassie. Stay with us." Logan tapped her cheek and she stared into his brown eyes, the color of the boat that would take him far away from her forevermore.

Chapter Fourteen

In a week from now her life would be altered completely with no more connection to her past. No more Cait, no more Callander and no more Logan. Sheena cried as Logan held her. She felt his hand rub her back. She heard his voice whisper hushing sounds as his breath swept her ear. She couldn't control her tears, but at least this time she didn't faint.

She would lose everything she ever knew within a week. She unearthed her handkerchief and blotted her eyes. She must stop this nonsense. She couldn't let Ian see her like this.

"I'm fine." She moved away from Logan, summoning all the strength she possessed. "Thank you." She blotted her eyes one last time and stored the handkerchief away. "Let's just forget, for today at least, that this conversation took place. We can talk about it later." She set her sights out the window, but saw Logan exchange an uncertain look with Cait. "Please," she spoke softly to

Logan and he nodded, moving back to his seat as Ian came into the carriage and sat beside Sheena.

After a quick glance in Ian's direction to appease him, Sheena steadied herself to remain looking out the window so Ian wouldn't notice her red eyes. Seeing her happy one minute and in tears the next, he would think her utterly insane.

Maybe she was going insane. If not yet, maybe she was headed in that direction. Insanity might run in her family. Her father suffered from it. Is this how he felt? Did it creep up on a person slowly? That seemed the case with her. These fainting spells were increasing at a worrisome rate and it continued getting harder for her to think clearly.

Worn out, Sheena finally arrived at her bedroom. Ian's family had invited what seemed like everyone in Glasgow to come and meet her before her departure tomorrow. The whole affair exhausted her. She greeted and talked to guests until their faces all blurred into one. Somehow she found enough residual energy to change into her white nightgown and tied the blue ribbon that pulled into a bow at the top. But without the ability to muster up some extra fortitude, she just sat on her bed, holding her hairbrush with her long unruly auburn hair falling into her face as she drifted off into thought.

Everyone had gushed over Ian tonight, forcing her to acknowledge her blessings. And considering the man could, just as easily, act like an unchristian miscreant, she agreed. Being already betrothed, he didn't need to impress her. She already belonged to him. And given that Jean held Tavia's best interest at heart when selecting a husband for Sheena, she didn't want to think about how much worse a man she could find herself betrothed to.

Throughout her life, Sheena heard stories of women treated more than unkindly by their husbands. Men who swore in front of God they would love and cherish their wives and afterward never even came close. She should count her blessings, and yet, a part of her still clung to her childhood and didn't want her future to proceed. That part still wanted her life in Callander to endure.

She'd always dreamed of growing old there and now the village would lose every trace of her family. She wouldn't even remain in the memory of her friends, for they wouldn't live there any longer, either.

She couldn't believe it. They wouldn't even live in Scotland. But what did it matter? She couldn't keep Logan as a male friend. And if Cait found happiness in the Americas, she should rejoice for her.

She shouldn't let her emotions run wild. But how could Logan and Cait have withheld this information from her? Sheena's temper rose thinking about this life-altering secret. And she found herself unable to sit alone any longer mulling it over. She needed to talk this out with someone before any more time slipped away. Only about a week remained. She didn't want to part with Logan and Cait on bad terms. And yet, she didn't know how to accept this news, either.

Sheena found the strength to rise and lay her brush on the vanity. No sense in fuming by herself any further. Cait had told her to go to her room whenever she needed to talk. Sheena would do just that. Time kept slipping away. And sooner than Sheena ever imagined, none would remain at all.

Wrapping her dark blue floor-length shawl around her white nightgown, she felt the cool wood beneath her bare feet as she picked up her candle before easing her door open and peeking into the hallway. Light still shone up from downstairs. She could hear the distant sound of muffled talking, but the upper floor remained deserted.

Stepping into the hall, she turned to close the door behind her so slowly it wouldn't make the slightest sound. Then she tiptoed next door. Standing in front of Cait's door, she hesitated for a moment. She should knock, and yet the noise could garner unwanted attention. And she did not want anyone seeing her in her nightclothes. Under any circumstance. What would her mother say? Sheena smiled at the absurdity before reaching out for the knob.

Hopefully, Cait wouldn't mind her coming in unannounced. As she closed the door behind her, she whispered into the darkness not yet lit up by her candlelight, "Cait." She could hear Cait rolling over in bed.

"Lassie?" Sheena saw Logan propped up in his bed. "What are you doing here?" He kicked his feet to the floor and took a few long strides to stand before her. Sheena stared at him. Her mouth went dry and she swallowed. She'd never seen Logan in his nightclothes before.

She closed her eyes and turned around, opening them

quickly to scramble for the doorknob. Finding it, she turned the handle. But before she could open the door enough to get out, Logan pushed it shut.

Her body froze. "Logan." She fumbled out his name, embarrassed, before looking sideways. Making sure not to meet his eyes, she kept her sight homed in on the buttons of his white nightshirt. "I thought this was Cait's room." She managed to look up into his eyes. And his deep, brown irises caught a hint of light making the flecks inside twinkle playfully at her.

"She's on the other side of you." He moved his body to lean his weight against the door, coming even closer to her. She could smell his freshly bathed skin.

"Oh." Her heart pounded in a rapid flutter until footsteps outside the door stopped it. She held her breath. What if someone found her in here? Horrified, she stood paralyzed looking at the light seep through the crack under the door. Logan's thinking seemed to merge with hers and once the light passed he quickly got his only chair and propped it under the knob to prevent the door from opening.

"I can't stay in here." Sheena didn't even direct her words at Logan. She just stated the fact.

"You'll have to until everyone is settled in for the night." He calmly walked over to his bed, glanced at it and then sat down on the floor to rest his back against it. "I might be your chaperone, but I am still a man and even though I don't mind you in here, others will most likely find that questionable. Especially if they see you emerge from my room in the middle of the night in nothing more than your nightclothes." He didn't hide his amusement, as he looked up over the length of her with a grin on his face.

Sheena pulled her floor-length shawl more tightly around her, which only made Logan's smile broader. Haughtily she stood, thinking just how like Logan to make light of the situation.

"Here." He reached up and grabbed his pillow. "Sit on this." He placed it down beside him. Sheena pursed her lips, grabbed the pillow and placed it across from him against the wall. Lighting Logan's candle for extra light, she set her candle down on his bedside table before sitting down in a hurry to avoid his all-too-encompassing gaze.

After making sure her nightclothes lay modestly, she grabbed her hair to wind it up. "Don't." Logan's low voice made her stop. "I like it like that." He stretched out his legs in front of him so they rested on the left side of her. A little too close for her sanity. "Carefree, wild, rebellious," Logan continued and Sheena shook her head at him in dismay, trying to get her hair quickly under control. Logan shrugged in defeat. "See. Untamable." He laughed, leaning over to rest on his right arm.

"Logan, you are enjoying this situation too much," she scolded him, realizing too late that her reaction would only incite him further.

"Lassie, I enjoy all the time we spend together." He winked. "I'll take what I can get." His audacity annoyed her.

"Logan, flirting with me is of no use. You would do

better to turn your attentions to someone else. Someone who could return your feelings."

Logan only lifted his eyebrows in response. And Sheena looked down at her shawl. That look could only mean one thing—Logan didn't think she could stand seeing him with another woman. Is that because he couldn't stand seeing her with Ian?

God obviously knew He must send Logan far away to the Americas to help both of them get on with their lives. He truly thought of everything.

"Why were you going to Cait's room at this hour?" Logan searched her face.

"To talk." She didn't know if her best recourse included opening up to Logan, so she didn't go further.

"Well, you've got me." He pushed up off his right arm to sit up straight. "Talk."

Again Sheena gasped at his forwardness. "I have been known to sit for hours by myself in quiet solitude. I don't have to talk. I could pass the time praying."

"Aye." Logan's face still had a wry expression. "I've no doubt." His confidence finally settled into a sincere look. "Please, let's talk. We have so few chances."

"That is exactly why I was going to Cait's room. I still cannot believe she is leaving me and going to the Americas."

"Leaving you?" Logan's face switched from shock to disdain. "You will be a newly married woman. Surely, you won't have time for her anyway. If tonight was any indication, you will have more social engagements than there are days in a month. And then, before you know it, you'll be a mother. And not once mind you, but several times over."

"You are very bold tonight."

Logan threw up his hands and lifted his shoulders. "What? Is that not how you see other people's marriages play out before you?" She squinted her eyes at him. He wasn't saying anything but the truth, and yet she couldn't imagine her life in such a clear-cut way. She couldn't see past her wedding day yet. Actually, she couldn't even imagine that.

"What will you do back in the Americas now that you are no longer an indentured servant?" She purposefully changed the subject. "Or are you going to become one again?"

"Nay." Logan ran his fingers through his locks. "Never again."

"That bad?" She'd never given him the opportunity to tell her about it and even now she didn't know if she could tolerate hearing about him getting mistreated. The whole five years Logan worked abroad plagued her with nightmares about the harm that could befall him under such dreadful conditions.

"Aye, but it would have all been worth it." He gazed into her eyes with an intensity that made her look down at her bare feet. "Your parents would never allow you to marry someone as poor as I was. I had absolutely nothing to offer you. I went and even worked two extra years to have enough to show for myself."

Sheena still didn't look up. "I never asked you to do that." And then she stopped herself from being so meek.

Anger flooded back and she glared directly at him. "In fact, I remember wholeheartedly asking you not to go."

Logan tilted his head, softening his features in the candlelight, but he couldn't soften her hostility. "I went for you. For our future."

"Really? Because it seems to me as if you left because you promised to marry me and then changed your mind."

"That isn't the truth, Sheena."

"It doesn't matter, Logan." Sheena looked out the window at the dark night sky.

"You didn't come home with as many silver coins as the stars I see shining down from the heavens, so you can't buy my dowry away from Ian."

Sheena stopped stargazing. "I'm glad God saw to your well-being, but you survived for some other fate God planned for you, maybe delivering those letters."

"Maybe, but you should know I did succeed." Logan straightened his back. "I worked hard."

"I never doubted you did." But Logan's expression conveyed thoughts of his doubt.

"I may not have made anywhere close to the kind of money Ian's family has, but I did secure myself a piece of land that I will be proud to call home." Sheena stared at him, speechless. "It's not going to be an easy life. But it will be life on my own terms."

"So your intention was always to live in the Americas?" Sheena's shock reverberated through her voice. She'd waited for Logan for five long years. Even feeling guilty when he returned, thinking he wanted to make good on his promise and marry her. And now he told her he never intended to live in Scotland, let alone their village. So even if her mother didn't betroth her to Ian, she wouldn't have lived out the plans she and Logan made anyway.

"My intention when I left Scotland was to make enough money to be able to ask for your hand when I returned. But when I was in the Americas, the opportunity presented itself and I thought it would be a good life for us."

Sheena's irritation rose. Why didn't women get any say in their own lives? "We must stop talking about the past and what you wanted and what you hoped to get. None of that matters anymore. I am glad you secured a good life for yourself. I hope you will be very happy in it."

"You don't understand, do you?" Logan sat up, kneeling in front of her, cradling her hands in his. "I will not be happy unless you are my wife."

"Logan, stop." Sheena pulled her hands free. "We are in Ian's home, of all places. You must stop all this foolishness."

"I am not a fool, lassie. I love you and I know you love me."

"I have never said so since you returned." He'd never said so since he came home, either.

"You don't have to. I know it in my heart. I can see it in your eyes." He held his hand over his chest as his honest brown eyes pleaded with hers to agree with him.

But she wouldn't. Didn't he care about the consequences of her breaking her betrothal? "Logan, stop. What you are saying to me is horrible. Assuming I am coveting another man while I am betrothed. Do you really think of me like that?"

Goose bumps ran up her arms. Pulling her legs in under her she hugged them, too terrified to let her mind register that Logan had just asked her to marry him.

"I apparently know you better than you know yourself." Logan grabbed a blanket from his bed and laid it over Sheena's lap.

The warmth calmed the goose bumps, but the shaky feeling didn't subside. "Then you must know that my mother is selling and packing up our house as we speak. Ian built a house for us…"

"Ian built a house for himself." Logan's nostrils flared as he sucked in a lungful of air.

"Logan, you are wrong." Sheena shook her head. "Why can't you see?"

"I am not wrong. Did Ian give you any say in where you wanted to live? Did you get to pick anything regarding the house? Nay and nay."

"That is just how men are. You would have dragged me off to the Americas. Ian is at least staying in Scotland." Sheena didn't like comparing Logan to Ian and yet, she didn't know how else to get through to him.

"Nay. I would never *drag* you anywhere without your consent. I fully intended to ask you and if you said nay, I would have stayed here and just given the land to my brother. And if he didn't want it, I would have sold it." Logan rubbed his thighs. "Drag you to the Americas? Do you see me dragging you anywhere now? Even though the thought has crossed my mind."

Sheena couldn't believe what he was telling her. She fiddled with the blanket. She needed to remain firm. "Logan. You can't be serious?"

"Why not?" He reached for her hands again.

Sheena hastily crossed her arms to avoid his touch. "Logan, you must stop."

"There has to be a way out of this. You cannot marry Ian. You don't love him." Logan leaned forward and rested his right hand on her shoulder. The touch sent a piercing pain straight to her heart and she brushed his hand away as if it actually did cause her physical torment.

"You are embarrassing me and especially yourself."

"I will not be embarrassed for speaking the truth in my heart. You love me and you belong with me." His tone intensified. "Stop fighting yourself."

"I am not fighting myself." Sheena combed her fingers through her hair before realizing they would get tangled in the impromptu hairstyle she gave herself. Freeing her hand, she tried twining the strands back into place.

"Nay? Then what's at the root of all this fainting all of a sudden?"

Sheena stopped grappling with her hair. "It may run in my family."

"Nay, Sheena, don't you realize that you are only fainting because, deep down, where you've hidden all your emotions away, you know the truth is that you don't want to marry Ian."

"Logan, that is entirely enough. I can't listen to any more." Sheena scurried to her feet, folding Logan's blanket in her arms until it became nothing more than a big heap of wool. In reaction to her movement, Logan sprang up, as well. "I am sorry this is how it must be between us." She pushed the bundle into his arms and then grabbed her candle. "I thought we could be friends."

Logan flung the woolen blanket onto his bed. "I can never be just friends with you, Sheena. I want to be so much more to you than that." He stepped closer, reaching for her hand.

"This is hopeless. You are not listening to me." She turned and walked toward the door. "Please remove the chair. I'm sure everyone is in bed by now. If not, I'll take my chances. I can't stay here any longer."

"Why? Because you may come to your senses?" She cast him an evil look. "Fine, take your chances. I hope someone sees you." Sheena's mouth gaped as Logan quietly pulled the chair free. "Infidelity is one of the conditions that would break your betrothal."

"I was not unfaithful."

"Someone who saw you leave my room in the middle of the night wouldn't think so." Logan crossed his arms.

"You don't know what you're saying. It's late." Sheena's heart thumped hard against her chest.

"You're only right about one of those things, lassie."

"Logan, please." Sheena held on to the doorknob, about to slip away into the darkness of the hallway.

"Fine, I'll leave it alone for now, but when we get home I'm going to prove to you how much I love you."

Logan held fast to both of her shoulders, but she wouldn't look into his brown eyes. Instead, she closed hers tight. "I love you, Sheena."

Her eyes burst open as she glared at him. "I'm not yours to love."

Chapter Fifteen

Logan laid his head against the papered wall. He'd finally professed his love to Sheena for the first time since he'd come back to Scotland and look at the result—she fled from him again as if he were a hunter and her a wild deer.

Of course she wouldn't marry him. She didn't know the real reason he'd left her in the first place. She wouldn't risk her mother's or her own welfare on a man she thought would only hurt her again. She wanted certainty and stability, and Ian, with his settled life in Glasgow, could give her that. She didn't know that Logan could, too.

Logan fought what she told him for far too long. As a good, virtuous, God-fearing woman, Sheena meant to marry Ian. Maybe she already loved him. She surely already respected Ian as her husband.

Logan pushed off from the wall and changed into his day clothes. Grabbing his bedside candle, he left his bedroom for the library. No point in going back to bed now—he wouldn't sleep.

He paused outside Sheena's door, but no light shone from underneath. Not that he would knock anyway. She'd made her feelings perfectly clear and he would accept them. For tonight anyway.

However, as things stood now, Logan doubted that even the letter would change her mind. She could still hate him for agreeing to her father's demands and keeping it all a secret from her. And maybe she would be right. Maybe he'd handled it all terribly wrong.

True to his word, Reed had left a stack of books in the library for Logan to peruse. But Logan couldn't bring himself to read the titles, let alone crack a spine. He needed some fresh air. Maybe that would help clear his head.

Treading quietly down the hallway past the large vestibule, Logan slipped out the front door and breathed in a lungful of crisp spring air. A walk would do him good. The quiet stillness of the night surrounded him as he walked around the side of the mansion.

"Logan?" He heard someone call his name and turned to see Finnean, Ian's driver, approaching.

"Do you always work until this hour, Finnean?" Logan reached out and shook the man's hand.

"Nay, but with the party running so late tonight I had to drive the last guests home."

"Why don't you come inside and have a drink before you go home? I've just come from the library and there are plenty of trays with food still out, as well."

"I really shouldn't."

Of course Finnean saw partaking in his employer's food and drink as an imposition. "Please, Finnean, as my guest. I could use the company since everyone else has gone to bed."

"In that case, I don't see why not." Finnean flashed a smile. And the two men walked back inside the estate house, through the grand entrance vestibule and into the library.

Taking their glass goblets, they each settled into high-back wingchairs that faced the fireplace and hid them from the sight of anyone entering the library.

"Logan, can I ask you something?" Finnean played with the decorative glass in his hands.

"Of course." Logan took a sip and then examined the fine detail embedded in the glass. Anything to take his mind off his argument with Sheena in his bedroom earlier.

"Are you and Cait a couple?" Finnean nearly dropped his glass goblet as he spun it between his fingers.

Logan raised an eyebrow. "A couple?" He huffed in a low laugh. If Finnean couldn't guess how much Logan loved Sheena after driving them around Glasgow these past couple of days, no one else would guess, either. Logan had done a better job of pretending to be Sheena's chaperone than he thought. "Nay, Cait's my brother's sister-in-law."

Finnean's head snapped to the right as he looked at Logan. "Is that so?"

"Aye. Why do you ask?" But Logan could see the

answer on Finnean's face. Finnean harbored an interest in Cait.

"Just wondering. Do you happen to know if Cait's spoken for?"

Logan couldn't squelch his grin now. "Nay, she's not. But she is set to sail to the Americas with her whole family, including me, in about a week."

That declaration sent Finnean in for a deep drink. And before he could say another word, two voices hissing at each other in some sort of disagreement erupted behind their chairs.

Neither Logan nor Finnean moved. Ian and Reed stood just inside the library doors, their hushed voices barely loud enough for Logan and Finnean to hear. Finnean certainly didn't want his employers finding him in their library, so Logan stayed quiet.

"Ian, this is lunacy." Reed's voice rang out with alarm. "You're betrothed to Sheena. She's upstairs as we speak."

"I know. I know." Glass clanked against glass as someone poured a drink.

"You can't be serious about Rona." More clanking as another drink got poured. "You're to be married to Sheena."

"I know that, but that doesn't mean I don't love Rona." Logan heard some shuffling, as if one of the men meant to leave. "Stop, I know it sounds terrible. I'm betrothed to Sheena while I'm in love with Rona. But it's not as if I planned any of this."

"I know, Ian, but people stand to get hurt."

"That's why I asked you to help me." A glass clanked down on a table.

"Aye." Another glass went down. "Of course I'll help you." Ian and Reed's voices died away as they left the library. Logan remained as still as a statue.

Who is Rona? And how could Ian love Rona while he remained betrothed to Sheena? If he loved Rona, then why didn't he break off the betrothal to Sheena? Surely he could afford to give Sheena's mother back her dowry and end all this. Unless he meant to marry Sheena and keep Rona as his mistress?

Either way, there was yet another reason Sheena couldn't marry Ian. Logan needed to tell Sheena what he'd heard. He couldn't let her get involved in this horrid love triangle. He would tell her tomorrow on the carriage ride home. She must know.

"Finnean, can I ask you a question now?" Logan turned in his chair, moving for the first time since he sat down. "What do you know about Rona and her relationship with Ian?"

Finnean cleared his throat. "I haven't heard that name mentioned around here in a long time. I thought Ian and Rona's relationship was over."

So Ian and Rona loved each other once. Logan watched as Finnean turned toward him, finally looking Logan in the eye. "I can understand your anger on behalf of Sheena. I don't want to be a party to any of this. If Ian still loves Rona, he has no business being betrothed to Sheena or marrying her." Logan nodded. His thoughts exactly. "Rona and Ian grew up together. But back then the Mackenzies weren't as wealthy as they are now and Rona's family didn't want her to marry Ian." How much this sounded like Logan's own life with Sheena. "One day, Rona just disappeared. I never found out where she went or why, but I suspected that it was to keep her away from Ian." Logan ran his fingers through his hair. "I wish I could help you more, but that's all I know."

Finnean set his glass goblet down and Logan thanked him, realizing they should retire for the night. Finnean needed his rest, since he would drive them back to Callander tomorrow. And Logan needed time to figure out how he would tell Sheena about all this.

"Logan, you don't look well." Cait held on to his arm after they bid farewell to Ian's family.

"Thanks," he said sarcastically, leading her toward the Mackenzies' private stagecoach, which would take them home.

"You know what I mean." Cait gave a little wave up to Finnean, who sat perched in front of the stagecoach, waiting for the journey to begin. Logan smiled at him, too, before yawning. "Didn't you sleep last night?" Logan didn't tell Cait about overhearing Ian and Reed's conversation—it was Sheena's right to hear it first. Let her decide what to do about the information.

And Logan wasn't sure whether he should tell Cait about Finnean's possible interest in her. Finnean had never actually said he liked Cait, but who knew what this trip home would bring. Logan wouldn't interfere.

If love was going to bloom, it would do so without his intrusion.

"If I slept, it wasn't much." Logan stopped before the stagecoach and turned in search of Sheena. By now, she had said her goodbyes to Ian's family and stood in front of Ian. "I am so glad to be getting away from this place," said Logan. Cait patted his arm, but no one besides God knew the turmoil raging inside him.

"Maybe we should wait in the stagecoach." Cait took him away from his thoughts.

"As much as I detest seeing them together, we are her chaperones, so we must stay out here." Logan willed Sheena and Ian to stop talking and part ways. But his ability to control events ended up being as pathetic as his talent for predicting the future. Ian held Sheena's hand and kissed it.

"Come on, Logan." He let Cait turn him toward the stagecoach as Sheena let go of Ian's hand. Logan stepped inside and dropped heavily onto the seat. Putting his head in his hands he readied himself to face Sheena.

Logan looked up when he heard Sheena enter the stagecoach but Sheena didn't even look at him as she sat down in the farthest seat from him. If it weren't for propriety, Logan knew she would prefer to sit out front with Finnean. Anything to distance herself from Logan.

Hatred seemed to ooze out of her every pore. Now didn't seem like a good time to tell her about Ian's conversation with Reed last night. But that suited him fine. Logan wanted to tell her alone, without Cait overhearing. Maybe that would lessen any embarrassment Sheena might feel being betrothed to a man who not only didn't love her, but loved another woman.

Logan would wait until they reached their halfway point and then try to speak to Sheena alone. Maybe by then she would at least look at him. He needed her to trust him and not think he would make this up just to get her to break off her betrothal to Ian.

Logan closed his eyes and leaned his head back; he would take advantage of his lack of sleep. *God help me get through to Sheena before she gets hurt by Ian.*

Awoken from his slumber, Logan's head hit the back of the stagecoach, sending a sharp pain through his skull. His eyes flew open just as Sheena and Cait screamed. They huddled together, peering out the window. Logan rubbed the bump on his head, looking past them to the window. He saw nothing except cream-colored dust.

Finnean drove the stagecoach like a madman and Logan placed a hand on each side of him to steady his body so he would remain in his seat. With no idea how long he slept or even how far along their journey they'd traveled, he hollered over the thunder of the Chapman horses' hooves, "What is going on?"

But before either Sheena or Cait could answer, a gunshot blasted through the air.

Chapter Sixteen

"Get down," Logan yelled, darting toward the window. But he couldn't see anything. The thick, smoky dust blocked everything from sight. The sound of horses' hooves pounding the dirt grew louder.

"What is happening?" Sheena's eyes questioned him, large with worry.

"Just stay down." Logan put his hand on her upper back to stop her from rising. "Someone must be pursuing us."

Cait's head shot up. "Highwaymen?"

"Stay down." He moved his hand back to the wall to steady himself as the stagecoach continued to jerk about and sounded as if it would crumble to pieces at this speed. "Finnean is trying to outrun them."

"He won't make it." Cait shook her head. "No one ever does. He'll get himself killed."

Sheena huddled close to Cait. "Pray." She held her, as Logan turned his attention back outside. Instinctively, he reached for his pistol, but remembered he didn't own one anymore. Having surrendered it, because of the Act of Proscription, he hoped the government's ban wouldn't lead to their deaths.

He vowed then and there to God that he would keep them all safe. He looked down at Sheena, sweat forming on his brow. The sense of protectiveness he felt for her didn't come from being her chaperone. He still loved her. He always would. No matter what.

Another gunshot exploded.

Logan sprawled on top of Sheena and Cait and no one moved until a bloodcurdling scream ripped through the stagecoach.

"Finnean." Cait tried getting up, but Logan held her down until the moment he felt the carriage stopping hard.

He got up. "We're surrendering. Stay close to me." Both women rose slowly. Sheena tucked in beside Logan and Cait followed right behind her.

Dear God, help me keep us all safe. Logan stole a look at Sheena. He would do anything to protect her. "I love you," he whispered, not knowing if she heard him before the door flew open.

"Get out," said a croaking voice, as thick dust flooded the stagecoach. Logan grabbed Sheena's hand and walked out first, holding her close behind him. He hoped she and Cait could jump down without any help, because he didn't want to take his eyes off the two burly men pointing pistols at them.

With his arms in the air over his head, Logan felt

Sheena and then Cait steady themselves against his shoulders as they jumped down.

"Hands up," the closest armed man hollered and Logan didn't even flinch, knowing full well Sheena and Cait would obey. Foolish courage didn't belong in a situation like this. These men were serious.

With a furtive glance, Logan saw Finnean lying on the dirt road near the horses with a third highwayman standing over him. The sandy dirt clumped together under the stream of crimson blood gushing from his arm. Logan sent up a hasty prayer, relieved the man hadn't been killed outright.

"Anyone else in that stagecoach?" the armed man shouted at them.

"Nay," Logan answered quickly, trying to shield Sheena and Cait.

"You." He pointed his pistol at Logan. "Stand against the stagecoach. And you. Go help your driver." He waved the pistol at Cait, pushing it into her shoulder. She hurried away from him over to the ground near Finnean, ripping her skirt to use as bandages for his gunshot wound. "And you. Come here." He threw his pistol to his left hand and grabbed Sheena's arm with his right, pulling her closer.

With the second highwayman still pointing his pistol at Logan, he couldn't do anything to stop him. "My, you sure are pretty." He held her chin and forced her face to look toward him. Putting the pistol on her back, he drew her to him. Logan lowered his hands, about to lunge for-

ward and strangle the scoundrel when another gunshot
jolted him. And he stopped.

"Don't move." The second highwayman glared at
Logan, his arm raised above his head. "Next time, I
won't let out a warning shot. Understand?" Logan
nodded, easing his arms back up over his head, but not
retreating a step. If the highwayman didn't notice, he
wouldn't voluntarily move farther away from Sheena.

"A fine specimen of a woman." The man buried his
nose in the hair at the side of her head as if oblivious to
the mayhem around him. "Now let's see what a pretty
young lady like yourself has on her." He said it so nicely
it jarred Logan's ears. This highwayman had singled
out Sheena, since she wore the most expensive clothing.
Her brown silk dress signified wealth to this highwayman's greedy eyes. "What a lovely brooch." His fingers
played with it clumsily, touching Sheena's chest where
the brooch lay. Sheena held her chin up, unflinching.

Logan couldn't stand by and watch Sheena get man-
handled. And yet being shot dead wouldn't help her,
either. *God, don't let her get hurt.*

"Take it from her already," the second highwayman
snapped angrily, but the crazed highwayman didn't seem
to change his temperament or demeanor—he simply un-
fastened the brooch. "A Luckenbooth." A wide smile slid
across his ragged face as he slipped it into his pocket.
Sheena's dark blue shawl fell open and she used both her
hands to pull the woolen fabric back into place and hold
it there.

"You won't be needing that." He took the shawl off

her. "Sure are pretty." He looked her over before searching her shawl for secret pockets. "What do we have here?" His eyes glistened with greed. "A stone?" He threw the shawl on his shoulder and rolled the stone between his fingers. "What is it?" He held it up to Sheena's eye level.

Logan fought back his emotions and stayed focused on the armed men. But he couldn't help marveling at the fact that Sheena had kept it. If he'd found out under any other circumstance, he would have done a Highland jig with glee. The green moss agate stone he'd given her before he left. A stone to stay with her and protect her. To give her strength to carry on in his absence.

"It's just a rock." Sheena looked past the green moss agate stone into the crazed highwayman's evil eyes.

"Now, my pretty, a woman like yourself does not carry around the landscape needlessly." He patted her on the top of her head. "I'll just put it with the brooch for safekeeping." He deposited it in his pocket, leaning in close to Sheena with a smile that showed off his yellow-and-brown-stained teeth. "Now where are you hiding your other valuables?" He stroked the right side of her face with his pistol. But when she didn't say anything he pressed it firmly into her cheek.

"She doesn't have any." Logan tried diverting the man's attention. But the highwayman didn't move away from Sheena or take his eyes off her.

"I wasn't talking to you," he practically sang out. "Please don't make me silence your friend here."

"I have a bag on the roof of the stagecoach." Sheena kept her stance firmly in place.

"Very good." He paused to smile at her, then grabbed her arm once more and abruptly turned to the second highwayman, moving his pistol around wildly in the hot spring air. "You heard her. Get up there and get it."

The second highwayman jumped up on the driver's seat and then onto the roof as the first man shouted to the one standing over Cait, "Leave her and get up there and get the loot."

Logan stood motionless as the third highwayman made his way onto the roof. Cait turned to look at Sheena and then Logan. He tilted his head to the right and she winked at him. He didn't know if she understood his meaning, but he couldn't wait to find out before acting.

Soon a bag fell onto the ground beside one of the horses, making her snort and kick her hoof into the dirt in annoyance. The horse's agitation transferred onto the one beside her and they both bobbed their heads and swished their tails in protest.

"Come with me." The villain tugged Sheena over to the loot.

The moment they crossed in front of Logan, Logan pushed Sheena. She fell into the thin, short man, sending him stumbling forward and her toward the ground. Cait lost no time kicking him in the groin. Logan grabbed his pistol as Cait kicked the man again, this time in the stomach. He fell backward into the horse's back leg. The horse kicked, knocking him toward the stagecoach door.

Logan grabbed him, pushing and shoving him up the steps into the stagecoach as more bags began raining down around them. The two other highwaymen took notice. One was about to jump down, as the other reached for his pistol.

Logan gave the man a final shove and leaped back as Cait hit the horse's rear end so forcefully it bolted. Diving to where Sheena lay, Logan used his body as a shield to protect her in case the man started shooting. But after a moment Logan looked up to see the two highwaymen on the roof holding on for dear life. The noise of the stagecoach faded away as the dust settled. The highwaymen wouldn't come back. Their fate lay in God's hands now.

"Sheena, did I hurt you?" Logan moved his body off hers. "I'm sorry." He put his arm on her shoulder and peered down low, trying to see her face. She turned and met his eyes, tears streaming down her cheeks. Body trembling, she rolled onto her side and after some hesitation sat up.

"Don't be sorry," she sobbed. "You saved us." She fell forward into his arms and he felt the electricity of love rush through him as he circled his arms around her. "Thank you," she cried, resting her head on his chest. Her chest heaved and he held her even tighter. She had gone through too much. This week alone she had gone through more ordeals than he ever wanted to see her exposed to in her whole life. So even though she spoke to him again, now still didn't present itself as the right time to tell her about Ian. He needed to wait.

Trying to comfort her, he rocked her. He would hold her forever if she'd let him. "I love you," he breathed into her ear, stroking her back. He knew now, beyond a shadow of a doubt, that she loved him, too, regardless of the walls she'd erected to keep him at bay. If holding her in his arms at this moment didn't prove it, the green moss agate stone she'd held secretly close to her heart all this time told him everything he needed to know.

The safety of Logan's arms couldn't last forever. Sheena jerked herself away. As a betrothed woman, she shouldn't act this way, no matter what the circumstances. She would only hurt Logan behaving like this. "Where is Cait?"

"She's fine. She's helping Finnean."

"We've got to help, too." Sheena put her hands on the dry dirt to push herself up.

"You're sure you're not hurt?" Logan stood way too close to her.

"I'm fine." She clasped her hands together, dusting them off. "Thank you." She might sound overly formal in her response, but it would do Logan good to remember what they meant and would never mean to each other. Sending grit into the air, she brushed her clothes as clean as she could and when she looked up, Logan stood before her with her shawl.

"I'm sorry the highwaymen took your brooch and agate stone." Embarrassment filled Sheena and she simply nodded. Logan now knew she'd kept it all this time. "But at least they didn't get away with everything." Logan held on to the dark blue woolen fabric in a way that showed he wouldn't just hand it back to her. Grudgingly, she thanked him and let him wrap the shawl around her before walking quickly to Cait's side.

Thanks to Cait, Finnean's arm rested under a heap of impromptu bandages. Only a tiny amount of crimson soaked through. Sheena touched Finnean's other shoulder. "I'm sorry."

"Not your fault." Finnean's strength of spirit shone through. "The highwaymen didn't see, but the bullet only grazed my flesh."

"Thank God." Logan reached down and helped Finnean to his feet. "Any thoughts on where we are?"

"We're somewhere around the halfway point."

"I'll just grab the bags and then let's hope those horses are tame enough to ride." Sheena followed Logan's gaze toward the highwaymen's three horses, standing around a river they now used as a watering hole.

Logan walked off, switching Sheena's focus. "He doesn't really think he's going to carry all those bags, does he?" Sheena looked after him. "Logan." She caught up to him a few yards away.

"Sorry I couldn't stop that highwayman." Logan kept his eyes on the bags strewn all over the ground.

"Don't apologize. You did put a stop to him in the end."

He glanced over at her. "I would have killed him if he hurt you."

Sheena saw Logan's knuckles turn white as his hand

squeezed hold of one of their bags too tightly. "Then I'm glad he didn't."

Logan raised an eyebrow, not meeting her eyes. "He was too close for my liking."

Sheena rubbed her chest, thinking about his rough hands and his yellow-stained teeth. "Mine, too," she said, and the serious look on Logan's face faded as she smiled at him. "My mother's going to need her smelling salts when she hears Ian gave me a Luckenbooth and I let it get stolen."

Sheena's smile widened. But Logan's failed to. "Are you joking?"

Her smile vanished now, too. "Nay."

Logan shook his head. "Do you really think your mother would be more interested in an object being stolen than your well-being?"

Aye. The answer popped into Sheena's head so fast she looked down in disgust. The sheer cost of the brooch would astonish Tavia. Meaning, of course, that when she recovered from the shock, Sheena would get an earful on her stupidity for not hiding her valuables properly while traveling.

Logan stopped abruptly. "Your mother should know that objects are just that. They're replaceable. People are not."

She leaned down to pick up a bag. Maybe the highwaymen stealing the agate stone had been for the best. She couldn't hold on to anything that reminded her of Logan anymore. Maybe God meant for it to happen.

To show her that she needed to embrace her future and forget about her past with Logan.

When they neared the others, Cait reached out her hand for a bag. "Here, let me take one."

"Me, too," Finnean echoed.

But Logan shook his head. "There aren't enough." He put down the bags he carried. "Can you help me charm those horses instead, Finnean?"

Finnean nodded and walked slowly with Logan toward them. Sheena and Cait looked on hopefully as Logan got closer to the horses and they kept their calm. Sheena didn't want to contemplate taking a ridiculously long and treacherous journey on foot through the countryside to get home to Callander.

"We're going to cause quite a stir when we get home." Sheena cast her amused eye over all of them individually. Finnean was streaked in blood and bandages, Cait in ripped and tattered clothes. She herself stood covered in dirt from head to toe with wee cuts and snags all over her brown silk dress. And Logan. She forced herself to assess him. He, however, only showed a few dirt smears. She rolled her eyes. How did he manage to remain relatively unscathed? Maybe his clothes just wore better? Nay. She smiled to herself. Pure Logan.

Cait chuckled, too, letting her hands linger on her frayed skirt while she evaluated her ruined clothes. "At least they'll believe our story about the highwaymen."

Sheena's blood boiled at the mention of them. "I hope they get caught and brought to justice." Sheena never took her eyes off the men winning over the horses. "Because of those thieves I owe Ian a stagecoach."

With a mocking expression Cait smiled. "I don't think Ian is that type of man." Sheena remained quiet. She agreed. He would concern himself more with her well-being and the fact that she made it away alive and unharmed. Unlike her mother, Ian wouldn't care about the Luckenbooth brooch.

Cait let her skirt drop. "I can't wait to freshen up." Sheena gauged her own clothes and sighed. She didn't even bother trying to fix her appearance. A lost cause.

Thank God she couldn't say the same for the horses, as Finnean now mounted the bay horse and Logan held a set of reins in each of his hands. He looked extremely comfortable wedged in between the two mountains of muscle.

"Can you take this horse over to that boulder?" Logan offered the reins of the chestnut horse to Sheena.

Taking the reins, she looked only at the horse facing her. Too fine a creature for such unscrupulous characters to own. She patted the horse's white muzzle and led him slowly to the rocks.

"Would you like the front or the back?" Logan came before the horse and rubbed her neck.

Sheena stepped back from the horse. "Excuse me?"

"Since neither you nor I can move as fast as a horse, we're not going to run alongside them, we're riding together. So, do you want to ride behind me or in front of me?"

"Neither." Sheena crossed her arms. "I'll ride with Cait."

"Sorry, she's all packed in." Sheena saw Cait mounted on a black horse that didn't seem to mind the weight of the bags strapped to its saddle. "And before you ask about Finnean, remember he's got a bad arm and he's got to deal with riding bareback so he can't hold on to you."

"I don't need holding on to."

Logan raised an eyebrow. "Have you ever ridden bareback?" Sheena glared at him. He knew the answer to that question. "So do you want to sit in front of me so you can hold on to the horse's mane or behind me where you'll have to hold on tight enough to me so you don't get bumped off her rear?"

"I'll take the front." Sheena walked to the horse's side. She didn't like seeming so frail. "You can hold on to me." That didn't come out quite right.

"Whatever you want." Logan winked, grinning as Sheena blushed.

"Let's just get going. I don't want to wait around for the highwaymen to come back." Logan helped Sheena onto the rock so she could mount the horse easily. Then he did the same.

"Ready?" he asked after steadying the horse. Sheena got her fists around clumps of wiry mane and nodded.

The horse galloped steadily under Logan's sure hand. And yet, no matter how she tried to lean forward she always jostled back against Logan. Even though she didn't seem to hurt him or push him off, she sighed.

Their village had better come into view quickly, because she couldn't stand being thrown together with Logan like this. Once she got home, she would make sure to put some distance between them.

The look in his eyes, his posture, his overall demeanor and mood had changed completely after the highwaymen stopped their journey. And she knew the transformation didn't come about because of a thrill for adventure or anything else death-defying. He read more into her holding on to his green moss agate stone than he should have.

And now he could very well become relentless in his pursuit of her. Because if he thought she still loved him he would act like a dog with a bone. And she couldn't tolerate that. She'd already hurt him repeatedly since his homecoming. She didn't want to keep doing that.

How silly of her to hold on to that agate stone and bring it with her on this trip. She'd never felt as if it brought her any protection or strength anyway. Only God offered her that. So she wouldn't get upset that she no longer possessed it. It didn't matter anymore. She would never get it back and she didn't need it. She didn't want it. Providence allowed the highwaymen to steal it and get it out of her life for good, just as Logan would vanish from her life in less than a fortnight.

"Logan, look." Something caught Sheena's eye and she pointed to it in front of them. "Do you think it's…"

Chapter Seventeen

Pulling back on the reins, Logan slowed their horse to a complete stop and waited until Finnean and Cait caught up to them. When they stopped their horses on either side of Logan and Sheena, Logan pointed toward Sheena's discovery in the distance. "Is that the Mackenzies' stagecoach?"

"I'd know those horses anywhere. They're ours." Finnean's head darted in every direction that the moor spread out around them.

"Is it a trap?" Logan looked around himself.

Finnean held still. "How could it be? They didn't know we'd head this way."

"But how did the stagecoach get there?" Cait's horse sidestepped under her nervous guidance.

"And where are the highwaymen?" Sheena strained to check their surroundings, too, but she saw nothing except rolling hills and rocks strewn everywhere.

"Come on," Logan moved his horse in front of the others' pulling his reins to the right. "I've got a plan."

Logan led the horses back along the dusty trail they had just come through and stopped behind the edge of a cluster of rocks. "You'll be safe here." He handed Sheena the reins. "Whatever happens, stay on the horse and ride away if anyone gets close." Sheena faced Logan, taking the reins hesitantly. After such a long ride, she knew she could ride bareback alone now. But as much as she wanted to get away from Logan, she didn't want it to come to this.

"What about you?" She couldn't mask her concern.

"Don't worry, I'll be fine and back before you know it. Just promise me you'll take care of yourself." Logan wrapped his arms around her. She didn't want to make the promise, but without a foreseeable alternative, she nodded. He pulled her closer to him and kissed her forehead before dismounting.

"Cait, please stay here with Sheena and don't get off your horse. Run at the slightest bit of trouble and don't look back till you get home."

"Aye. Then we'll send an army to get you and take care of the thugs properly." She sounded much more confident in Logan's ability to stay alive than Sheena did.

Sheena squeezed the reins, listening to Logan talk to Finnean. "You good enough to come or do you want to stay with the women?"

"After seeing what Cait did to that highwayman, I'll be more use to you." Finnean dismounted, lopping his reins to Cait and winking at her.

"Good. Let's sneak over to the stagecoach and make sure the highwaymen are long gone." Logan stole one final look at Sheena. She couldn't look away and yet she didn't want to encourage him any further. "Don't worry. We'll be back shortly." He shot her an amused expression before ducking out in front of the rocks and disappearing.

Sheena couldn't just sit and wait. If she must remain still, she needed to take her mind off worrying about Logan. *And Finnean, too,* she corrected herself. "Cait, we never really talked about your plan to have Logan replace Boyd as my chaperone." Being this close to home, Sheena needed to know what to expect when she got there.

Cait laughed off the question. "I wouldn't call it a *plan*. We never actually made one."

"What?" Sheena glared at her, urging her to continue.

"Nay. We didn't think past being with you as your companions. We never thought we'd get to Glasgow. Although, we did tell Boyd that if he didn't hear from us to watch for a stagecoach today so he could go back to your house as if he went on this trip with you instead of Logan."

Sheena's mouth gaped open. Cait and Logan never expected to reach Glasgow. Surely, Logan found himself ill-prepared to see her with Ian, then? Oh, Logan. Sheena's stomach lurched. How much torment Logan had endured on this trip.

Cait finally grew serious. "I was certain you'd realize you loved Logan, end your betrothal to Ian and return to Callander without ever stepping foot in Glasgow." Sheena rolled her eyes. "I guess I was wrong."

"Terribly wrong."

"Sorry, Sheena. I know you're betrothed. And now I know Ian's a fine man and his family are beyond wealthy. But even though I doubt you'll be mistreated, I don't think that's enough. Your heart belongs to Logan. You'll never be truly happy."

"Enough, Cait." Sheena didn't like the way this conversation was headed.

"Nay. It's not enough." Cait moved her horse so she faced Sheena. "I have to say this. Then I'll never bring up the subject again." Sheena put her head back and rolled it from side to side, feeling the tension build in her shoulders as she listened. "You're going to kill a part of Logan if you marry Ian."

"*When* I marry Ian." Sheena made sure to emphasize the first word, even though she knew it made her sound callous.

Cait waved her hand in protest. "Let me finish. He's always thought of you as his soul mate. He wants to marry you. Begin a new life with you in the Americas. I know you don't want to break your betrothal and the commandment to honor your parents, but you're condemning Logan to a life of misery without you. You will crush Logan if you marry Ian."

"He will recover." Sheena rubbed her neck. "I did when he left."

"He won't. And I'm not so sure you recovered, either." Cait's suspicious look annoyed Sheena. She didn't like Cait trying to figure out what she felt in her heart.

"Are you finished?"

"Nay. Stop denying your feelings and run away to the Americas with Logan. Start a family with him."

Sheena shook her head. "Run away? I can't do that. Do you know how many people I would hurt? My mother, my aunt and uncle, Ian's family, Ian. And he doesn't deserve that."

Cait raised her voice, nearly squealing. "Ian doesn't deserve a wife who doesn't love him, either."

"You're correct. But I've already told you, love can develop with time. So what Ian really doesn't deserve is me deserting him. He's never done anything wrong. Imagine how embarrassed he'd be if I ran away. He has such plans for our future."

Cait furrowed her brows—she obviously didn't care about Ian if it meant hurting Logan. And that bothered Sheena because she didn't want to hurt Logan, either.

Sounding even more irritated than earlier, Cait told her, "I've heard this all before."

Sheena didn't want to look at Cait anymore. Somehow, if she kept her out of sight, this conversation might seem less pressing. So she focused on a cloud getting blown by the wind to cover the sun, removing not only the warm rays, but all the shadows. However, only too soon the sun emerged and Sheena turned from its blinding light to face Cait.

"Why can't you see the chaos that would ensue if I ran off with Logan?"

Cait looked at her with a hopeful glint in her eye. "*If* you run off with Logan? Don't you mean *when?*"

Sheena rolled her eyes at Cait for throwing her words

back at her. "Ian and his family are tobacco lords. They own just about all the ships that come and go to the Americas or, if they don't, their friends do. My mother would figure out that I chose to go with your family to the Americas and she would have Ian's family pick us off the ship so fast I wouldn't even have time to get seasick."

"Sheena, your mother forced you into this betrothal without your knowledge. She shouldn't have given that dowry to the Mackenzies before she asked for your consent to marry Ian."

"Of course. I can't deny that, but if I break my betrothal, my mother will lose the money she gave the Mackenzies for my dowry. Our next step would be homelessness and dependence on the charity of others. I can't live with the guilt of that."

Cait nodded in agreement. Maybe she finally understood something Sheena said. "If your mother made a mistake she needs to own up to it."

"Cait, that's all fine and good, but you're assuming one very big thing."

"What's that?"

"That I love Logan and want to marry him instead of Ian."

"Of course I'm assuming that. You've always loved Logan."

"That is before he left me and sailed to the Americas. Leaving without a reason, not sending word for five years. I didn't know that he would come back to Scotland. I thought he'd abandoned me. Lied to me about everything he ever told me our whole lives. I can't trust him now. Don't you see that? He could disappear again. Fill my head with empty promises and then I'd have to live with being lied to a second time. Nay, I can't risk that when it is not only my life I am risking, but my mother's way of life, as well."

Apparently, Cait didn't understand her. What could she say to get her to see the impossibility of the situation? The risks? Sheena turned her head away. "I can't talk about this anymore. I'm not going to get upset with you, Cait. I know your heart is in the right place and I love you—I do. I hope all your romantic notions pay off for *you* someday. You've been the greatest friend to me. But you have your opinion and I have my beliefs and because of that I don't want you to come to my wedding to Ian."

Cait gasped. "But it's your wedding."

"Cait." Sheena turned back to look at her. "I can't have you there knowing how you feel."

Cait smiled sheepishly. "Fair enough. But I'll be there in spirit."

"I know." Sheena reached out her hand and met Cait's. Squeezing it tightly. "I don't want you to come home with me now, either. You've got a little over a week left in Scotland. I won't let you waste it stuck in our house working. Cherish the time you have left."

"Thanks, Sheena." Cait squeezed her hand in return. "I've always considered myself a part of the McAllister clan and thought you would have made a great addition."

Sheena drew away. "Cait." She shook her head, smiling at her dearest friend. "You're relentless."

Cait shrugged. "I'm going to miss you."

"I know." Sheena smiled. "Me, too."

"Wait. Listen." Cait put her finger to her lips and waved her hand around. "Did you hear that?"

Sheena stopped breathing. Getting so entangled in this troubling conversation, she'd lost sight of why they sat hiding behind these rocks.

Danger lurked in the moors around them. She straightened, careful not to rouse her horse as she strained her ears to hear. The hills blocked much of their view, as did the rocks.

Crack.

Their heads jerked to the right. Sheena's hands gripped the reins tighter and she moved her legs out, prepared to kick her horse into a run and bolt out of there.

"Logan." Sheena let out a sigh of relief the moment she saw his face. His grin meant good news and his brown hair swayed around his shoulders as if cheering him on while he walked.

"Couldn't see any sign of the highwaymen." Logan went over to Cait and took Finnean's reins from her. "I don't think they're anywhere near here." He mounted the bay horse. "Looks like they all jumped off. The horses must have kept running until they tired or wanted to eat. Who knows?"

"Where's Finnean?" Cait looked around anxiously.

"He's with the stagecoach, waiting for us." Logan

turned his horse around. "Go on, Cait. We'll catch up."
Logan looked over at Sheena. "Think you can manage
to ride that horse by yourself?" His smile teased her.

"Aye." Sheena didn't wait and moved her chestnut
mare with her chin stuck out high in the air. Logan drew
up beside her in a flash.

"We're stopping just outside the village, so you and
Cait can get into the stagecoach for your ride home."
Logan winked at her and then let his horse start walking slowly. Sheena knew he went slower than usual to
make sure she really could ride her horse and wouldn't
hurt herself. How very protective and sweet of him. She
smiled down at her horse. He could behave like such a
good man when he wanted to.

The Logan she knew five years ago seemed perfect
in her eyes and she saw hints of his fine character this
whole trip. Coming to Glasgow in case she needed him,
even though it hurt him to see her with Ian, delivering all
those letters and promising to take responses back to the
Americas, and saving them from those armed highwaymen. If only she could trust Logan. But how could she
when he'd promised to marry her and then abandoned
her?

"Logan, Cait's not coming home with me." The sunlight shone on his brown hair, making it gleam. "I want
her to enjoy her last week in Scotland, not spend it working." Logan's smile looked like the one she just avoided
letting him see. Did he think of her as protective and
sweet, too?

Riding as if she always sat bareback, Sheena kept

her horse beside Logan's while Cait cantered beside Finnean's stagecoach ahead of them. The journey didn't stretch out long enough for Sheena to consider it unbearable. And, thankfully, they reached the edge of Callander without any more personal injury.

With Finnean and Cait already tending to their horses, Sheena brought her horse up beside Logan's. "Here." Logan appeared below her, reaching up to catch her around the waist so she could dismount. She didn't fight him. No point. They would see each other at church on Sunday, but this marked the last time they would be alone together for the rest of their lives.

"Thanks." Sheena pulled her hands away from Logan's large shoulders, but couldn't pull her eyes away from his or even take the appropriate step to put space between them.

"Sheena." Logan took hold of her hands with a warmth that held her firm. Rubbing the top of each of her hands with his thumbs softly, he confessed, "There's something I have to tell you."

Chapter Eighteen

Logan looked down at Sheena's hands, flipping each one over to rub his thumbs into her palms. The gentle caress made her hands relax. After squeezing the horse's reins for so long, it felt wonderful.

"I've been trying to think of a way to tell you this since last night, but there's no time left so I just have to say it."

As good as his hand massage felt, Sheena pulled her hands away and rubbed them herself. "Logan, please, let's not go over this again. Let's part as friends. I don't want to argue with you." His earnest face fixed upon hers and she felt as if a weight pressed on her chest.

"I know you don't trust me. And I understand why you don't. You see me as a man who promised to love you and marry you and then broke all those promises when I entered into an indenturement and left for the Americas against your wishes, even staying on two extra years to obtain a land grant. You're looking at me as if it doesn't matter, but it does. You need to know the truth about everything."

Sheena nodded her head. If this was the last time they would ever talk, she could at least listen.

"Sheena, there's something I need to tell you. Something that can't wait. Something I actually have proof of so I can tell you now without worrying about you thinking that I'm a liar." Sheena looked up into his deep brown eyes, speechless. What could he have to say? "It's about Ian." Logan took a deep breath. "Last night after you left my room I went for a walk and met up with Finnean."

Sheena didn't want to think about last night anymore. She looked down at the dirt beneath her black shoes. She didn't want to think of herself hurting Logan so much. Refusing his offer of marriage, maybe even breaking his heart because she couldn't return his love.

"Finnean and I were sitting by the fire in the library having a drink when Ian and Reed came in." Sheena looked up into Logan's worried face. "Ian and Reed didn't know that Finnean and I were there and we overheard their conversation."

"Logan," Sheena scoffed at him. "Eavesdropping?"

"Sheena, we didn't mean to. We couldn't help it. They came in so fast, talking, not even bothering to look around, and then they left just as quickly."

"I don't want to hear anything you found out through eavesdropping. Of all the things to do, Logan." Sheena turned to leave, but Logan blocked her.

"Sheena," he blurted out. "Ian is in love with another woman."

Sheena's head jolted up. "What?"

She could barely grasp Logan's words. And her mind spun. Would Logan make something like that up? She could just go ask Finnean—why would he lie to her to help Logan? And then she realized that maybe Logan spoke the truth.

Unable to say anything else she listened to Logan fill the empty air. "I'm sorry I told you like this and I'm sorry to actually have to tell you this. Her name is Rona. Apparently, Ian and she have a past together and he still loves her. I don't want you to get hurt in some twisted scheme of Ian's."

"Is Ian going to break off our betrothal?" Suddenly shivering, Sheena wrapped her arms around her waist. She hadn't expected this. How did her aunt not know about this when she found Ian as a possible husband? How could her mother betroth her to a man who loved another woman? "Maybe you misheard?"

Logan shook his head. "I don't know what Ian plans to do, but it doesn't matter—you can't marry a man who is in love with another woman. He won't treat you right." She agreed. If that was truly the state of Ian's mind. She searched Logan's gaze, looking for any sign that would show he was lying to her now. But she didn't see one.

She turned her back to Logan. When she felt the heat from Logan's hand on her shoulder, she turned with a glare. He couldn't possibly think she would just fall into his arms now. Forget all the hurt he'd caused her.

Didn't Logan know that his decision to leave Scotland
had caused all this to happen? If he'd stayed and married
her, she would never have been betrothed to Ian. And
she wouldn't have to figure out how to handle the news
that Ian was in love with a woman named Rona.

She needed to get away from Logan. She needed
time to think. She scrambled past him and flung herself up into the stagecoach, not bothering to look at Cait
or Finnean. Finnean. Ian's driver. She hung her head in
her hands. What would become of her now?

"I'll take her home," Sheena heard Finnean saying
outside the stagecoach. "You take the highwaymen's
horses. Sell them and use the money to start a good life
in the Americas."

"Finnean, we can't," Cait protested.

"Aye, you can," Finnean sounded completely confident. "You both saved our lives back there. You deserve
it."

Sheena moved her hands to cover her ears; she didn't
want to listen anymore. She wanted to think. But before
she completely blocked out the world, she heard Logan's
low voice. "I'll leave you two to discuss this."

The door of the stagecoach burst open. "Sheena."
Logan came in and shut the door behind him.

"Leave." Sheena dropped her gaze and picked at a
fray in her brown silk skirt.

Logan sat in front of her. "I know you're scared. You
and your mother will be left with nothing if you don't
marry Ian. But how can you subject yourself to a marriage with a man who is in love with another woman?"

He leaned so far forward he practically sat in her seat. "Let me help you."

He took her hand and pushed her chin up to look at him. "I won't let you get forced into marrying a man like that. I know I hurt you when I left Scotland. And because of that you don't trust me now. But I'm going to change that when we get home. I buried something in the ground before I left five years ago that will change your opinion of me."

What on earth would Logan need to dig out of the ground? Worms wouldn't exactly change anything between them or right their past together. "Logan, I don't understand what you're talking about."

Logan seemed to wrestle with a strange notion in his mind. "I just hope you'll believe me." But Sheena couldn't guarantee him that. She didn't know anything about this buried treasure of his.

"I know you didn't want me to get indentured and you still haven't forgiven me for that, but your father thought it would do me good."

"My father?" Sheena didn't avert her eyes anymore. "My father told you to risk your life? To sell yourself?"

Logan nodded. "I never told you I went to see your father five years ago before I left Scotland. I wanted to do everything the right way back then. I wanted to ask him for your hand in marriage before I asked you. Your mother may hate me, but your father liked me. And I told your father how much I loved you."

Sheena stared at Logan. "You never told me that. My

father never told me, either. You actually told my father you loved me? What did he say?"

"He told me to prove it. And I wanted to do whatever I could to impress him so he would let me marry you."

Tears dropped from Sheena's eyes. She always thought Logan just hadn't loved her enough to stay with her. And now he told her he had suffered through an indenturement for her. Could everything she thought about Logan since he left Scotland five years ago be wrong?

If so, her father had caused Logan too much pain. "I'm so sorry, Logan." She took out her handkerchief and blotted her eyes.

"Don't be." He rubbed her arms before wiping a stray tear off her cheek. "Before I left that meeting with your father, he gave me a Montgomery family heirloom box."

"The one with leaves carved into it?" Logan nodded. "My mother has been searching for that box since my father died." How would Logan know about that wooden box?

"I have it. Or at least it's buried somewhere in the ground around my family's home. Your father wrote me a letter and stowed it away in a hidden compartment inside that box. I couldn't take the box with me to the Americas and I didn't want to risk the letter getting destroyed, so I buried it near my family's home."

"Logan, I want to see the letter."

"So do I." He laughed. "I've dug in the place it should be, but I haven't been able to find it. So I left Angus to search for it. Hopefully, when I get home he will have found it. If not, I'll start digging again and as soon as I find the box I'll bring it to you."

Sheena nodded, looking into Logan's deep brown eyes. Could she trust Logan again? Five years of doubt didn't dissipate so quickly. She needed time to think about everything he'd just told her. And seeing that letter would confirm Logan's every word. "Aye, please do bring me the letter as soon as you can."

Too quickly, the stagecoach neared the Montgomerys' house. Sheena didn't feel any sense of homecoming. Unlike the warm welcome she'd received from Ian's family, Sheena knew not to expect anything besides indifference here.

Since no one came out to greet her, she left Finnean outside to tend to the horses and the stagecoach while she made for the drawing room to announce her return. Taking a deep breath, she braced herself and walked in.

"Hello, Mother, Aunt Jean." Sheena bent to kiss her mother first.

"Don't kiss me." Tavia pushed her away. "You are absolutely filthy. And don't sit down." Tavia ran her hand over the empty upholstered seat beside her as a blockade. Sheena stood stock-still. With everything else on her mind she'd forgotten how horrible she looked. "What happened to you?" Tavia asked with disgust.

"We were attacked by highwaymen somewhere around Stirling." Sheena held her dirty hands behind her back.

"Did they take anything?" Jean sipped a cup of tea.

"A couple of trinkets. But *everyone is fine*. The Mackenzies' driver, Finnean Munro, got shot, but the bullet just grazed him. He'll heal fully, although maybe he'll be left with a scar." Sheena rambled on, not sure if they even cared to hear the details. But she couldn't help herself, seeing as Logan's words rang true. They did care more about material possessions. And they shouldn't. Why didn't they ask about everyone's well-being?

"What *trinkets?*" Tavia perked up.

"It doesn't matter." Sheena wrung her hands. Tavia rolled her eyes and puffed at her insolence.

"Your mother asked you a question, child." Jean clanked her teacup down into its saucer. "She deserves an answer."

As annoyed as Sheena became, she knew she must answer the question. "They took my shawl, but we got that back, so they only got away with a rock and my Luckenbooth brooch." Sheena nearly whispered her answer.

"Luckenbooth," Jean and Tavia exclaimed in unison. "Ian gave you a Luckenbooth." This time it didn't surprise Sheena that this is what drew their attention.

Tavia's hands clapped together and her eyes sparkled. "Do you know how much they cost?" She could barely remain seated.

"He'll get her another one." Jean winked at Tavia.

"And hopefully a new wardrobe?" Tavia scowled at Sheena's appearance. "But what was that about a rock?"

Sheena felt a lump form in her throat. "It was nothing

valuable." It hurt Sheena saying that. She considered it invaluable. "Just a protection stone."

"That green moss agate stone of yours?" Jean narrowed her eyes.

"Aye." Sheena looked down at the floor. She didn't realize her mother and aunt even knew about it.

The two sisters eyed her as if examining an oddity. "Sheena, go wash and change. I'll be up to see you soon." Sheena knew Tavia had sent her away so they could return to their private conversation. She'd already overstayed her welcome. On a normal day, Tavia and Jean never wanted her around for longer than propriety dictated or they got whatever information they wished to squeeze out of her. But Sheena found relief in their behavior today and spun around to leave.

"Wait, Sheena." Jean's voice made Sheena stop. What now? She slowly turned. "Where's Cait?" How little of an explanation could Sheena get away with? Mentioning the green moss agate stone didn't seem like the wisest move.

"She no longer works here. I've let her go." Sheena's answer came out so vague it pleased her.

"You let her go?" Jean smiled wryly. "Maybe you do have it in you after all." Her chest swelled with pride as she stirred her tea. Sheena knew the time had come for her escape. Without a second pause, she raced to her room.

But her relief was short-lived after she realized her

mother had said she would come up to see her. In her bedroom? That almost never happened. What did Tavia need to see her about in private?

Chapter Nineteen

"Looks like your plan didn't pan out." Angus chuckled at Logan's messy appearance when he entered their home at last. "Ian and his men rough you up?" He sat back, relaxing in his stool.

But then Cait walked in, after Logan and Nessia rushed to her. "What kind of *men* would hurt a woman? Only monsters would do that."

Angus's face fell and he jumped to his feet. "What happened? Are you all right?" The stool fell backward with a thump to the floor.

"We're fine." Cait pushed Nessia's wandering hands away. "Stop fussing, please," she told her sister. "We're not hurt."

"We were overtaken by three highwaymen." Logan walked around them, picked up the fallen stool and sat on it.

"Highwaymen?" Nessia shrieked. "You could have been killed." She wouldn't let Cait push her away now that her worries had become real. "Sit." Nessia led Cait by the shoulders to the stool she'd just vacated. "I'll get you both something to eat before we get you washed up." She quickened her pace to the black cauldron steaming over the open fire, while Angus found a stool for himself.

Logan looked around the one-room dwelling, glad to sit at home among his family. Ian's family would be astounded if they ever stepped foot in a home like this. After only a couple days' visit, he knew their lives were worlds apart. Even Sheena, who didn't live nearly as rich a life, would be shocked to find herself here in this dimly lit room surrounded by dirt for the roof, walls and floor. Many things Ian and Sheena took for granted were missing in this hut, like fireplaces to house flames instead of letting them blaze from the open hearth in the middle of the floor, upholstered furniture, proper beds with pillows and so many more modern conveniences.

Could Sheena leave the comforts of the home she'd always known and live in a rustic cabin in the woodlands of the Americas? Could she even imagine the squalor awaiting every passenger aboard the cramped ship setting sail next Saturday to take them across the Atlantic Ocean to the New World?

But shouldn't her love for him mitigate the treacherous conditions that lay ahead? He believed it would. He would spend his life making her happy, if she gave him the chance.

With a clang, Angus placed his empty pewter tankard on the table and Logan snapped back to the present. "So these highwaymen, are they still out there somewhere?"

"Aye." Cait looked tired and that fact didn't escape Nessia's watchful eye as she brought her sister a warm bowl of broth.

"I'll spread the word tomorrow. If those thieves show up around here, they'll be sorry." Angus shook his finger angrily at no one in particular.

"Aye." Nessia brought another bowl for Logan and then put her hands on Cait's shoulders. "Come. Let's get you cleaned up. Then you must rest. A good night's sleep will do you good." Cait nodded, rising slowly from fatigue and carrying her broth with her. A look of gratitude in her eyes.

With the women gone, Angus turned to look sympathetically at Logan. "I'm sorry, Logan, but I didn't find the box."

Logan sipped his hot broth.

"I thought as much when I didn't see it. Thanks for looking. I'll resume my search tomorrow."

Angus clapped him on the back trying to ease his mood. "So you ended up in Glasgow?"

"Aye. Ian was perfectly nice. Perfect in every way."

Angus laughed. "That bad? No third eye or anything?"

"Unfortunately, he had money, looks and good manners, too."

"You sure know how to torture yourself, Logan. But what does Sheena think about him? Did she fall for him?"

Logan smiled. A quick and easy grin as he leaned

forward, resting his elbows on his knees. "Surprisingly, I don't think so."

Angus put his arm on Logan's shoulder. "I don't think it's surprising at all." Logan smiled at his brother's encouraging compliment.

"At least I hope she didn't already start getting feelings for him, because last night before we left I found out that Ian is in love with another woman." Angus's eyes bulged and Logan pushed off his knees after his last spoonful of broth.

"What? He can't marry Sheena if he loves another woman. That's not fair to Sheena, himself or this other woman."

"I'm hoping either Sheena or Ian will break off the betrothal." Logan gave his brother a sly look. "I've asked her to marry me and come to the Americas."

"You did?" Angus waved his hands for more details. "And?"

"*And* she said nay, but that was before she knew about Ian. I didn't ask her afterward. I only just told her about Ian loving some woman named Rona. The news struck her hard. It shocked her. She's been through so much." Logan ran his hand through his hair.

"And so have you, Logan."

"Sheena." Tavia knocked on her door, opening it at the same time. Sheena shot up. She could count the number of times her mother had come up to her room.

Tavia looked around it aimlessly, and Sheena went to sit on her bed, leaving the chair free in case Tavia preferred to sit. But Tavia didn't move farther than a foot inside the doorway.

"I didn't want to have this conversation in front of Jean." Sheena stared at her mother. What conversation? And whyever not? She would most likely tell her sister all about it afterward anyway. The two of them told each other everything. Why should this conversation be different? "First, tell me about Ian's home."

Sheena moved her hands from her sides to fold them in her lap. If Tavia got straight to the point, Sheena wouldn't mince words, either. She didn't want this conversation to take any longer than absolutely necessary. Her nerves lay in knots already. "It's three stories high, richly decorated and full of merriment." She threw in the last bit as the most important contrast to their house.

"Are they indeed rich, then?" Tavia became all too transparent. Where were the questions about her health or mental state after getting attacked by highwaymen? Didn't her mother want to hear about how they got away from the highwaymen safely?

Obviously not. Sheena answered with a scowl, "I never met with their bankers."

"You know well enough what I mean." Tavia's hands flew to her hips. And Sheena simply nodded. Her mother smiled with obvious delight before she continued her interrogation.

"Where will we live once you marry Ian?" It came as no surprise to Sheena that Tavia intended to live with her rather than Jean. Why, Sheena didn't quite know. Surely, Tavia would love the company of her sister, but

Sheena suspected her mother hated the idea of people considering her as her sister's dependent and wanted all of Glasgow to see her as the matron of a rich household. Maybe Tavia would even garner satisfaction from being wealthier than her sister.

"I have not seen the house. Ian is keeping it as a surprise. All I know is that it is down the street from his family's home and should be finished in time."

"That's wonderful." Her mother nodded as if her agreement in the matter actually mattered. But it didn't. Ian had already forged ahead with all his plans.

"Is Ian taken with you, Sheena?" Sheena shifted on her bed. "Answer me. Is he keen to wed you?"

"Mother, you don't understand. Someone overheard Ian tell his brother, Reed, that Ian loves another woman named Rona."

Tavia paused for a moment. "You say they *overheard.* Well, they heard wrong. I paid your dowry. Ian agreed to marry you. Unless he returns my money—you are marrying him. He will grow to love you and forget all about this other woman, if she even exists."

Sheena took a deep breath and slid off her bed onto her feet. "Mother..."

But Tavia wouldn't listen. "I've told you before, I will not have you ruin this and I mean it." Tavia held firm. "Why did you have that green moss agate stone with you anyway?"

Sheena faltered. And Tavia jeered at her. "I know all about it. That ridiculous fairing that Logan lad gave you." She almost laughed. "Do you think I'm blind? I remember how listless you were after Logan left five years ago. I know that's when the green moss agate stone appeared. I remember you always holding it and rubbing it. I just hadn't seen it for a while. I thought you'd given it up. Apparently, I'd made a mistake. But I won't be making any more of them."

Sheena leaned back against her bed again as the candle's flame flickered low. Did her mother sympathize with her? Did she hate Logan for hurting her?

"It's just as well that agate stone was stolen. I was looking for it, meaning to throw it away myself." Sheena's mouth fell open. "Saves me the trouble of sneaking in here while you're sleeping." Sheena couldn't help shuddering, as a chill ran through her body, thinking of Tavia standing over her while she slept so vulnerably.

"Mother…"

Tavia interrupted her again, putting her hand up to silence Sheena. "I don't want to hear it. I saw the way that Logan lad looked at you at church last Sunday. The nerve of that man." Sheena couldn't believe it. Tavia had guessed Logan's feelings for her. Did he show them so clearly? Sheena had missed them completely.

"I don't care about Logan. You will marry Ian."

Sheena pressed her lips together firmly, unable to utter a sound as a maid came into the doorway carrying a tray. "Ma'am." She addressed Tavia.

"Set it over there." Her mother stepped slightly to the side, making room for the maid to place the food tray on Sheena's bedside table. Sheena looked at the unappetizing food on the tray as the maid left. Her stomach churned. She didn't think she could eat with all the worry twisting inside her.

"Jean saw Boyd yesterday." Tavia's cold, lined face spat the words out and Sheena knew the shock registered on her face before she could hide it.

"Mother, I don't know what Boyd told you..."

Tavia raised an eyebrow. "You had another chaperone. That Logan lad." Sheena merely looked at her mother. "Boyd's been fired thanks to you. All those years of service. I hope you're happy with yourself." Sheena kept herself in check, even though she felt terrible. She must hold back her tears in front of Tavia. "You could have ruined your meeting with Ian. Did you consider the consequences of that?" She stepped farther back into the doorway, darkness engulfing her wee frame. "I'm not letting you out of my sight again." She grabbed the doorknob. "Consider yourself confined to your bedroom, you'll be staying in here until your wedding day."

Tavia slammed the door shut.

Sheena sank down in front of her bed and bent her legs up to hug them. Staring straight ahead, she rested her head on her knees.

"Are you trying to dig to the Americas?" Nessia smiled, with the lads and Cait trailing behind her. Logan raised his hand to wave. Laughing, he shook his head as they passed on their way to yet another friend's house for a final visit before they all left Callander for good.

But Logan didn't hesitate a moment more before

thrusting his shovel back into the earth. Their ship sailed in days.

"You've been at that all morning," Angus called. "Time for a break."

Wiping sweat from his forehead, Logan leaned on his shovel as Angus handed him the family's pewter tankard. Logan downed the water at once. "Thanks." Angus took the tankard back without a word as he surveyed the holes surrounding them. "Do you need help with anything, Angus?"

"Nay, I wouldn't take you away from this. I know how important it is that you find that box with Sheena's father's letter in it." Angus threw his hand around, pointing at the holes. "And besides, I'm just going to give away some more of our stuff."

Logan knew the people of Callander didn't have much money to spare to buy their belongings from them. And that probably suited his family just fine, since a better life awaited.

"Shouldn't take me long anyway—we didn't have much to begin with." Angus chuckled. And Logan joined in agreement.

"I'll leave you to it, then." Angus began walking away, but stopped to call over his shoulder, "Promise you'll stop when the sun goes down?" Logan smiled. He couldn't promise that. He must keep going until he found the wooden box.

He thrust his shovel into the dirt again. This is where he'd buried it before he left for the Americas five years ago. Why couldn't he find it?

* * *

Sheena didn't even look up as her mother stepped into her bedroom on Saturday. "Good morning." Sheena's anger hadn't subsided since last night. How could her own mother not care that her future husband may love another woman? How could she just shrug it off? Sheena surely couldn't. "How did you sleep?"

"Not well." Sheena stood before her mother and took a more direct stance. "The man you betrothed me to is in love with another woman."

Tavia scratched her cheek with her wiry fingers. "You have no proof of that. And besides, if Ian thinks he has feelings for another woman it is simply prewedding nerves. He's probably just a wee bit nervous before the wedding. If there's anything in his system he'll get it out before the wedding takes place."

"How can you be so sure, Mother?"

"I've seen a lot of things in my forty-six years, Sheena. You really could learn a few things from me if you'd pay attention." Sheena'd heard that before and each time the smug, self-righteous lecture felt akin to scratching an itch with a thistle. "Now let's not let this get in the way of the future we have planned for ourselves. We both will live very well with Ian as your husband. Be sensible. Ian is wealthy beyond measure."

Sheena shook her head. Tavia shouldn't just dismiss it as meaningless and hope it would go away. They should face it head-on. Confront Ian. Find out the truth. If her mother wouldn't, Sheena would before she ever walked down that aisle with Ian.

"Do you really see me as such a vile mother? A woman concerned with her own well-being at the expense of her own children? If you do, you are wrong. I won't deny that I like the finer things in life, but God knows I want what is best for you."

Sheena didn't answer. Shocked by her mother's words she weighed whether they rang true or not. Did her mother mean to come this close to telling her that she loved her? Or was she just saying that to try to manipulate her further?

"Sheena, I have lived in this cruel world longer than you. I truly loved your father. And because of my experiences with life, I am, as your mother, going to make sure you do not repeat my mistakes."

"How can loving Father have been a mistake? I remember the two of you when I was younger—you were happy. Completely content. And utterly in love. What more is there in life?" Sheena stepped forward, eager to debate this topic with Tavia.

But Tavia wouldn't let her get any closer. She retreated and sat down on Sheena's bed. Like a child, her feet barely touched the ground. She let out a long breath. "Life changes, but the one thing that never does is the need for money. One cannot live happily in this world without it. Look at me now. God rest your father's soul. Heaven knows I look forward to seeing him again, but he left me to fend for myself in this world. He left me entirely at the mercy of others. If Jean didn't find Ian for you, I don't know what we would have done. We can't afford our home anymore. And even after selling it, that money won't last long. We would become dependent on the charity of Jean and Kyle."

"Mother, if things were different, Aunt Jean and Uncle Kyle would happily take us in."

"Aye, they're too nice. I'm sure I'll spend most of my time with them anyway, but being dependent on others would have lowered your ability to marry well and that is the most important job a mother has—to make sure her children form beneficial attachments." Sheena didn't argue about the things she thought a mother should do, like forming a loving relationship with her children.

"Mother, how can I marry Ian when he is in love with another woman?"

"Come now." Tavia ignored Sheena's assertion. "It just so happens I have wonderful news. Would you like to hear it?" Sheena looked at her mother with a vacant expression as she dropped off Sheena's bed. Tavia would do whatever she wanted to anyway. "All right, I'll tell you. Nay, wait. I'll show you." Tavia clasped her hands together excitedly.

And Sheena moved to stand by the window, the farthest spot from her mother, as Tavia called in a male servant. He placed a large box on Sheena's bed before leaving.

"Open it." Tavia's excitement hung in her words. But Sheena didn't budge. She knew exactly what that box housed. "Very uncooperative." Her mother tsked at her, but it didn't seem to ruin her mood. She opened the lid and pulled out yards of delicate fabric. Her mother's wedding dress. "Isn't it gorgeous? This is the most expensive silk fabric. A family could live off the cost of this material for a couple of years." Her mother glowed as she hugged the dress against her. She looked young again and Sheena saw for a brief moment a wide-eyed young lass.

"I want you to wear it when you marry Ian." Sheena knew the mother-daughter moment she dreamed about all her life was actually happening, but given the circumstances it fell completely short of the ideal. And her mother didn't seem to notice or care. Tavia just talked on, perfectly happy with a one-sided conversation.

"We have a seamstress coming in less than an hour. I expect you to clean yourself up by then. We're going to get this dress to fit you somehow." Her mother crossed the room to hold the dress up in front of Sheena. "We'll need a miracle." She said it so matter-of-factly that Sheena scowled. "Maybe I should have the cook cut down on the food she serves you." Sheena's mouth fell open in response. "Never you mind. We don't even have a week. Not much we can do in that time anyway."

Appalled, Sheena stopped herself from telling her mother that her size seemed about the same as every other woman her age, but her mother wouldn't listen anyway. Tavia had already formed her opinion and wouldn't change it.

"Doesn't matter. Ian's already seen you and he agreed to marry you." Sheena couldn't listen to any more of this without going insane. She stepped away from Tavia and the dress. "Don't get any ideas," Tavia said, turning sharply to face her. But Sheena didn't understand what she meant. "Two men are waiting right outside. You are not to set one foot outside this room." Tavia glared at her. And then Sheena understood, remembering her punishment for the chaperone swap.

"Mother, did Father ever mention to you whom he wanted me to marry?" Sheena knew better than to bring up Logan's name. But she couldn't help asking, in case her father had told her mother about his meeting with Logan and the letter he'd written Logan. "Did Father ever tell you that someone asked to marry me?"

"Nay. He only wanted you to marry well, and now you are. So, come. We've wasted enough time talking. The seamstress will be here very soon and you need all the time you can get to improve your appearance." Tavia went to the door. "Don't just stand there gaping at me. Get moving," she ordered, before shutting the door behind her.

Sheena complied. She would need to wait until church on Sunday to see the secret letter for herself. If it existed.

The sun sank in the sky and the misty fog rolled in over the moors as Logan threw the shovel's blade over his shoulder like a rifle and trudged a few steps to start digging in a new spot. He prayed with every shovel full of dirt he flung over his shoulder.

"Logan." Angus's tone sounded like a reprimand and Logan stopped digging. "You've been at this all day now."

But Logan didn't want to admit defeat.

"I know I put it here by this rock before I left Scotland five years ago. And between the two of us we've already dug up everything in every direction and I still can't find it. I've gone deeper than I know I dug in the first place. And nothing. It's got to be here. I've got to find it." He started digging again.

"What's Uncle Logan doing?" Duncan stood beside his father.

"He's looking for a box he buried."

"A wooden box?"

"Aye." Angus raised a brow, and Logan stopped digging.

"Why did you guess a wooden box, Duncan?"

"Because Ewan dug one up years ago."

Logan and Angus exchanged looks.

"Ewan." Angus's voice rose so loud it carried through their home and beyond. Ewan stopped in the middle of a game near their home and spun around in the direction of his father's voice. Even Nessia and Cait poked their heads outside to see why Angus had raised his voice.

"Ewan. Come here." Angus yelled almost as loud, but no anger shaded his tone and Nessia and Cait went back inside, as Ewan raced over.

"Ewan, your uncle Logan is looking for a wooden box. It's about this big." He mimicked the size with his hands. "It's wooden, and has carvings of leaves all over it." Ewan tensed at his father's words. "Do you know what I'm talking about?"

Logan stood baffled. The lad knew about his secret box?

"Is that what you've been digging for?" Ewan raised his eyes just enough to look into Logan's.

"Aye." Logan tried to answer calmly, repressing his anxiety.

"I'm sorry, Uncle Logan." Ewan kicked at the dirt. "You won't find it here."

Logan steadied his voice before speaking to Ewan, making sure he didn't scare the lad into silence. "Why not?"

"Because when I was little I saw you dig a hole and put something in it before you left and I dug it up. I'm sorry, Uncle Logan, I shouldn't have done it. It wasn't mine, but I just thought since you were gone it didn't matter and it was better if I had it than if it was lost in the earth forever." Logan took a long breath. Here stood yet another person with no faith that he would come back to Scotland from the Americas. Logan winced at how much trouble that disbelief caused.

"It's fine, Ewan. I'm not mad. Just tell me where it is."

"I thought it was going to have something fantastic in it, but it was empty, so I gave it to Duncan." All eyes turned to Duncan and the lad's eyes grew large in alarm.

"Why would you bury an empty box, Uncle Logan?" Ewan rubbed his chin as if trying to solve the biggest mystery of his childhood.

"It wasn't empty." Logan bent down so he could put both hands on his thighs and remain at the lad's eye level. "It had a secret compartment."

"Neat." Ewan's eyes gleamed. "You're like a real pirate."

"Nay, I'm not." Logan straightened a little too

abruptly making Ewan and Duncan freeze. "Most pirates are not good people and I follow the Lord. I don't hurt others or steal things that aren't mine. Now would one of you please tell me where my box is? It's very important."

"Duncan?" Angus put a hand on his son's shoulder, giving him the courage to speak.

"I gave it to Ma to sell last week."

Angus looked back worriedly into Logan's face.

"Who did she sell it to?" Logan prayed for the answers as he tried to remain optimistic, realizing the new owner had acquired it less than a week before so they probably hadn't figured out the secret compartment yet. At least Logan hoped they hadn't thrown out Sheena's father's letter.

Duncan shrugged his shoulders.

"Thanks, lads." Logan let his shovel drop. "We've got to ask Nessia." They all walked to the house.

"I'm sorry, Logan. While you were in Glasgow we got rid of whatever things we could, trying to get ready to leave Scotland. I was out here digging so much, I must have missed it."

"Not your fault, Angus. Just pray that Nessia knows who she sold it to and that it's not halfway to Ireland by now."

They all crowded into the one-room dwelling behind Angus. "Nessia, do you remember selling a wooden box with leaves carved into it last week?"

Nessia stood by the fire, wiping her hands on her apron. "Aye, that is actually the only thing we sold."

She laughed before Logan cut in. "Who bought it?"

"Tavia Montgomery." Nessia dropped her apron. "Sheena's mother."

Chapter Twenty

Pulling his brown sleeveless vest over his white shirt, Logan set off toward Sheena's house with Cait in tow.

Tavia buying back her family's heirloom containing the letter Sheena's father gave Logan seemed like a direct blessing from God. It was right by Sheena, not lost to them forever. Finally, Sheena could open it and read for herself why Logan had never told her about his secret meeting with her father or the reason he took that indenturement in the Americas.

Hopefully, all of Sheena's mistrust for Logan would be laid to rest. And Sheena and her mother could read for themselves that Sheena's father had wanted Sheena to marry Logan when he returned to Scotland.

The sun shone brightly on this beautiful spring morning. Logan had wanted to go straight to Sheena last night, but thought better of it. It was too late. But this morning maybe Cait would be able to see Sheena if Logan couldn't. At least he prayed for that outcome as they walked through the moor.

"Logan, Cait." Boyd's voice flew across the moor and they waved at the Montgomerys' butler.

"Thanks again for switching places with me and going to Glasgow as Sheena's chaperone, Logan." They shook hands when he reached them.

"It is I who needs to thank you, Boyd. How's your father?"

"Still ill. I guess everything worked out for the best though, seeing how much my family needs me on the farm while my father's ill and can't work."

Logan exchanged a quick look with Cait and saw confusion on her face, as well. "Boyd, how are you working on the farm and at the Montgomerys' house at the same time?" he asked.

"I'm not." Boyd looked between them. "Tavia found out about us switching places as Sheena's chaperone and fired me."

Terror gripped Logan. If Tavia knew about the switch, how much punishment had Sheena endured?

He could barely walk. He wanted to run. They left Boyd with barely a farewell. And when he saw Sheena's house, his determination rose even further until he saw the Mackenzies' stagecoach. He fought back the glimmer of hope that Sheena sat inside because, however much he wanted that, he knew the difference between fantasy and reality. His jaw clenched.

"I was on my way to find your home." Finnean jumped down from the driver's seat, bowing in front of Cait and shaking Logan's hand. "Where are you headed?"

"We're actually here to see Sheena." Logan eyed the stagecoach packed to its brim.

"I'm sorry. The Montgomery house is empty—everyone's gone to Glasgow." Logan's heart sank. This couldn't be happening.

Logan wanted to leave for Glasgow right away. He just couldn't wait any longer, realizing that every hour that passed brought Sheena closer to walking down the aisle with Ian. What if her mother moved up her wedding day? If that was the case, even if Logan left right now he might arrive too late to stop the ceremony. Logan still couldn't fathom how Tavia knew he had switched places with Boyd.

"Did Sheena look well when she left?" Finnean nodded. Questions fired through Logan's mind. "Is this all the Montgomerys' belongings?" Logan wondered if Finnean had stored the heirloom box in the Mackenzies' stagecoach.

"Nay, there were other carriages. They left with Sheena and her family."

Logan examined the stagecoach. "Finnean, did you happen to load a wooden box with leaf carvings?" Finnean shook his head.

"I was the last to bundle up my coach and thought I'd come by to see you before I headed back to Glasgow myself. Maybe offer my services in case any of you needed a lift to Glasgow. Seeing as I have room for a passenger." Logan looked from Finnean's gaze to Cait's blushing cheeks. He knew Finnean meant to direct his invitation to Cait.

"That passenger will have to be Logan. I can't possibly go to Glasgow right now." Cait curbed the tension with her refusal. Logan knew Cait had offered for Logan to go instead of herself for more than the obvious reason of not traveling alone with a man unchaperoned. She always tried to help Logan with Sheena. "My sister, Nessia, still needs me to help get the lads ready for the move. But Logan is all ready to go. He can get things settled for us before we arrive." Logan couldn't feel more thankful to Cait.

"Sure." Finnean bowed to Cait. "I do hope to see you in Glasgow, though." Cait nodded with a huge smile on her face.

"But, Finnean, if you wouldn't mind, Cait could use a ride home before you and I set off to Glasgow." Finnean nodded with a grin that spread rapidly across his face. Cait squeezed Logan's arm in appreciation for giving her time with Finnean.

With a look up the crag that nestled Sheena and his special waterfall Logan knew no time remained for him to hike up there and see it one last time. Just as well, he thought. He didn't want to stand up there without Sheena.

Arriving home, Logan went inside to find his canvas bag. He didn't own much, nor did anyone in his family. They could all ride on the three highwaymen's horses to Glasgow with less than a bag each for their belongings.

As everyone waited outside for Logan to reemerge, he picked up his bag. The same one he'd just returned to Scotland with. He took a deep breath. He knew he'd never step foot through this door again.

Knowing this home, this village and the rest of his homeland remained etched into his memory already, he didn't regret leaving. He'd tested his memory when he'd gone to the Americas the first time and he knew it wouldn't fail him. He could get back here in a second by simply closing his eyes. "Goodbye," he said, walking out of the darkness and into the light.

Kissing Nessia, Logan leaned down to hug the lads, before standing to embrace his brother. "We've been talking and we're going to leave this afternoon, so we'll be there just after you, Logan."

"Have a safe trip."

Angus nodded solemnly. "Don't worry about us. We'll make it to the inn. You just concentrate on getting your wife." Angus grinned. "Now go. And Godspeed."

Logan found Cait standing by Finnean and threw his bag up on the seat before hugging her in farewell. "We'll meet up with you at the inn. Finnean's agreed to put you up for the night until we get to Glasgow and you can join us at the inn tomorrow," Cait told Logan, making him smile.

"You're a godsend, Cait." He kissed her cheek before climbing aboard to give her and Finnean a moment together before they set off.

When the inn Sheena and Logan had visited last week on their way to Glasgow came into sight, Logan real-

ized how differently he would have done things if he'd
known then what he did now.

Leaving Finnean to tend to the horses for the last half
of the trip, Logan went in search of materials to write
Sheena a letter. The idea had struck him on the way here.
Since Finnean worked as a driver for Ian, a chance might
present itself for Finnean to get close to Sheena. And
if that happened, Logan wanted to make sure Finnean
could give her a letter from him.

God willing, that would work and Sheena would
know that her mother actually had the box in her pos-
session. But if that didn't work, Logan figured he would
just have to get to Sheena himself. Somehow.

Finding a spot outside, Logan sat down to write:

Dearest Sheena,
If you get this note, it is because I could not get
to you myself. Please know that I am in Glasgow
looking for you.

I do not know why you left Callander so suddenly without saying goodbye or waiting to see the
letter. I can only hope it was not your choice to do
so. But I hope you will not let your mother force
you into a marriage with Ian if he still loves Rona.

I also must tell you the whereabouts of the
secret letter your father wrote, promising that you
could marry me if I came back to Scotland after
my indenturement in the Americas. Your mother
has it.

She bought the Montgomery family's heirloom

box from Nessia. I don't think she knows about the hidden compartment the box contains, so she probably has not seen the letter.

I hope you will find it. If you open the box and push down hard on one side of the bottom, the other side will rise and the letter should be underneath in the hidden compartment.

After you've read it, I hope you will remember what we shared and what we meant to each other five years ago. I also hope you will forgive me for obeying your father and leaving you to secure our future together.

On our last night in Glasgow, I asked you to marry me and I want you to know I still want to marry you. I love you, lassie, and my heart is indentured to you forever. Logan

Folding the letter, Logan prayed Finnean wouldn't need to give it to Sheena. It would turn out that much better if Logan found Sheena himself.

In a cloud of dust, a carriage passed in front of him. When the dust settled, Logan saw the driver—an employee of the Montgomery household. Logan jumped to his feet. Sheena must be inside that carriage.

He ran after the carriage, shouting, "Sheena." But the carriage drove on. He kept running, yelling and waving his arms. *Please, God, stop that carriage.*

But it didn't stop. It bounced along the rough road until it turned and he saw her looking out the window.

He waved and yelled again. Her head shot out the window, a mass of auburn hair flew in the breeze.

Could she see him? She must. *Please, God, let her know who's waving at her.* He needed her to know he'd come after her. She waved a white handkerchief until it escaped her hand and floated to the ground. Logan stopped running when the coach moved too far down the dirt road. Finnean and he would set off quickly enough. They would arrive in Glasgow soon after Sheena did. Relief fluttered through him as he walked toward her white handkerchief. He squeezed it in his hands. God willing, he would return it to her while she still remained a Montgomery.

Chapter Twenty-One

~

Walking far behind Tavia and Jean, Sheena left the Mackenzie home as slowly as she could. She hadn't been able to ask Ian for a private conversation tonight to inquire about Rona. But she did request a private conversation with him before the wedding and he agreed.

Lingering in the street, she looked around her, but saw nothing besides the enormous houses and carriages lining the street. No one who looked like Logan.

She knew she'd seen Logan at that inn after their carriage started off on the dusty road to Glasgow. At first, she didn't know if she'd heard Logan call her name or if her mind had been playing tricks on her. And since everyone inside the carriage slept, there was no one to ask. Not that she would have anyway. But when she looked out the window, a male figure ran after them waving at their carriage. It had to be Logan. No one else would care to pick up the handkerchief that accidentally blew out of her hand. Logan had probably found the letter from her father and would bring it to Glasgow to show her. He might already have arrived in Glasgow. Hopefully, he would find someone to help direct him to her aunt Jean and uncle Kyle's house where she and her mother resided now.

"I know I've said this before, but what a fine estate house the Mackenzies' own," Tavia said, prancing toward Jean's waiting carriage, completely oblivious to how close her decision to enjoy a leisurely dinner at the inn came to letting Sheena meet Logan. If only Sheena had known to eat even more slowly and extended their dinner well past one o'clock in the afternoon, then maybe Sheena would have bumped right into Logan. Sheena hoped for that now as she followed her mother, stalling as much as she could and putting a fair bit of distance between them. First, her shoe needed fixing, then her shawl needed adjusting, then something on the ground needed her attention, and so did something off in the distance. And when she couldn't think of anything else to stall with, she started the process over again.

She thought if she stalled long enough Logan might just find her in front of the Mackenzies, since he knew where Ian's house stood.

She breathed in the night's cool, salty, ocean air, wishing she could run down to the docks and watch the waves lap the shore.

"I will like getting accustomed to this lavish lifestyle." Tavia's voice speared that peaceful thought.

Jean took her sister's arm. "I did not overexaggerate at all, did I?"

Tavia hugged her sister's arm tighter. "Nay, you

did not. Bless you." Sheena shook her head wondering how the Mackenzies could miss seeing the greed in her mother's eyes.

She couldn't help thinking her mother should marry Ian herself. If an age difference didn't divide them, Sheena knew her mother would gladly change places with her.

With no further way to stall, Sheena arrived at the carriage and entered behind her mother and aunt.

As the carriage strode steadily toward Jean's home, Sheena sat quietly, listening to Tavia and Jean prattle on about the Mackenzies and whomever else caught their fancy. But without the word *Logan,* no topic piqued Sheena's interest.

"Sheena, are you feeling ill?" Tavia's question took Sheena a moment to grasp, since it intruded into her thoughts.

"I'm fine, Mother."

"Good, because this is no time for you to fall ill. Your wedding is tomorrow."

Of course her mother only concerned herself because of that. Wait a minute. "Tomorrow?" Sheena thought the wedding wouldn't take place until next weekend.

"I talked it over with Ian's parents tonight and they agreed. We will just have the three banns of marriage announced tomorrow before the ceremony. No one will object to that. Now, when we get home I want you right up to bed. I'm not taking any chances."

Neither would Sheena. If she confirmed that Ian loved another, she would break the betrothal herself and not marry Ian. Only now, Sheena needed to find a way to corner Ian fast, because obviously he didn't know about the accelerated plans their parents had made for them. Sheena turned to look out the window. How would she get to him?

"The womenfolk have returned." Uncle Kyle's booming voice filled the front hall before he kissed his wife's cheek. "Hope you enjoyed a pleasant evening, my dearest?"

"We missed you tonight," Tavia told her brother-in-law, handing all her outer clothes to the nearest servant.

Kyle chuckled. "Such is the life of the law." He led Jean into the drawing room.

"Be that as it may," Jean said, as she sat beside her husband on the sofa, "you work much too hard. Too many long hours."

"My dearest, if I did otherwise we could not afford all this," he bellowed and Jean patted his knee.

"You are a good man." Tavia sat opposite them in an armchair. "Jean forgets that a couple cannot live on love alone." Tavia smirked, but Jean did not.

"Now Tavia, how could I forget that, since you saw fit to prove your own theory?" Sheena didn't sit down—the tension in the room pushed her to stand by the fire and keep her back to the rising tempers.

"Very well," Tavia didn't defend herself or her marriage, which irritated Sheena to no end. How could her mother talk so disrespectfully about her late father? "That mistake will not be repeated in the next generation." Sheena felt all eyes prick her back as she steadied herself more firmly in front of the fireplace.

"Nay. I dare say." Kyle chuckled. "The Mackenzies put everyone to shame."

"Sheena will have the best of both worlds, as do we," Jean agreed and Sheena felt suddenly light-headed.

"Aye. Sheena will not repeat my mistakes," Tavia spoke hoarsely.

"Now, now Tavia," Jean softened her voice. "Your marriage was blissful."

"Nay, you were right in what you said before, Jean…"

"Nay, Tavia. What I said was in anger…"

"Hush, hush. I am where I am today because of the foolishness of youth. I know that as well as anyone."

Sheena turned. "Love is not foolish, Mother."

"Not if it's properly placed," Tavia replied evenly and Jean interjected. "You are lucky to have Ian, child."

Sheena flushed from anger.

"Never mind reasoning with her, Jean. Why do you remain, Sheena?" Tavia grimaced. "You have paid your uncle Kyle his due respect, so now off to your room."

Kyle stood and walked over to Sheena. Kissing her cheek, he squeezed her hands with his big, thick fingers. "Bless you. You do look tired. I'll send up some tea for you."

"Thanks, Uncle." Sheena kissed his cheek back. Since arriving, she thanked God on numerous occasions for her uncle's caring presence. And this time proved no different.

Sheena said good-night to Tavia and Jean, as Kyle lit

a candle for her to take up to her room. Quiet solitude quickly became her sole companion as she approached her darkened bedroom.

Before she entered her bedroom though, she heard a knock on the entrance door and a servant answer it.

Sheena stood still, listening, but she couldn't make out any words, just muffled sounds. Who would call at this late hour?

The journey to Glasgow from the inn took much longer than Logan had anticipated. He thought they might catch up to the Montgomerys' carriage, but they never did. Between the horses and the bad roads, they never got their speed up. And now with the sun set, darkness cloaked Logan as he stood on Sheena's aunt's doorstep.

"If you could please tell Sheena Montgomery that Logan McAllister is here to see her," Logan said to a servant. He knew he had knocked on the correct door due to Finnean's detailed directions.

"I'll handle this," Tavia hissed at the servant and stood before Logan, her anger an almost tangible block at the doorway.

"Please, Mrs. Montgomery, I must give this letter to Sheena." Logan held up the letter to show Tavia and she snatched it, keeping it firmly hidden behind her back.

"I'll make sure she gets it. Good night." But Logan knew not to believe Tavia's promise.

"There's a letter from her father…" But he never got a chance to finish.

* * *

"Mother, who was that?" Sheena raced down the stairs, her candle flickering in the wind she created. She thought she'd heard Logan's voice.

"No one of importance," her mother huffed. But Sheena doubted that.

"Then show me what it is you're hiding behind your back."

Tavia turned, trying to move the letter Sheena just saw her reading from behind her back into her shawl without Sheena seeing, but she did.

"Mother. That was Logan, wasn't it? He gave you a letter, didn't he?" Sheena set her candle down on a table and approached her mother. "It's a letter from my father stating that Father wanted me to marry Logan, isn't it?"

Tavia's mouth fell open. "Sheena, your father wrote no such thing. I would know if he had. Logan is lying." Tavia folded her arms, concealing the letter further. "It was Logan who told you about Ian loving another woman, wasn't it? That lad just wants to make trouble. Doesn't he realize what a wonderful future you will have with Ian? And here he is going out of his way to destroy it. The fool."

"Mother, if it is not true, then show me the letter." Sheena held out her hand.

But her mother never even looked at her hand, let alone contemplated for a fraction of a second handing the letter over. She turned abruptly and stalked into the drawing room. Jean gasped as Sheena ran in after her.

"Nay, Mother." Sheena lunged for the letter, but her mother flung it into the fire.

"I will not have that lad filling your head with nonsense. Now go to bed." Sheena stared at the letter erupting into flames before glaring at her mother.

Forget the letter. Sheena didn't need it. In addition to confronting Ian before the wedding ceremony tomorrow about the possibility of his loving another woman, Sheena could also track down Logan and find out from him what the letter said. If only she could go out now, but she would never get past the front door. And even if she did, a lady didn't go outside in the city unaccompanied at this time of night unless she wanted to invite danger. For now she needed to put her trust in God to work all this out.

Disappointment surged through Logan as he realized his letter in the hands of Tavia was now as good as gone. He would need to formulate a new plan to get Sheena, and it didn't include standing on Sheena's aunt's doorstep all night. Walking down the street to the Mackenzies' mansion to meet up with Finnean, Logan unfortunately passed Sheena and Ian's future home. He could do without seeing that.

Reaching the Mackenzies', Logan leaned on a light pole across the street. No lights beckoned from inside. Only a few muffled sounds in the distance reminded Logan of just how large a city he stood in. And only the odd carriage rode past him. No one walked about.

"Logan?" He turned to see a man running up the street to him.

He pushed off the light pole. "Finnean."

"I'm afraid I've got some news you may not want to hear."

"What is it?" His body tensed in anticipation.

"Sheena and Ian are set to marry tomorrow morning at eleven o'clock at Glasgow Cathedral."

Logan clapped Finnean on his shoulder. "As long as they're not married yet I have time to see her again. He ran his fingers through his hair with relief, but stopped, suddenly catching sight of someone coming out of the Mackenzies' front door.

Grabbing Finnean's arm, he pulled him back away from the streetlight into the shadows. "Look."

"It's Ian," Finnean whispered, even though his voice couldn't possibly carry across the street.

"Where's he going at this hour?" Logan squinted his eyes, more in thought than out of any need to see better. "Does he usually take walks at this time of night?"

Finnean shook his head. "No one sets off for a walk this late at night. The guards are about to get everyone off the streets soon."

Logan didn't take his eyes off Ian, who hesitated at the bottom of his walk before turning right and setting off at a quick pace. Logan moved sideways. "I've got to follow him."

Chapter Twenty-Two

"I'm coming, too." Finnean followed Logan, who could barely keep from running after Ian.

When Ian turned onto another street, they quickly crossed their street and caught sight of him again. On and on they followed as fog rolled in from the harbor and thickened around them. Up and down endless streets that all looked the same to Logan they crept along.

Hearing the waves crash against the rocks and smelling the sea air, Logan realized that they had traveled to the docks. And from experience, he knew the docks weren't a good place for law-abiding Christians at night. Some didn't even qualify during the day.

"We've got to get closer," Logan told Finnean as they inched along a cold stone wall to get a better view. Ian stood by the water's edge, the sea mist covering him. He just stood there looking down at his feet.

Why had Ian come here? Logan couldn't make sense of his behavior. The night before his wedding day, a man shouldn't roam around in the darkness attracting harm to himself. Did Ian consider suicide? Impossible—he possessed everything good in life and besides, he hadn't come with anything heavy to tie around himself. And yet, Ian stood on the edge of the pier as if he thought about diving into the roiling waters.

Logan ducked his head a little lower as footsteps sounded on the dock. Ian heard them, too, and his head shot in their direction. A woman's silhouette came into view as the fog lifted. She walked with determination straight up to Ian. "Thanks for meeting me here." Her voice sounded soft and out of place in such a foreboding area of Glasgow.

"I wouldn't miss it, Rona." So this was Rona, the woman Ian had told his brother he loved. "It's been a long time."

She moved closer to Ian and took his hand. "I'm glad to see you well, Ian."

"Rona, I'm betrothed." Ian's words stunned the woman for a moment.

But she continued on in her soft, cheery voice. "Do you love her?" Ian crossed his arms across his chest. But the woman didn't seem to feel rejected. She simply smiled and laid her hand on his forearm.

"I love you." She stepped closer to him again and smiled up at him. "Did you hear me? I said, 'I love you.'" Logan's mouth fell open in shock. And then a hand covered it as another one wrapped around his throat. Someone pulled him back and he struggled.

The sound of his muffled yells turned Ian and Rona's attention to him and his eyes locked with Ian's. Grabbing Rona's hand, Ian ran off with her into the blackness, leaving Logan and Finnean to face this fight on their own.

How could Ian just run away? Surely, if he didn't remember Logan, he would recognize his own driver. How could he leave them in such danger, knowing they could get beaten or killed? Couldn't he fight? Didn't he help his fellow man?

Logan saw another attacker fighting Finnean before Logan's attacker knocked him over the head and Logan fell to the ground.

Logan stayed low, waiting for his attacker to come closer so he could grab him and bring him down. As Logan kicked and thrashed his body against his attacker, they rolled along the dock. At some point he punched the man's nose so hard it gave him time to jump to his feet and pull Finnean's attacker off him. Together, they stood staring at their attackers.

"You can either make this easy on yourselves or hard." The one attacker's face looked impish. Logan kept his fists raised and his senses locked on the closest man.

The attacker took out a knife. "Give us your money and no one gets hurt."

The two brutes approached, trying to circle them. But Logan and Finnean kept moving, keeping them in front.

"If that's the way you want it." The knife-wielding attacker lunged forward, swiping at Logan's stomach. Logan jumped back so the blade missed.

The second attacker cracked his knuckles into his

other palm. "Last chance, lads." The man let out a sadistic laugh before leaping forward at them.

In midair, a whistle blew and both attackers turned toward the sound. Logan didn't look toward the whistle as he kicked the first attacker's hand, sending the knife flying toward the water.

If the knife made a splash, Logan didn't hear it, nor did he see what happened to Finnean as an attacker pounced on him. Pain shot through Logan's body in each spot he took a blow. Luckily, he didn't stay under the attacker long, because a man pulled the attacker off him.

Logan braced himself, watching as two night guardsmen handcuffed the attackers. Blood trickled out of Logan in too many places to stop any of it and Finnean looked as if he suffered just the same. Logan couldn't stand yet.

"Those are the attackers," Ian told the night guardsmen as he vouched for Finnean and Logan while Rona looked on by his side. Logan realized Ian and Rona had gone for help. He owed them his gratitude now.

"This isn't the first time these lads have been in trouble with the law, but it'll be the last," the night guardsmen assured them by roughly moving one of the attackers.

Trying to stand up, blood rushed to Logan's head, nearly knocking him down again as he watched the guardsmen with the criminals fade into the distance. This left Logan and Finnean to stand uncomfortably in the presence of Ian and Rona.

"Thank you for helping us." Logan broke the silence as Finnean relayed his thanks as well and both Ian and Rona shrugged off the gratitude.

After formally introducing Rona, Ian tried to explain. "I know as Sheena's chaperone you are probably wondering why I'm at the docks the night before my wedding to Sheena."

Logan nodded silently, hoping to draw Ian out. "Rona was the love of my life. Four years ago we tried to elope, but her father found out and stopped us. Then he sent Rona away. I thought they'd shipped her off in one of their boats to the Americas and married her off. At least that's what her father told me. But apparently, she was living with relatives in southern England."

Ian paused to steal a glance at Rona. "You must understand, my family didn't have wealth back then, but her family did. Her father thought I only wanted to marry her for her money. And he threatened my family and me if I ever went looking for her. A foiled elopement would hurt everyone and my family's reputation would suffer to the point that people wouldn't do business with us. I couldn't bring that torment down on them. We wouldn't be where we are today if I had."

"Hey, what are you doing out at this hour? Return to your homes." Another night guardsman approached them and they began to depart, as Ian kept explaining.

"This past year I began to question if Rona did indeed marry someone in the Americas. I sent out investigators with every one of our ships that sailed across the Atlantic and no one ever located her. Rona's father caught wind of my search and arranged with my father to have me married off before I found Rona."

"So they arranged for you to marry Sheena?" Logan asked, walking on Ian's right, while Finnean stayed to Logan's other side, coming to walk beside him or falling behind depending on the width of the walkway.

"Sheena's uncle Kyle is my cousin," Rona piped in from Ian's left side before Ian continued.

"All I knew was that Rona's father threatened to interfere with my family's trade if I didn't marry. So I agreed. However, I increased my hunting endeavors and just recently found Rona and brought her back from southern England."

Logan stopped and stared Ian straight in the eye. "Am I to assume that you want to break your betrothal to Sheena and marry Rona instead?"

Ian nodded without a moment's hesitation. "I will repay her mother the dowry she gave my family and I will even give her extra money for all her trouble, but I don't know how I can break the betrothal without hurting Sheena." Ian glanced at Rona. "I don't want Sheena to get hurt in all this. She is a sweet lass." Rona nodded and smiled thoughtfully.

And Logan appreciated their compassion. Although, as he told them, "Hopefully we won't have to worry about that."

With or without any of the letters, Logan prayed above all else that Sheena would trust him again. If she trusted him, none of this would come as a shock to her. And if she could forgive him, then maybe she could love him again.

* * *

Sheena sat with her hands folded in her lap staring at her wedding gown. All alone and feeling small within her bedroom at her aunt and uncle's house, she noticed every minute that passed and it made her more nervous. She unfolded her hands and pressed her skirt with them. She knew she couldn't sit there much longer. Someone would come for her soon to take her to the cathedral where they planned to dress her.

Sheena jumped at the sound of the knock on her door. It couldn't be time already. She took a deep breath and braced herself on the arms of her chair. Slowly she stood and looked toward the door.

She felt hot and started to sweat. The air she breathed felt thick. She tried to take another deep breath, but she couldn't. Her breaths came short and rapid. What if after she opened that door she couldn't get away from whomever she let in? What if they dragged her to the cathedral, forced her to put on her wedding dress and pulled her up to the altar?

Logan rolled over and awoke to a pain shooting through his leg. He groaned, sitting up in bed to survey himself. The damage didn't look too bad. Nothing that wouldn't heal in a few days. Luckily, the attackers hadn't broken any of his bones. But if Ian and Rona hadn't run to get the guards, things wouldn't look so bright now.

Logan rubbed his bruises as he went in search of Finnean.

"We'd better get going," Finnean said. "I've sent a message to the inn telling your family we'll be at Glasgow Cathedral in case they've already arrived in Glasgow and want to meet us." Finnean held the door open. "I've got the horses all ready."

"Anything you ever want, my friend, I'll be there for you." Logan patted Finnean's shoulder as he stepped out into the cool morning air. And Logan knew how bad he must look after seeing Finnean, whose black eye and scrapes clearly showed his involvement in a fight. But Logan didn't care about his appearance. Not while he was on his way to see Sheena. "I owe you my life, Finnean."

"I thought it was I who owed you my life." Finnean mounted his horse.

"We've got to stop this." Logan threw his leg over his horse. "I can't keep track anymore." They both laughed.

Logan wanted to run his horse full out to the cathedral, but the city streets wouldn't allow it. Too much traffic. "There is something you can help me with." Finnean patted his horse's neck before sitting up straight. "Can you convince your family I'm a good match for Cait?"

Logan's head whipped toward him.

"I know I'm a bit older, but I love her and she loves me and…"

"I understand. Trust me. I understand." And Logan wanted to reach out and shake the man's hand, but a clearing opened up in the traffic and they pushed their horses a little faster.

"Sheena?" Cait's voice whispered from the other side of the door. Sheena sprang forward, opened it and pulled Cait in.

"How did you get here?" She hugged Cait.

Cait squeezed her back just as tightly. "The usual way—horses."

"You know what I mean." Tears formed in Sheena's eyes. "Not Glasgow. How did you get up here to my bedroom?"

"I used to work for you, remember? I have friends in all the right places." Cait grinned.

"The staff snuck you in?"

Cait nodded. "The gossip mill at the inn we're staying at knew every detail of your wedding. I can't believe it's in a few hours."

Sheena kept hold of Cait's hands as they went to sit on her bed. "I need to talk to Ian and see Logan before I do anything today."

"I know, Sheena. Logan told me everything. He's in Glasgow. Have you seen him?"

Sheena shook her head. "He was here last night with a letter. Probably the one from my father, but my mother burned it before I could read it."

"It couldn't be the one from your father, Sheena. Logan doesn't have it."

"He doesn't?" Sheena's heart sank. "He didn't find

the box?" Now she would never get to read what her father had told Logan.

"Sheena." Cait smiled at her. "He couldn't find the box because you have it." Sheena's eyebrows jerked together. She didn't understand. "Your mother bought the Montgomery family heirloom box from Nessia."

"My mother has it." Her hand flew to her chest. "Maybe that's what Logan wrote in the other letter. Maybe he thought he could slip a letter to me telling me about its whereabouts. But Cait, if that's what happened and my mother read Logan's letter before she burned it, then she would know about my father's hidden letter." Sheena jumped to her feet. "What if she finds my father's letter and burns that, too?"

She raced to the door with Cait and then snuck quietly across the hall to Tavia's bedroom.

"It's not here," Sheena concluded after they'd searched everywhere.

"Where else could it be?" Cait nervously exited Tavia's room and Sheena followed. Neither of them wanted to get caught in there.

"It must still be downstairs with all the things we never unpacked."

Cait led Sheena down the servants' back stairs so her family wouldn't see them.

"In there." Sheena pointed at the storage room and they began their frantic search.

"I found it." Sheena held up the wooden box with leaves carved all over it.

"Logan said if you push on one of the sides on the bottom the other side will pop up."

Sheena took off the lid and gave it a try. "It's not working." Sheena pushed harder as Cait came to lend her force. And then the bottom edged up. Sheena thrust her hand in and pulled out the envelope. A tear escaped her eye. Logan hadn't lied about the box or the letter. She ripped it open.

"What are you two doing?" Tavia's shrill voice cut through the room.

Sheena held the letter behind her back. There was no way her mother would get her hands on it.

"We found the letter from Father. The one Logan said was in this box."

"Impossible." Tavia stepped forward and Sheena moved back, not letting her mother get any closer to her. "There can't be a letter from your father in that box. Logan lied about all that. Your father never wrote him a letter."

"He did, Mother. It's right here in my hand."

Tavia looked at her in disbelief. "I didn't even check the box." She stumbled on her words. "Let me see the letter. I would know your father's writing anywhere. If Logan forged that letter and lied about this, I'll know." She held out her hand, but Sheena didn't concede.

"Mother, I'm going to read this letter aloud and then I'll let you see it." Sheena took out the paper and began reading as Cait stood like a wall between Sheena and her mother.

"'Logan, countless times I watched you with my daughter, and I saw the way she looks at you. You told me of your intentions to marry her, but I must be sure you truly love her and are not just marrying her for the money.

Accepting an indenturement to prove yourself worthy of my daughter goes a long way with me. And I am sure it will convince Sheena's mother that you are the right man for Sheena.

A love that would withstand the torture of an indenturement and still pull you back on another sea voyage home is one I would gladly wish for my Sheena.

If you loved her enough to do all those things, then, Logan, I give you her hand in marriage. Come see me, dear lad, and we will start the festivities.

Mr. Arthur Montgomery'"

Tears streamed down Sheena's cheeks. Her father had made Logan suffer so much these past five years. How she wished she could have spared Logan. She wiped at her tears with the back of her hand. At least she had her father's blessing to marry Logan now.

"What do you think about that, Mother?" Sheena stepped toward her.

"It sounds like your father." Tavia leaned against the wall and dabbed at her face with her handkerchief.

Sheena held out the letter, never releasing it from her grip. These were the last words she had from her deceased father and she would cherish them all the days of her life.

Tavia scanned the letter, then looked up at Sheena with a blank expression. "That's your father's writing."

Hearing her mother admit it lightened Sheena's heart. "I didn't know anything about this. Your father never told me." She twisted her handkerchief in her hands.

"Mother, I'm not going to marry Ian."

Tavia nodded before she began to cry. Real tears. "God knows I loved your father and I won't go against his wishes now."

After hitching the horses up, Logan surveyed the cathedral. Guests arrived in fancy carriages and everyone looked like royalty, wearing such exquisite clothes and jewels. Ian's family stood at the main entrance, greeting people as they came in.

Impulsively, Logan rubbed at an ache before ducking out of sight with Finnean. *God, please make this work.* Logan had never entered a cathedral before and he didn't have time to now. He needed to go to the spot behind the cathedral where last night Ian had said to meet him.

Turning the corner, Logan slowed his pace until he stopped in astonishment. There in front of him stood more than just Ian and Rona. Tavia, Jean, Kyle and their sons, along with Angus, Nessia, Ewan, Duncan and Cait—all stood close to Sheena.

How lovely she looked in a cream silk dress with her auburn hair cascading over her shoulders.

But why were they all standing back here together?

* * *

Sheena stepped forward toward Logan, smiling at Finnean when he passed her on his way to stand by Cait. "Logan." She looked up into his deep brown eyes that stopped darting around at everyone and now bore into hers. "Ian and Rona told me about your fight last night, but look at you."

She touched his face, close to where a bruise lay. She knew it must feel a little sore. But as much as she wanted to take his pain away, she couldn't. God would help, though, and time would heal his wounds.

"We picked up your family at the inn." Sheena turned to smile at them. Logan's hair swayed gently in the warm breeze and Sheena smiled at the shocked expression he still wore. She needed to explain everything before that look of uneasiness would disappear.

"I've talked to Ian and Rona and it seems our situations are more alike than I ever imagined. But you already know that, so why don't I tell you some things you don't know." Sheena couldn't help the smile that overtook her face.

"Cait helped me find our Montgomery family's heirloom box this morning and we all read the letter my father wrote to you." Logan's eyebrows shot up and Sheena's grin grew wider. He was starting to understand.

Tavia approached them. "Logan, my husband made you a promise, and I intend to honor it. Even if it does leave me with nothing." She shook her head and pursed her lips in distaste.

"Come, come. It's not that bad, Tavia." Jean put her arm around Tavia's shoulders. "We're glad to have you live with us."

"And you won't be left with nothing, Tavia." Ian joined them, holding Rona's hand and everyone followed behind until they stood in a circle around Logan and Sheena. "I'll give you back your dowry and Rona and I will even make sure Sheena, Logan and the rest of the McAllisters get to the Americas on one of our ships so they get a little extra-special treatment." He winked and Sheena thanked them.

Taking Logan's other hand, Sheena held them tight and a smile from Logan's lips finally grinned down at her. "Ian and Rona are about to get married. Do you have something to ask me, Logan?" Sheena could hardly contain her happiness as she teased him.

And she felt him squeeze her hands. "Lassie, I love you." Logan's words warmed her heart. This time she could accept them freely. She loved the man who stood before her. She always had. She always would. And she trusted him with her life. Everything he did, he did for her. For their future. She knew that now and she forgave him for agreeing to keep everything a secret between himself and her father. She understood why he felt he needed to do that and she loved him more for his sense of honor.

"Lassie, will you marry me?" Sheena barely gave him time to finish asking her before she told him, "Aye. A hundred times aye." Logan scooped her up in his arms and twirled her around a few times, hugging her tight as everyone clapped.

"Then what are we waiting for?" Ian asked. "Let's go have a double wedding."

"Wait." Finnean stopped the crowd as he took Cait's hand in his.

"He's a good man," Logan told Angus and Nessia, whose eyes, like Sheena's, never left Cait and Finnean.

"I love you, Cait. I've loved you from the first time I saw you wide-eyed and innocent. I loved you more each time I drove you around Glasgow and almost confessed it to you when you helped me with my gunshot wound. You are an amazing woman and I hope you'll take me for your husband."

Cait's hands shook. "I love you, too, Finnean."

Angus and Nessia looked on, dumbfounded, and Logan beamed, while Sheena laughed. She couldn't imagine a time when everyone she loved glowed so happily, especially Cait. Love blossomed before her, but she'd gotten so caught up in her own life that she didn't even notice Cait and Finnean falling in love.

"Another one for the ship." Ian clapped Finnean on the back in congratulations.

"And another couple for the alter." Logan squeezed Sheena's hand before bringing it to his mouth to kiss it as he looked into her face.

Seeing his brown eyes sparkle, Sheena told him, "I love you, Logan." And he kissed her. The love of her life. Her Logan.

* * * * *

Dear Reader,

I hope you enjoyed traveling back in time to a tumultuous period in Scotland's history. The struggles endured by those living in the eighteenth century are astounding and awe-inspiring, given that these people still rose above it all. What a true testament to the human spirit.

It simply amazes me to think of all that our ancestors persevered through, and yet we must acknowledge that we continue that legacy today. How wonderful it is to share in the continuity of life, love and God. I hope you realize you are here today because of the enduring love passed down through previous generations. And I hope that thought gives you comfort and the courage to face any challenges in your life.

I would love to hear from you. Please visit me through my website at www.EvaMariaHamilton.com. I look forward to meeting you.

Keeping you in my prayers,
Eva Maria Hamilton

Questions for Discussion

1. Logan appears like a ghost from Sheena's past. When have you experienced a surprise from the past? Did it alter the path of your life in some way? If so, how?

2. Sheena and Logan faced a division between wealth and poverty that threatened to separate them. How has a difference in wealth figured in your experience?

3. Sheena and Tavia do not have a close mother-daughter relationship. How does your relationship with your mother or daughter(s) compare to theirs?

4. Both Logan and Sheena find it difficult to tell the McDougalls about their son Gordon's death. Have you ever had to be the bearer of bad news? If so, how did that affect you?

5. Sheena's father swore Logan to secrecy. Has someone ever asked you to keep a secret? Did you keep it? Do you think you made the right decision? Why or why not?

6. Logan is a very determined young man. When have you challenged yourself and pushed yourself to your limit to accomplish something important to you? Did you succeed? Was it worth the effort?

7. Sheena's father's death greatly impacted her life. How has a loved one's death affected your life?

8. Logan searches fervently for the secret letter from Sheena's father. Have you ever lost something of extreme importance to you? What was it, and did you eventually find it? If not, how did you handle that?

9. Cait wants a husband and family like her sister, Nessia. Do you have anyone you look up to? Why do you want to emulate that person?

10. Sheena knew that people might be hurt if she broke her betrothal to Ian. Have you ever been faced with a decision that could hurt those involved? How did you handle it? What was the outcome?

11. Cait always considered herself part of the McAllister clan. Who do you consider part of your family, even though they may not have any genetic link to you?

12. Tavia ultimately chooses to follow her husband's wishes and agrees that Sheena should marry Logan. When have you encountered someone who has changed in light of new information or circumstances?

13. Ian and Rona promise to give the McAllister family some special treatment on one of their ships to the

Americas. When have you done something kind and generous for someone? How did it make you feel?

14. At the end of the novel, Cait and Finnean's relationship takes Sheena by surprise. Have you ever encountered a shocking situation that, in hindsight, you realize you should have been aware of, because the signs were there all along?

15. Sheena changes her life drastically when she agrees to marry Logan and move from Scotland to the Americas. When have you faced such a life-altering change?

INSPIRATIONAL

HISTORICAL

COMING NEXT MONTH
AVAILABLE APRIL 10, 2012

THE WEDDING JOURNEY
Irish Brides
Cheryl St.John

BRIDES OF THE WEST
Victoria Bylin, Janet Dean & Pamela Nissen

SANCTUARY FOR A LADY
Naomi Rawlings

LOVE ON THE RANGE
Jessica Nelson

REQUEST YOUR FREE BOOKS!

2 FREE INSPIRATIONAL NOVELS
PLUS 2
FREE
MYSTERY GIFTS

Love Inspired
HISTORICAL
INSPIRATIONAL HISTORICAL ROMANCE

YES! Please send me 2 FREE Love Inspired® Historical novels and my 2 FREE mystery gifts (gifts are worth about $10). After receiving them, if I don't wish to receive any more books, I can return the shipping statement marked "cancel". If I don't cancel, I will receive 4 brand-new novels every month and be billed just $4.49 per book in the U.S. or $4.99 per book in Canada. That's a saving of at least 22% off the cover price. It's quite a bargain! Shipping and handling is just 50¢ per book in the U.S. and 75¢ per book in Canada.* I understand that accepting the 2 free books and gifts places me under no obligation to buy anything. I can always return a shipment and cancel at any time. Even if I never buy another book, the two free books and gifts are mine to keep forever.

102/302 IDN FEHF

Name	(PLEASE PRINT)	

Address		Apt. #

City	State/Prov.	Zip/Postal Code

Signature (if under 18, a parent or guardian must sign)

Mail to the Reader Service:
IN U.S.A.: P.O. Box 1867, Buffalo, NY 14240-1867
IN CANADA: P.O. Box 609, Fort Erie, Ontario L2A 5X3
Not valid for current subscribers to Love Inspired Historical books.

Want to try two free books from another series?
Call 1-800-873-8635 or visit www.ReaderService.com.

* Terms and prices subject to change without notice. Prices do not include applicable taxes. Sales tax applicable in N.Y. Canadian residents will be charged applicable taxes. Offer not valid in Quebec. This offer is limited to one order per household. All orders subject to credit approval. Credit or debit balances in a customer's account(s) may be offset by any other outstanding balance owed by or to the customer. Please allow 4 to 6 weeks for delivery. Offer available while quantities last.

Your Privacy—The Reader Service is committed to protecting your privacy. Our Privacy Policy is available online at www.ReaderService.com or upon request from the Reader Service.

We make a portion of our mailing list available to reputable third parties that offer products we believe may interest you. If you prefer that we not exchange your name with third parties, or if you wish to clarify or modify your communication preferences, please visit us at www.ReaderService.com/consumerschoice or write to us at Reader Service Preference Service, P.O. Box 9062, Buffalo, NY 14269. Include your complete name and address.

LIH11B